EASY STREET

BY

J. GREGORY SMITH

EASY STREET

OTHER TITLES
BY J. GREGORY SMITH

Thrillers

A Noble Cause (Thomas & Mercer, Kindle Bestseller US, UK, and Germany)

The Flamekeepers (Thomas & Mercer)

Darwin's Pause (RedAcre Press)

The Reluctant Hustler Series

Quick Fix (Book 1, RedAcre Press)

Short Cut (Book 2, RedAcre Press)

Easy Street (Book 3, RedAcre Press)

The Paul Chang Mystery Series

Final Price (Book 1, Thomas & Mercer)

Legacy of the Dragon (Book 2, Thomas & Mercer)

Send in the Clowns (Book 3, Thomas & Mercer)

Young Adult

The Crystal Mountain (RedAcre Press)

Short Stories

"Heroic Measures" (Amazon StoryFront)

"Blenders" (*Insidious Assassins*, Smart Rhino Publishing)

"The Pepper Tyrant" (*Uncommon Assassins*, Smart Rhino Publishing)

"Something Borrowed" (*Zippered Flesh: Tales of Body Enhancements Gone Bad*, Smart Rhino Publishing)

"Street Smarts" (*Stories from the Ink Slingers*, A Written Remains Anthology, Gryphonwood Press)

"Powder Burns" (*A Plague of Shadows*, Smart Rhino Publishing)

"Short Order Crook" (*Asinine Assassins*, Smart Rhino Publishing)

Published by RedAcre Press

Cover design by Ebook Launch

Printed in the United States of America

First Printing, 2022

ISBN 978-1-7353889-1-5

For Julie

CHAPTER 1

Fishtown, Philadelphia, Pennsylvania

What a mess.

I closed up the laptop on the dining room table after completing the checklist of tasks for what I thought of "Businessman Kyle's" world. It felt like I was somehow preventing the legit part of my life from seeing what I was up to on the hustler side.

I glanced at the picture of my friend Ryan that sat on a shelf nearby. A simple headshot from high school. No reason to keep it there, then again, no reason not to, as this was his house. Sort of.

Used to be.

Ryan was dead, but the outside world didn't know it. I'd been there the night he was killed and by default dumped all the problems of his weird empire on me. Along with this house.

"This is all your fault, you know." This was by no means the first time I'd spoken to this photo. As always, Ryan just smirked back at me. "I never wanted to run a shipping port."

I doubt he would have wanted to do it, either, but things had a funny way of working out.

"Wipe that damn grin off your face, why don't you? Those psychos from your smuggling op came right after me, Ryan. *Hard*. Really appreciated that." I slammed the flat of my hand onto the table. "I didn't want *any* of this crap. Were you *trying* to get me killed? What, are you lonely on the other side?"

I know I sounded nuts yelling at an old photo, but sometimes I just couldn't help it. The bastard needed to hear it.

1

"Those goons didn't get me, but their massacres over in the Sand Box sure put the kill shot on Delivergistics. What were you thinking, working with them?"

To be fair, Ryan and another co-worker, Tom Thumb, stopped doing any side hustles with the mercenaries once they realized their bloodlust. "Look, I get you couldn't have known the port would go for sale, but if *I* could see it as an opportunity for Ali to invest some of those riches, you sure would have."

Maybe. Half the time I still wanted to kick Ryan's ass, but the other time I just wished like hell he could talk back. When he finished laughing at what he'd landed me in, I know he'd have some ideas worth listening to. The guy could spot an angle and work it. Yeah, his hustles had dragged me into this life, but it was those hustles that were getting me through the trouble they caused.

"Bet you wouldn't have set it up as a legit operation," I told him. "Ali wants a fresh start, and with his backing, I'm the face of Global Imported Crafts." I flashed one of the business cards in front of the picture.

Sometimes I could almost hear Ryan speaking to me in my head. Right now, he was saying, *Sounds boring.*

"It's working, man. Just because it's legit doesn't make it stupid. Ali brings in high-end furniture and crafts from all over the Middle East, and we truck it to him in Ohio."

Thrilling.

"Steady income is never dull." Ryan always saw through my lies. "Fine. So, I don't exactly burrow down into the day-to-day management details. The port was kind of turnkey, and our old boss Cliff handles all the tedious crap."

Now Ryan's smirk had a "told you so" quality.

"Whatever. Most of all, I wish you'd told me how easy one thing leads to another. Seems like I always need a new scheme to keep existing ones from crashing down."

The picture was a head shot, but if I could have seen Ryan's shoulders, I imagined they would have shrugged. Some days it felt like he'd dropped me onto a running treadmill and the only way to avoid falling was to keep going.

The late morning sun glinted off my watch. "I'd love to stay and chat about the finer points of working with Customs, you asshole, but Sandy's waiting for me."

CHAPTER 2

Old City, Philadelphia

I loved the location of Sandy's physical therapy shop. She'd managed to find an old factory converted to office space right off of Arch Street near the historic Betsy Ross House. I had to walk down one of the cobblestone streets that was so narrow I didn't want to try to drive it with the new company truck. With my luck, I'd scrape the barely dry Global Imported Crafts logo right off the side. Parking down there was a nightmare, but rank had its privileges and I had a reserved spot at a small parking lot around the corner. I'd done a small favor for the owner when he got into a zoning argument six months before.

Sandy met me at the door. I could see the two assistants were already helping clients and the shouts of encouragement alternated with pain-filled growls and muttered obscenities. "Been there, done that," I said after Sandy gave me a smooch.

"You're never done; didn't you read the fine print?" She smiled. "Just because you can walk without limping and run without needing crutches for a month after doesn't make you graduated."

"Good. I may need a fallback if things don't, you know, work out." She tagged me in the ribs and led me back to the cobblestone street.

"Where did you want to go eat?" I asked.

"Can't. No time today." She took my hand. "Let's just walk for a bit."

She hadn't called me across town just to take in the city air. "Everything okay?"

"Not me. It's one of my clients. He's a really sweet old guy, making great progress coming back from a crushed pelvis."

"Sounds good so far." I waited for the rest.

"He told me he has to stop coming for treatment."

"Pelvis has left the building?" It came out before I could shut my mouth. When she didn't laugh, I saw I'd better pay attention.

"He needs to keep up his therapy or he'll lose the mobility and strength we've built. And he wants to. He says just can't afford it anymore."

Ah.

"I get it. Insurance ran out? And he needs a loan?" I don't know why she didn't just say so in the first place. She knew that I got involved with local finance, another Ryan-linked arrangement. I always kept it as low-key as possible, but it got hard to explain all the cakes and cookies dropped off at the house, not to mention all the honks and waves in our neck of the woods.

But she shook her head. "It's not that simple. I'm not even sure he'd accept a loan."

"Then why . . ."

"Let me finish." Sandy stopped and faced me. "Clarence Penney and his wife were in a horrible car wreck almost five years ago."

"Okay."

"Both were severely injured, and the truck driver was found at fault."

"And they sued?"

She nodded. "The wife found a lawyer, Clark LeSuer, who took them on and convinced them to accept a settlement."

"But?"

"You'll have to get the details from Clarence, but the big picture was that they were receiving a structured payout, then the wife passed away and LeSuer said the company had a modification offer, which Clarence felt pressured to accept."

"I'm not sure I understand. Did he accept the new terms? I take it, for less money?"

"Correct. Enough less that now he says it's impossible to afford therapy, even with the discount I've offered."

"If it's important to you, I could cover the cost, I suppose. At the discounted rate, of course. I can't afford to be seen as too easy a touch, not even by my girlfriend."

"You're sweet. But I don't think that's the real issue. Again, you'll have to talk to him, but Clarence thinks LeSuer scammed him. His wife trusted the guy and Clarence trusted her. They were both in bad shape, remember. That original settlement should've been in the millions, not a pittance doled out to the two of them over the years. And now he's left with a pittance of the pittance."

"But if that's the case, why me? There are whole departments devoted to helping victims." Though to be honest, my ears had perked up at the word "scam."

"I asked him about getting a better lawyer. He said he'd tried and the state blew him off like he wasn't even there."

"I'm assuming he didn't confide in you because he knows you and I are dating."

Sandy pursed her lips together. "Hell of a coincidence, but I also think he didn't have anywhere to turn."

It sounded rather self-serving on his part, but I was willing to hear him out. "I can talk to him, but what do you think he expects from me? For that matter, how about from you?"

Sandy resumed walking. "I know you don't like to get into your . . . side deals with me, but you sure did help me out with the whole Barnaby Bones fiasco. I was thinking you might have some nontraditional approaches to his problem."

"You do have a way with words. I hope you don't think that means you think I have some goons available to send a message."

"God no. Nothing like that." She went pale. "You don't use people like that, do you?"

"I do know them." I tried to gauge how surprised she looked. "But using them isn't my style." I saw relief in her eyes. "Sometimes the direct approach is the best way to go, but for me, I get a lot more mileage out of people worrying that I *might* use such people."

She nodded as much to herself as to me, I think. "That makes sense."

"There's a lot of ways to persuade people. It can take some creativity, and it isn't always easy finding leverage in a way that I can live with."

She squeezed my hand. I noticed she didn't step in here to tell me not to intervene on behalf of her Clarence.

"I'll talk to Mr. Penney," I said. "It may well be there's nothing I can do for him, at least not what's in your comfort zone."

"Thank you."

"Please remember if I do go forward that discretion is key—and, for your part, ignorance isn't just bliss, it's a sound legal strategy."

"I changed my mind," she blurted out.

I hadn't seen that coming. "You sure?"

"Positive." Sandy grinned. "Let's get lunch."

CHAPTER 3

Fishtown

It was just as well that Sandy hadn't wanted dessert after lunch because when I went home, I saw enough baked goods on the porch to make a Girl Scout troop blush. I might not be getting rich with the small loan racket, but if I wasn't careful, I was sure going to get fat.

I carried the stack of boxes inside, opening the door with my hip after I'd unlocked it. The scent of apples and chocolate trailed after me into the house. I appreciated the appreciation, but cash was still king. Actually, most of these older families did make good on their debts. The ones who had no ability or intention to repay the loans didn't leave cookies. They tended to avoid me altogether. My friend Rollie helped me keep things in perspective and told me to file the deadbeats in the "good riddance" write-off column.

I didn't like it, but it was better than trying to enforce a harsh penalty. At least they didn't try to borrow again and anyone dumb enough to ask would be told to try their luck with the Irish Mob. I was only in this racket to repay a favor they did for me.

One of my burner phones chirped. There was a text message with a one-word message: *Outside.*

I peeked out the window and saw a dark sedan with tinted windows. Not a great sign.

Who dis? I replied, trying to sound casual. I edged closer to an end table with a hidden compartment containing a loaded pistol. I was no heavy, but sometimes threats didn't respond to nuance.

NOW.

I rarely did business from the house but whoever this was had one of my private numbers. I decided to leave the pistol behind and stepped outside.

The car sat still, the exhaust curling out of the tailpipes making me think of a recently fired double-barrel shotgun.

Was it too late to go back for the piece?

Yes. The tinted window slid down to reveal a hulking figure with a huge, thick skull and piercing ice-blue eyes.

Kevin "Killer" Cullen.

"You're not here for the Cal Ripken, Jr. rookie card we talked about, are you?" I forced my tone to be as light as possible. We knew each other: he worked for the Irish, earning his nickname. He also collected baseball cards, sometimes from me. Go figure.

"No. Get in." He was all business today.

"Um. Is that a good idea? Your nickname isn't 'The Driver,' you know."

"I wasn't asking, and you're wasting time. They want to see you."

"Dead or alive?" I blurted out. My nerves were jumping.

"Last time I'm telling you, or I stuff you in the trunk." His face was like stone.

I reached for the rear door handle and decided that if there was another goon waiting in the back, I'd put my rehabbed knee to the test and dash for the house.

The back seat was empty. I climbed into the car. "What's going on, Kevin?"

He pulled away from the curb. "I'm taking you to see them."

"Them" meant the O'Brien brothers, head of the Irish Mob in this neck of the woods. I couldn't imagine what I might have done to make them mad enough to send Cullen.

"Just so you know, I don't have the Ripken yet, so, if I wind up in that trunk after all . . ."

"I'm only driving. If it was another kind of visit you wouldn't see me coming." He spoke over his shoulder to me. "Just so *you* know."

I shut up for the rest of the short ride.

* * *

We pulled up in front of Heather Bakery, the worst-kept secret in Fishtown. The place made only two kinds of cookies but all kinds of deals in the backroom apartments where the O'Briens conducted business.

Cullen pulled into the reserved parking spot, and right away I noticed there were more people milling around the front area than usual and now that I looked, also on every corner. The other thing I noticed was that everyone's eyes were darting around more than a Secret Service detail's.

I opened the door. "You coming in?" I asked.

"No."

Most of the people I saw as I approached the bakery looked vaguely familiar but no more than one or two I could name. I never dropped by for fun. The door opened, and I saw it was held by a thinly built ginger who'd been the one to pat down visitors and show them to the inner sanctum for as long as I'd dealt with the O'Briens.

"Hey, Red. You still stuck with groping duty? Recruiting falling off or something?" I tended to jabber when a strange guy was about to feel me up.

"Worry about your own career, asshole." Red glared at me.

That was a switch from his usual bored contempt.

I stepped in and the old, dusty display cases along the front showed clean spots, as if a bunch of people had been leaning on them to stare out the plate glass window. Stale cigarette smoke hung in the air, dominating the remnant sugary odors of not-so-freshly-baked lace cookies. The interior trapped the late summer heat.

"This way," Red said, like I hadn't been here a bunch of times. Never without an invite.

Something was missing. "What, no strip-search?"

He shrugged, a lid back on his emotions, it seemed. "Must be your lucky day."

I was barely exaggerating. In the past they'd gotten me down to my skivvies and made me wear a robe (stolen, of course, from the Four Seasons). Over the last year, their level of trust in me, if you could call it that, had improved to require nothing more than a cursory pat-down. One of the perks of having mountains of dirt on each other, I supposed.

I followed Red up the back stairs and encountered a pair of big guys I recognized as straight-up soldiers. I never dealt with them, but they knew who I was and stood aside at the sound of the buzzing lock.

I glanced up at the camera above the door and turned up my palms to show my cluelessness.

Inside, the O'Briens had made a posh apartment suite and filled it with comfortable leather furniture and a bar with high-end cut crystal tumblers for their equally high-end whiskey. The air conditioning felt chilly compared to the stuffy hallway.

"Get yourself a drink; you know where everything is," I heard Charlie call out from another room deeper in the apartment. He had a booming voice that suited his beefy, barrelhouse frame.

Charlie was the brawler of the pair, but anyone who mistook his rough demeanor as unintelligent fell right into his trap. His brother William was slender by comparison and every bit as smart as he appeared.

I picked up one of the better Irish whiskey bottles. I knew because I'd been the one who gave it to them. It was always fun to score stuff they couldn't get themselves.

When the two of them walked into the room, the first thing I noticed was that William hadn't shaved. Charlie was always kind of rumpled looking, but William was downright fastidious.

"Thank you for coming on short notice." William shook my hand.

Charlie headed to the bar in silence.

"I don't recall getting a choice," I said.

"Be that as it may," William said. "We needed to speak to you right away."

I didn't bother to point out the convenience of a phone. They were kind of big on discretion. "So," I said, "where's the fire? Are you guys okay?"

"You got your ear to the ground," Charlie said. "What have you heard? What have you seen?" He took a big belt from his tumbler and readied a second. I was drinking for taste and declined a refill.

"Can you be a little more specific?" I asked.

William spoke. "New faces in town, lemonade stands popping up without permission, things like that."

I assumed he meant unauthorized activity within their area of control. "I guess I'd have mentioned it if I had. You don't think I'd be involved in anything like that behind your back?"

Charlie shot me a look, but William raised his hands to indicate calm. "Of course not."

"Then why the big production? And what's with sending Cullen to drag me over here?"

Charlie finished his second drink. "Cullen was for your protection."

"Huh? From what?"

William looked over at his brother, then nodded. "We're not sure. We were hoping you might be able to help us understand."

"Enough. What's going on here?"

William spoke. "What would it take to get you to move some packages for us? Through the port or otherwise?"

Cold anger soaked through me. I knew what they meant by "packages." Methamphetamine. "You know better than to ask."

"We're asking anyway." Charlie slammed his fist down on the bar, making the tumblers jump like he'd startled them. "Short term. Very short term. And this wouldn't be a favor. Name your price."

"You both know how I feel about that shit. I'd never get in your way, but my direct involvement was *not* part of the deal."

William spoke in a calm voice. "We know. And you should appreciate how important it must be for us to ask."

"But why me?"

Charlie took a deep breath and exhaled. "We've lost several of our messengers, along with their 'messages,' in the last couple weeks."

Meaning their mules and the drugs they carried.

"And we have no idea who or what is responsible."

"I don't know. Not busted, I take it?" I wouldn't recognize their mules if they knocked on my door.

"Not unless the law is executing them at the drop points."

"That's not in the news," I said. Grisly murders were always top story fodder for the media.

"We got there first," Charlie said.

I assumed he was referring to the shadowy "Shamrock Sanitation" crew that made messy problems disappear. "Any ideas?"

"Not for lack of trying," William said. "We just know it's not the law, nor our Italian colleagues, though they have been reluctant to go any further to help."

"Interesting," I said. "First, I have to say no, again, to the movement of product. I understand what you are asking and you need to appreciate that I say no with all due respect." Charlie's jaw clenched. "That said, I'll put out feelers through my network. That doesn't include the Italians. I stay away from them, and you'd know anything before I would on that front."

"I'm not sure that's true, but it isn't your concern. All right," William said. "Cullen can take you home."

Yeah, no. "Thanks, but I'll get my own ride."

"Suit yourself." Charlie poured another drink and turned his back to me without shaking my hand.

CHAPTER 4

Fishtown

I waited in front of Heather Bakery after making a quick call. The guys out front gave me the side eye but avoided any small talk. Fine with me. Cullen must have gotten the word on my way down because his car was nowhere to be seen.

Before too long I heard a distinctive "a-*wooo*-ga" car horn, and an electric blue VW Beetle rolled into view, complete with an authentic Bentley grill, complete with the chrome-winged "B." My personal Uber had arrived.

The driver pulled in where Cullen had been, and two guys started forward.

"It's for me," I said, and the guys stepped back.

The door opened and a short, pudgy guy with lips reddened by cherry juice waved at me. "Hi, Kyle!"

"Hey, Beet. Thanks for coming." Short for his full nickname, Beetle Bentley. He had a close-cropped haircut and a blue shirt with a sparkly gold Starfleet Federation insignia on the chest.

I heard snickering and a reference to an old kid's show, *The Wiggles.* I turned to the rough-looking guy who'd produced it. "No, no. Think older. He's Spock, from the original *Star Trek.*"

Beet overheard me. "Not me." He pointed to his ears. "Do these look pointy?"

"A little pointy?" I wasn't sure what answer he wanted.

"But I am in the science division." He flashed the amused goons a Spock split-fingered salute. "And I speak fluent Vulcan."

I squeezed into the front passenger seat. Beet closed his door. "So," he said, "where to?"

14

"Home." Then I remembered. "I mean Ryan's place." Beet knew Ryan was not around, but I don't think he'd worked out that it was a permanent situation. I'd "inherited" him when he got into debt trouble and I had to get the Irish to run off the old loan shark.

"Oh, okay. I thought I might get to see Rollie."

"I'm sure he's up for a checkers rematch sometime."

Beet grinned. "Gonna whip his butt."

"I believe you will. How's Cliff down at the port?"

"Great. Really busy." Beet paused. "But not *too* busy, if you need me for something."

"Just the ride for now, buddy." I was so proud of how far he'd come since losing his father. The old guy had been his world, and Beet had been kind of lost for a while.

* * *

Back at the house I saw another box of what I figured to be baked goods waiting for me. If I ever went away on vacation, I'd probably need to hire an exterminator for all the ants that would have invaded in my absence. Sure enough, more cookies and a note in tall cursive. "K, Thanks for your patience and understanding."

If they ever made a movie about me, it would be called *The Diabetic Loan Shark*.

I said goodbye to Beet, then went inside the house and shut off the alarm. That was a new touch insisted on by Rollie and VP.

Funny thing about the system, it wasn't monitored by an alarm company. It was monitored by VP herself, and Rollie would get a call and he could reach others if I needed the cavalry. They'd agreed with me that I wasn't looking for an excuse for the cops to come busting in. Yes, I was careful and did try to keep all "side gigs" at arm's length from the home. Still, no reason to look for trouble.

I set the boxes down and tried to remember which shelter hadn't seen me for a while. I'd drop something off regularly. No reason for such good food to go to waste. I'd even established a nice little network of informants, all based on cookies and brownies.

The security system chirped. I'd turned off the alarm, but VP had tuned the system to motion-detect and alert me to someone approaching from the front or back, along with specific tones for each. This time it was the front door.

There were buttons around the house that allowed me to lock the place down in case of trouble, like hitting the key fob for a car. There was a whole war room VP had a blast making fitting out with cameras and a more secure interior space. It felt like engineering overkill, but Rollie and VP were so pleased with the results I chose to think of it as more for them than for me.

Instead of racing to the bunker, I risked a glance out the window. I saw an old guy with a large aluminum cane, the kind with the four rubber-tipped feet, making his way across the porch with a manila folder under his arm.

I was halfway to the front door when he rang the bell. I waited a beat before opening the door, not wanting to startle the guy.

He didn't look familiar, but with his white hair and worn sport coat, I had a good guess. "Hi, can I help you?"

"Good afternoon, sorry to bother you," he said in a low, but steady voice, "but are you Mr. Logan?"

"How did you know to find me?"

"I was told by Sandy that you agreed to speak to me?" His deference made me uncomfortable. Maybe it was the age difference.

"It depends. What's your name?"

He switched his grip on the cane and held out his hand. I shook it and found the grip stronger than the papery skin would suggest. "Clarence Penney. I would have called first, but Sandy said—"

"Please come in." I stepped back and let him make his way inside. "The dining room table to the right, please."

"Thank you."

"As you can see, I don't exactly keep office hours, but I do prefer to discuss things in person."

"I understand," he said, though I doubted it. Still, he'd reached out to me for a reason. That he'd come by so soon told me it was important to him.

I offered water, which he declined, and then we got down to business. My kind of guy.

"Sandy told me in broad terms what is going on," I said. "You have my sympathies, but what were you hoping I could do for you?"

"I've lived in this neighborhood all my life. Probably will die here, too, just like Isabelle." Penney licked his lips. "My problem is, if things keep going like this, I'll be dead broke first."

"I understand you think your settlement isn't right."

"It's not a settlement; it's a crock of shit."

"I don't mean to sound blunt, but didn't you and your wife agree to those terms a while ago?"

Penney turned a deep shade of red. "Which ones? That slimy bastard keeps changing them. And he thinks I'm stupid."

"I'm not defending anyone, or blaming you either." The last thing I wanted was to give the guy a heart attack. "I promised Sandy that I'd hear you out." I ran down what I knew from her.

"She's a good listener, and a good therapist." Penney smiled. "This goes deeper than just being able to afford her torture sessions."

I mentioned my rehabbed knee, and we shared a smile. "Deeper how?" I asked him.

"See, LeSuer told me that the company was hard-assed about settling. Their offer was a couple hundred grand cash payout or fifty grand a year for twenty years. I thought that was too low, but he told Isabelle it was the best we could hope for unless we wanted to fight it out in court for the rest of our lives."

"So you took it."

"Dumb, but yeah. We took the fifty a year. And we had to agree to no publicity and all that crap. Long story short, after Belle passed away, LeSuer came to me and said they had an offer to lower the payment to thirty-five a year but they'd extend the payout for another five years."

"Why would you do that? It's less than the original offer." I wasn't a math whiz, but something didn't add up.

"LeSuer said that the settlement had been for the both of us. With me as sole survivor, the company could have grounds to petition for a reduction. He said we were lucky they were willing to extend the payments if I waived going back to court."

Now I thought I saw where this was going. "Big of them."

Penney nodded. "If it was them making the offer. Once LeSuer said I should sign, I got the strongest sense he wasn't representing my interests." A polite way of saying his own lawyer was trying to screw him.

"Sandy said you'd tried to open up an official complaint?"

"Tried. I think the son of a bitch at the Disciplinary Board of Pennsylvania round-filed my complaint before the elevator reached the lobby after I left his office."

This guy may have had money trouble, but his spirit sure wasn't broken. I leaned forward, no longer wanting to find a gentle excuse to send him on his way. "Do you remember the Disciplinary Board guy's name?"

Penney reached into his manila envelope. "I can do better than that; here's his card." He handed it over.

I held the card up between two fingers. "Before I go any further, we need to be clear on a couple points, and then we need to be vague on some others. Do you get me?"

He paused. "Yes."

"First off, you didn't come here for a loan. What are you hoping I can do?"

"Help me sleep."

"Excuse me?"

"It's not right," he said. "A guy like that lawyer can take advantage of people and get rich. But I bet he sleeps like a baby."

"Probably."

"Nobody else will help me. I don't know where to turn."

"But what did you think I could do?" I needed to hear it.

"If I knew, I'd do it myself. If I could." He seemed to crumble. "Justice," he said, in a small voice.

I hated to see a strong man look like that, but this was important. "Mr. Penney, are you asking me to . . ."

His eyes opened wide. "No. Not that. I know how to pull a trigger. That won't help, not that I'd piss on him if he were on fire. But that way, he'd go out with his reputation intact and I'd just be some senile nut-job."

Interesting. "Thank you. Now we're clear on that. If I agree to work with you, I need a free hand and you are out of the whole thing unless I say otherwise."

"You know I don't have a lot of money."

"Let me worry about that. You give me everything you know, and I will look into it. If I can help, I'll let you know. If I can't, same deal and you don't owe me a thing. Fair enough?"

"How long?" he asked, and I knew I was in.

"Keep going to see Sandy. I will cover you for it. It won't be long. And if I can't do anything else, you just owe me a small favor for the therapy. Okay?"

He shook my hand.

* * *

I heard the *tap-tap-tap* on the door soon after the backyard warning buzzer sounded. It was getting dark out, but I didn't need to look to know the knock belonged to VP, who'd agreed to come out to the house. We still did a lot of business over burner phones, but sometimes it was just easier to lay out details in person, especially when we were starting a new project.

She had a new apartment after moving out of her folks' place. She was in her twenties and a self-described hermit. I knew where she lived but had never set foot inside the place. That she allowed me to know that much about her was a big deal, and she never shared anything about her parents. I still didn't know her real name, though at this point I liked to think that this was more out of habit than trust. "VP" suited her well enough, but I wasn't going to call her Vox Pox except when I needed to reference her in business. That kept her gender in the veil of secrecy.

I opened the back door, and she stood there in her standard uniform looking like a millennial ninja with her hoodie obscuring her face. "Duuuuude." She raised her fist for a greeting bump.

I obliged and let her in.

She looked around the kitchen. "Coming along. I still see the seventies peeking through here and there, but it's getting better." She opened the fridge and helped herself to a MonStar energy drink.

"If you ever get tired of being a hacker—"

I stopped when she pulled back the hood and shot me a look with her unique crooked grin, a leftover of the stroke suffered during her teenage years. I raised my hands in mock surrender.

"Pardon moi. Data manipulation artiste." I led her into the dining room, where I had the information Clarence Penney had given me. "But you could be a great interior decorator, I was going to say."

"No thanks. The sales side would kill me." VP turned to the papers. "So, what have you got?"

"One of your favorites," I said. "At least, I think. Possible dirty lawyer ripping off an old man disabled in a car wreck."

"Spill." She took a seat while I ran down the particulars. Her head kind of nodded like she was hearing music while I spoke.

"Does this Mr. Penney know how we work?"

"No, and I didn't press the guy on how he knew to come to me. But after he got blown off by the state, he arrived ready to listen. Like a lot of our . . . clients"—I still wasn't sure of the right term for the people we helped—"he's more focused on results."

"Cool." She looked down at the papers. "Tell me about the target."

"What you see is what I got. Clark LeSuer."

"His name is The Sewer?"

"I guess so, yeah."

"I like it already." She looked at the table again. "So, we have his work address, and props to the old boy for getting his home address. Is it good?"

"I haven't had time to check it."

She'd already pulled out a laptop, and her fingers flew across the keyboard, then she sat back a stared at the screen. "If this is him, my apartment could fit inside his pool house. Twice." She spun the laptop around, and I saw a Google Maps satellite view of a sprawling house in Bucks County.

"I know where the office is," I said. "Near City Hall. Big building, lots of offices and cameras and whatnot."

VP didn't answer. She'd spun the laptop back around and was typing and scrolling at a frenetic pace. "Blah, blah, blah. Award-winning law firm, we win or you pay nothing. Let's try this." More staccato keyboarding, then she looked up at me. "About what I figured. His above-board presence is a polished social media and professional pillar of the community, for an ambulance-chaser, anyway."

"I think I know what comes next." I smiled. Lately, VP had become more interested in helping with fieldwork.

"Pretty please?" She held the second word like a note, and I wondered if she ever did any singing. I bet she'd be decent if she wasn't so shy.

I held out my hand. "No promises. I'll get the house and office scouted and see if we have a shot to slip this in during business hours." VP handed over one of her custom-designed infiltration programs loaded on a memory stick. I still hadn't a clue how it worked, other than that it uploaded itself onto a system and circumvented all but the most sophisticated antivirus and malware protections.

The only downside to her program was that it required direct physical input to the target system. Once infected, it gave her access to run amuck from a distance, at least until it was discovered and the security was reconfigured. Usually by then she had whatever we needed copied and redirected. That said, it wasn't always easy to sneak up on the sneaks. Cyber-savvy crooks tended to be paranoid. Also, we had to be careful, because it went without saying that the hacks were illegal as hell, not to mention what we might do with the information.

"If you get lucky and plant that, let me know right away," she said while flipping through some of the other printed pages. "Jeez, did you see the pictures of the old couple's wreck?"

"They were lucky to live," I agreed.

"Oh, is this the last-straw guy, Mahoney?"

"Yeah, he's the one from the Disciplinary Board of Pennsylvania."

"Lemme guess. Is that where a bunch of lawyers who couldn't get better jobs let other lawyers off the hook?"

"Sounds about right," I said.

VP got to her feet. "Let me know what you find out, and in the meantime, I can get started building profiles of these two," she said. "I'll also see what I can learn about the insurance company."

"Careful," I said. "Do you need a lift home?"

"Nope." She pulled up her hood and slipped out the back.

CHAPTER 5

Fishtown—Kyle's place, three days later

I'd called a morning meeting of what was loosely known as our brain trust to figure out the next steps on the Clarence Penney case. It always sounded strange to me to use the term "case," like we were a team of lawyers or something, but in a real sense we were going to represent the man's interests, so maybe it worked.

As luck would have it, one of the remote members was able to get to town on short notice. Dozan Thomas Sabri, a.k.a. "Tom Thumb," was using one of the guest bedrooms while in town. He was based in Ohio and split time doing projects for me and acting as a liaison for our investor Ali, who was the guy who'd made the purchase of the Delivergistics Port possible in the first place. Tom spent the rest of his time getting up to whatever mischief he could find. He was an old-school hustler whose ties throughout the Middle East and no doubt now in the American Midwest kept him busy with his own side gigs.

Tom's diminutive stature, five-foot three tops, explained his nickname, but I always thought the reason he never objected to it was that it encouraged people to underestimate him.

Tom had been one of Ryan's guys back when we all worked for Delivergistics over in the Sand Box. He'd proven himself many times over there, when we shifted work stateside, and ever since Delivergistics went out of business and we'd ramped up activities.

His soft footsteps pattered down the stairs. "About time for the rest of the blokes to arrive eh, mate?"

"Yup, soon," I said. "I put water on. I have some tea in the cabinet if you forgot to bring any."

"I'd sooner forget my shoes." He grinned. "No offense." Tom's tea snob reputation remained as strong as his mostly British accent. I say mostly because, while he'd been schooled in overseas UK schools, traces of his diverse background crept into his speech. The only time it didn't was when he was putting on a voice as part of a scam.

The front yard security buzzer sounded, and I glanced out the window to see my friend and former landlord Rollie. I opened up before he had to ring the doorbell. No need for him to drop the pizza he carried.

"Hey, kid, I hope you meant it when you said you'd provide the beer." Rollie still called me that despite me being in my late thirties. Then again, he was in his seventies, not that he looked it. The former Marine sniper kept in shape and could outwork most people half his age.

I heard the kettle shriek, but Tom was on it before I could head for the kitchen. A moment later, Tom emerged from the kitchen with a couple beers in his hands.

"Uh-oh, they sent in the little guns." Rollie took the beer and gave Tom a bear hug. He'd seen Tom's courage firsthand.

"Always with the shooting," Tom said. "All right, mate?"

"Can't complain. What have you been up to the last few months?"

"I could tell you, but then I'd have to—"

"Yeah, yeah, I know the rest." Rollie took a pull from his bottle. "Nothing for you?"

"Steeping."

We all turned at the sound of the backyard alert.

"That'll be VP," I said. "Can you let her in while you get your tea, Tom?"

"No worries." Tom went to the back of the house.

It was nice to be able to refer to VP in her actual gender. The four of us had been "in battle" together, and Tom was familiar with her.

* * *

After I caught Rollie and Tom up on the basics of Clarence Penney's situation between bites of pepperoni with mushrooms, it was "movie time," as VP called it.

"I wanted to keep everyone here clean for the next phase," I said, "so I used Steve for the initial recon."

"Starving Steve?" Tom asked, and I nodded. Steve was a resource from VP who, in addition to being great with remote camera installs, had shown a real flair for fieldwork. He went by his moniker because he was a self-described starving filmmaker. "Mr. Penney gave us some great starting points, and I wanted to both verify them and then get a feel for where we might find weaknesses."

"A lot of effort for one down-on-his-luck bloke," Tom said.

"Stick with me," I said. "I didn't volunteer you for any charity work."

"Too right." Tom was strictly a for-profit kind of guy.

"We sent Steve out to the target, LeSuer's place, to get a look at his house and to get a read on his patterns." I hit PLAY on the video file. Right away the picture showed a "Steve's eye" view from one of VP's Cam-Caps.

"The steady-view is kicking, isn't it?" VP beamed with pride.

Steve walked around a large property mostly obscured by a high wall. Most of the shoot was quiet, but Steve narrated as needed. "Already spotted several security cams," he said. "You'll see the property in a sec when I go by the gate." Sure enough, the iron bars let us see a large field-stone property with rolling grounds and a glimpse of a pool in the back.

Tom spoke up. "Why didn't you say the mark was a deep-pockets?" He was leaning forward now that he was satisfied that I wasn't wasting his time.

Steve kept walking, making sure not to attract attention. "I could come back with a drone," he said quietly, "but with all the security I just saw, I don't recommend it."

I paused the video. "Anyone see anything different? The main house looks like a challenge, to say the least."

"I could just shoot out the cameras," Rollie said. "Right, Tom?"

"Let's stay on point," I said. Nobody objected, and the video cut to Steve's point of view behind the wheel of what appeared to be a van of some sort.

"Day two," Steve said. "I stuck a game camera on one of the side-walk trees by the entrance gate. I want to see what time he leaves and what he drives. Oh, and I'm a lawn care truck, in case you're wondering."

The view chopped from an edit and Steve went on. The shot was through the van's windshield, probably from his baseball cap camera. "That's the main gate buzzer. I'm around the corner and I got him. Black Lexus, one of the big SUVs." Steve kept a discreet distance. "No need to spook the guy; we know where he's going. I'm just going to stay close enough to see where he parks."

We watched in silence while I fast-forwarded through LeSuer's commute. I'd looked earlier and nothing indicated that Steve had been spotted.

Once LeSuer was in the city, the van followed several cars back. Steve passed the Lexus when it turned into a parking garage next to the building where the man's law office was located. "I hate street parking down here," Steve groused, and we all understood. At that time of day, there wasn't usually any parking available except for the lots.

Steve pulled over, blocking a fire hydrant. Not a long-term solution. "You can see the car from here. Lucky guy, he's got a spot right by the entrance. Hang on, he's crossing the street. Damn, cop coming, gotta move." I liked how Steve didn't sound rattled.

"Ah, got him," Steve said. "He's going to the coffee shop." We could see the shot in the rearview mirror.

"'Bean There, Done That,'" VP read off the screen. "Isn't hipster humor just the best?"

We zipped through while the video showed Steve finding a space in a paid lot. Out of the van, Steve crossed the same street and headed for the busy coffee shop. Inside, the place buzzed with caffeinated customers. Steve spoke in a whisper, but VP's mic captured it all. He took out a phone and pretended to talk to someone. "He's to my right. The place is packed, but there had to be a table waiting for him." He glanced in the direction, and we got a clear shot of LeSuer with his back to the wall and taking out a laptop. He was in a nice suit and with his executive-style silver hair looked every bit the big-shot attorney.

Steve joined a line, and he panned over to show that customers picked up the orders themselves. One of the baristas broke away with a cup and a muffin and worked her way through the line. "Here you are, Mr. L."

"What did I tell you?" LeSuer's voice was faint, but we could still make out the words.

"Sorry, um . . . Clark." Steve kept the camera on them. LeSuer only had eyes for the barista. He held out a folded twenty to her like he was tipping a stripper.

"Seems our boy is a regular," Rollie said.

"Yeah, regular asshole," VP said. "He's the only one getting served, acts like he owns the place." I wondered if she had any customer service in her background. She'd read this guy quick.

"Maybe he does," Tom said.

Steve eventually got his coffee and stood at a little counter along a wall while he drank it, getting a good view of LeSuer without seeming obvious. LeSuer worked on his laptop the whole time.

"Notice how he's about the only person in the place not on his phone?" I said.

"Yeah," VP said. "I mean, he can surf or whatever on the PC, but you'd think he'd take a call or two."

It hit me. "Despite the chaos, this counts as peace and quiet for him. He can concentrate in there."

"How long does he stay?" Rollie asked.

"Not much longer," I said. "There he goes." Steve got footage of him packing up and heading across the street. Steve took his time and tossed the paper cup in the trash before following him onto the street. "He's going in now. I'll give him a few minutes. Just long enough to presto-chango my outfit."

The screen went black and picked back up with Steve about to enter the office building. In the reflection from the glass doors, we could see he was dressed as a guy from a messenger service.

On the tenth floor he got out and walked to the door of the law firm.

He opened the door, and there were several people in the waiting area. They looked like regular folks, and I was sure each had a tale of woe that they hoped Clark LeSuer, Esquire, could rectify.

Steve nodded to the group and pretended to take in the charm of the foyer while he panned the camera for us. Nothing interesting so far.

"Can I help you?" a rough feminine voice called out.

Steve jumped, or at least pretended to be startled. He turned and revealed the speaker was a no-nonsense-looking woman with dark eyes and a steel-gray short haircut. "Yeah, sorry," he said. "Pickup for Davidson?"

"Who?"

"Davidson, like Harley-Davidson?" Steve stepped forward, and the camera gave us glimpses of rooms in back and a long wooden conference table. I noted one security camera by the ceiling and a computer terminal on the reception desk that the woman hovered over.

"Nope," she said. "No pickups at all this morning."

"Are you sure?" Steve leaned forward and extended a pointer finger to the computer screen. "Can you check?"

"Don't touch that," she snapped.

I thought I heard Rollie chuckle.

"Sorry, I . . ." Steve stammered.

"Do I *look* like I'm not sure? I run this office, and I'd know if we had a pickup." She had a good glare. "Are you sure *you* didn't make a mistake?"

"Mr. Silverstein? Suite Eleven Sixty-Five?"

"You're on the *tenth* floor. Think that might just be the problem?" she said in tone so icy the Flyers could have skated on it.

"It sure might," he said. "Sorry." Steve beat a hasty retreat.

I turned off the video. "That's about it. Steve said he asked one of the coffee shop workers if he could reserve a table like that guy, and they shot him down. Said that was a special arrangement."

"The house looks tough," Rollie said. "So does the office. God knows I don't want to tangle with that dragon lady."

Everyone else nodded.

"Yup," I said. "I think we know where the smart play is. Tom, are you thinking what I'm thinking?"

Tom grinned. "The Good Samaritan?"

"Definitely," VP said. "I call point," she said, and looked at me like she was daring me to say something.

Perfect call. "You got it."

CHAPTER 6

Downtown Philadelphia, the next morning

I nursed a large coffee, my second, as I'd arrived at Bean There, Done That early to stake it out. Steve was out in the burbs keeping tabs on LeSuer's departure. We all got the sense we were dealing with a creature of habit, but it was always good to have some reassurance.

I'd gotten the text that said only *On the way* and figured we had about thirty minutes to set up. Plenty of time.

All the coffee had me wired, and I took the opportunity for a much-needed trip to the restroom. When I came out, the barista we'd watched from the video was shooing away customers and setting up the same table. I texted to the crew that we were on.

Not long after, VP strolled in wearing her trademark hoodie and blending in with the younger workers who weren't in business attire. It was about a fifty-fifty mix, so she'd be able to hide in plain sight.

Like most everyone else, I stared at my smartphone while we waited. VP was across the room, and we never acknowledged each other.

Eventually, LeSuer sauntered into the shop and set up at his reserved spot. He didn't appear to take any notice other than a casual look at the room and a more pointed glance toward the servers. The same barista came out from her station with the coffee and muffin ready without taking an order. A creature of habit, indeed.

I couldn't help but notice a slight head shake from VP when the guy made a show of his tip again. LeSuer turned his attention to his laptop as soon as she left.

VP caught my eye and pried the top off her coffee cup. I immediately texted: *Green*. When I got the response from the others, I took off my Phillies cap and wiped my forehead to signal her.

VP sauntered forward, with her head bopping like she was lost in some music. She weaved through the crowd and ended up near the table. She caught her foot on another guy's and stumbled forward, catching herself on the edge of LeSuer's table.

"Dude!" she cried as her coffee popped out of her hand and tipped over, spilling just past the computer but straight across the surface and into his lap like a brown mocha waterfall.

"Damnit!" LeSuer tried to scoot back but the wall had other ideas, and he just stood up, half bent over, trying in vain to avoid the deluge. Too late.

I was glad to note that he yelled in surprise and frustration, but not pain. VP had been careful not to scald her mark.

"Sorry. Are you okay?" She kept her head down so it was hard to see her face at all.

"Idiot!" LeSuer pulled most of the napkins out of a holder and began to blot his ruined pants.

"I tripped, man. Are you hurt?"

"I'm fine, my suit isn't. At least you didn't get my computer." He grabbed another wad of napkins.

"Yeah, I did." VP snatched the laptop off the table and snapped it closed. "Yoink!" She pivoted and bolted for the door.

LeSuer moved faster than I expected. He made it around the table and shoved a confused kid in a suit out of his way. VP reached the door and slid through just as LeSuer sprinted across the room now that the commotion had cleared a lane. He flew through the open door just as another person was trying to enter and what followed was a smack that sounded like a good open-field tackle. Except the two bodies hit the sidewalk, and I could hear the cry of pain from across the room.

"My ribs!"

I joined the rest of the customers in the doorway and muscled my way to get a better view.

An old man in a baggy, worn suit lay sprawled on the sidewalk. His thick glasses were askew, and his gray hair would be turning white soon. Despite the cries of pain, somehow, he had a firm grip on LeSuer's jacket.

"Help me," the geezer groaned.

"I can't." LeSuer craned his neck to get a better view of VP racing down the block.

A young man ran up. "I saw what happened! Stay with him, I'll get your stuff back." With that, the short young lad sprinted off to chase VP around the next corner.

"Hard . . . to . . . breathe." The old guy was struggling to get air.

"I didn't see him," LeSuer said to the crowd, or maybe himself. "Stay down, sir."

Someone in the crowd shouted, "Call an ambulance!"

"I think he's okay," I said, and like magic, the guy sat up.

"That's better," he said. "You knocked the wind out of me, son. What the hell were you thinking?"

"Some kid ripped me off and I was just . . ."

"You were just about to get sued back to the stone age if you'd really hurt me." The old guy sounded stronger every minute.

I kept my eyes and ears tuned for the sound of an approaching siren of an ambulance nobody needed.

LeSuer stood up, and I thought it looked like he might have gotten the worst of the exchange. "Can you get up?"

The old guy rose to his feet without any assistance and took a couple deep breaths. "I'll live. I used to be a football coach. Decent tackle, but don't forget to wrap up with your arms next time." He began to dust off his battered clothing.

LeSuer looked relieved, probably because he wasn't going to be sued after all.

"Yo!"

We all turned and stared down the block. The short guy had rounded the corner with the laptop held high and a huge grin on his face. He jogged back. "Here you go. It got a little scraped when the thief dropped it. I hope it still works."

LeSuer took the laptop. He turned it on and watched it boot up. He grinned. "It's fine. I can't thank you enough." He reached for his wallet and gestured to the old man. "Both of you, let me give you something to thank you and apologize to you."

The old guy waved it off. "No harm, no foul. Good job, kid. You ever play ball?"

"Only soccer."

"Wrong football. I better go, the guys at the American Legion won't believe my morning." The guy walked away, nodding and reassuring the remaining onlookers. He stepped on my foot, but I didn't say anything.

LeSuer pulled out a hundred-dollar bill and extended it to the young guy. "Really. Please take it."

The guy hesitated. "It goes against my religion, but if it makes you feel better, it was nothing." The cash disappeared in his grip.

"I'm Clark LeSuer. And you are?"

The guy shook his hand. "In the right place at the right time. Rather not give out my name." Then I heard him whisper, "No green card." He jogged back down the block.

LeSuer stared after him, and I took the opportunity to stroll away as well.

* * *

Kyle's place, an hour later

We all met back at my place.

"Guys, that might have been one of the cleanest operations we ever ran," I said when the brain trust had assembled inside.

"Considering none of us were shot or slashed, it's an improvement," Rollie said. His hair was still covered in the gray-going-silver theatrical spray. He looked like the old geezer still, but he moved like a younger, fit version. About right.

"You sure you're okay?" Tom asked him. "That was a cracking good hit you took."

"I'm just fine, sonny. I know how to take a shot. I'm just glad he bought it."

"I hope he bought it all, or this was just a good-looking exercise." I turned to VP, who'd already tucked into her first taco. I'd stopped off to pick up celebratory Triumph Tacos, not to be confused with the Planning Pizza from the other night. "How long until you know if it worked?"

"Depends. If he's paranoid and runs a bunch of spyware scans, my program will go dark until the coast is clear."

"But it *is* spyware, isn't it?" Tom asked.

"Do you think all tea is the same?"

Tom smirked at her.

"There you go," she said. "I make the finest chameleon-style spyware in the game. My own custom blend, if you will." She took a big bite and finished her taco. "If I worked at that food joint, I'd be five hundred pounds. These things rock."

"But you were saying?" I asked.

"Yeah, the program loaded, no sweat. That was fun."

"It's really a blast when they're trying to kill you," Rollie said.

Tom nodded in faux agreement. We all knew better.

"Anyway," she said, "the ghost is in the machine. I designed it to hide from scans, but if it is doing that, it can't phone home. I better get back and monitor." She washed up.

"What's next?" I asked her.

"Once I get in and can poke around without fear of detection, I'll figure out what this guy has been doing."

"What if the old man was wrong?" Rollie asked. "What if the lawyer is just incompetent?"

"Mate, did you see that house?" Tom asked. "You don't get a wee cottage like that if you're not good at your job."

"I bet it'll be like the old Mae West line: 'Goodness had nothing to do with it,'" I said. "But if that's the case and the guy's legit, we leave him alone and break it to Mr. Penney."

"We should know soon enough," VP said. She moved toward the back door. "Gents, always a pleasure."

CHAPTER 7

Philadelphia Port, Global Imported Crafts

The next morning, Tom and I drove over to the port so he could make sure the latest shipments coming out of Customs were as expected. I wasn't concerned because my old boss Cliff always ran a tight ship, no pun intended. I tried to stay out of their hair as much as possible.

Cliff knew I had lots of "independent projects" (his words), but as long as he didn't have to get involved and they weren't going on at the port, what he didn't know wouldn't hurt him. Fair enough. Our investor Ali wanted a legit operation, so I didn't have to fight off any pressure from Ohio.

"Should make for a dull morning," Tom said cheerfully, "but that's what pays the bill, doesn't it?"

I parked the truck and stepped out. "I'll see what I can do to keep you entertained," I said, then drew up straight as the hackles on the back of my neck stood up. I pivoted to face the street.

I learned long ago never to ignore my instincts.

There were cars parked along the side of the street, but down here it wasn't congested like it was in the main city. I saw sedan and trucks, most likely belonging to dockworkers and assorted waterfront businesses. A van and a couple cars had tinted windows, preventing me from seeing inside. It had never bothered me before, but it sure was now.

"All right, mate?" Tom had been watching me and looked across the street. He was alive a dozen times over because he never ignored his instincts either.

"I guess so." I scanned the row of vehicles. One of the blacked-out ones, a white sedan, had the engine running. The exhaust curled around the back fender and vanished into the morning air. When I took a step toward it, it pulled away from the curb. It didn't roar off—there wasn't any dramatic screech of tires—it just drove away.

I was fifty feet away, maybe more. It could have been anyone. "It's nothing," I said.

Tom's expression told me he didn't believe me. I wasn't sure I did, either, because as soon as that car had pulled out of sight, my hackles lowered.

"I'm getting jumpy in my old age." I smiled.

"Being jumpy is why I'm going to *be* old. Someday," Tom said. "You know that car?"

"Never seen it before," I said. "Or I see it all the time, but no it doesn't mean anything special to me." I shrugged, the feeling gone like vapor from the tailpipe.

* * *

"So that's pretty much everything," Cliff said. "Whenever you're ready, we'll walk across the street and you can inspect the latest containers off the boat. The last one cleared Customs yesterday afternoon."

"How long before they can go on the trucks?" Tom asked.

"If we hustle, as early as this afternoon. If you need the whole shipment right away, I can call in some extra help; otherwise, we ought to be able to get it all to Ohio in less than a week."

"No need for an all-hands-on-deck," Tom said. "I thought I might catch a lift with one of the drivers, since he's going that way. I can return my rental car here."

I tuned out the rest of the routine shoptalk. It didn't sound like anything that needed me to get involved.

"Hi, Kyle!" This was Beet, coming out of a breakroom. He was dressed in Global Imported Crafts coveralls, and by the looks of them, he'd been doing cleaning.

"Hey, Beet, did you just hold a handle and have one of the guys push you around the floor like a broom?"

"Ha, ha," he said. "We're clearing out some of the leftover cargo containers. They're pretty dirty." I'd feel bad for giving him such crappy duty, but he seemed thrilled to be doing helpful projects others avoided.

"Say, Beet. You haven't seen anything odd around here lately, have you?"

"Nope, just me!" He laughed. "That was a joke."

"And a good one," I said. "No, I mean outside the property, like on the street. Maybe strange cars?"

"You're worried?" Beet had a tendency to pick up moods from others like a sponge.

"Nah, it's fine. I'm just being careful, you know?" If *I* didn't know what I meant, how the hell would he?

"You always say you can't be too careful. Want me to keep an eye out?"

"That'd be perfect."

"Which one?" He winked at me.

* * *

Strawberry Mansion, Philadelphia

I'd left Tom at the port to finish up and was now headed to a run-down section of the Strawberry Mansion neighborhood. I was meeting Rollie before noon to help him fix an oil furnace in one of the houses that I guess you could say I partly owned. The irony that I'd come into the properties after driving off the slumlord owner wasn't lost on me. The row homes were packed with people from multiple families, and both the houses and the residents were pretty beat down. I knew better than to think that we could solve all their problems, but they at least deserved to have the heat, water, and electricity in working order.

The manager of the properties, Franklin Smith, had worked for the prior owner. Franklin was no saint, he even pulled a gun on me back then, but after the guy signed over the title to the places to Franklin (with me providing the financing), we got along just fine.

Rollie pitched in with maintenance, and I helped out when I could. The sweat equity helped to lower costs, but even so, I hadn't stumbled on some magic ethical way to make money on low-income housing with top-level amenities. I tried to find other opportunities for the families to branch out and avoid overcrowding. That didn't always work out, but sometimes I did manage to find work for people. For others, I was able to chip in a bit to make rents more affordable. Those situations built a hefty reserve of favors, and I quickly developed a nice underground network on tap. Of course, sometimes people just trashed wherever they went, and I wasn't shy about having Franklin toss them out.

The previous slumlord had skirted all those pesky laws by paying off the corrupt inspector assigned to the area. We fixed most of the code violations, but when the same guy tried to put the squeeze on, we gave him a choice: work with us at a reduced rate, or enjoy the exposé we'd prepared for a reporter friend, which would've ensured his firing and probably some jail time. He wasn't dumb.

I saw Rollie's car out front. On the outside, the Blue Bomber looked like a powder-blue Oldsmobile Delta 88, the kind a grandmother might drive. Total camouflage. Under the hood, Rollie had dropped in a crate motor with upwards of six hundred horsepower. He knew how to drive it, even though my life tended to flash before my eyes whenever he took me for a ride and decided to "blow the carbon out."

I parked the truck behind him. Several members of the Lopez family greeted me on the front stoop, and I knew our vehicles were safe from mischief. The places stood out, with fresh coats of paint and unbroken, functional windows.

Rosa Lopez, the matriarch of the place, gave me a big hug. After we'd chit-chatted for a minute, she nodded at the front door. "Señor Rollie is downstairs."

Inside, the furniture was ratty and I could smell the last few days of cooking, but the smoke detector we'd added hadn't been ripped down again and the wall outlets all had cover plates.

I went down to the basement, a spare but functional space. The hot-water heater worked, and there was no longer a rusty puddle underneath the unit.

"Your timing's impeccable, kid." Rollie peeked up from the back of the oil furnace, soot smudging his face like warpaint. "I'm almost finished."

"I can come back in a few minutes," I joked.

We installed a fresh burner and then confirmed everything worked.

We said goodbye to each other, and I ignored the scowling teenager who peered down from the top of the steps. He knew I'd okayed Franklin to read him the riot act about breaking stuff and impress upon him the fact that the things we'd made right were on them to maintain or they'd have to leave. I assumed his mother took care of the rest.

Once we finished fixing everything, and had renters who paid on time (more or less), I hoped to transition everything over to Franklin eventually. For now, we were making a bad situation better and for the residents, far preferable to getting the places condemned.

* * *

Kyle's place

VP called in the early afternoon. That she gave me no information over the phone told me that she had plenty to deliver in person. I asked her if we'd want the entire group, and she said no.

The backyard motion buzzer alerted so soon after her call that I wondered if she'd been around the corner. I went to the door off the kitchen and looked out only to see no one.

We'd installed hidden cameras to cover the front and rear entrances. I stepped over to the bat cave, flipped on a monitor, and rewound the last five minutes of recorded footage to see what had tripped it. If the system was faulty, I wanted to know. If not, what the hell set it off?

I scrolled through and slowed the replay when it got close to the time log of the alert.

Ah. Henry was early, that was all. The orange tabby from up the block normally patrolled at dusk or sometimes would pop over the fence to say hello when we were in the yard, if he was in the mood.

I relaxed, not realizing until that moment how tense my shoulders had been. I also stopped thinking about making sure the shotgun stored in the hidden compartment was still in there and loaded.

I waited for VP in the cave, just to make certain the system picked her up.

She slipped through the back gate and across the yard a short while later. I couldn't see her face. She had a knack for avoiding cameras, even when she hadn't been the one to install them. But she moved like no one else.

I met her at the door. "Thanks for making the trip."

"All good. May I?"

I nodded and she hit the fridge.

"So whatcha got?" I said once we were settled.

She pulled some folders from her backpack. "This guy's really paranoid and takes his security seriously."

"That doesn't sound good," I said, except VP had that cocky, crooked grin on her face that gave me hope.

"To most amateurs it would be the proverbial brick wall." She arranged her folders in a fan on the dining room table. "But in this case, his arrogance was my edge."

"Explain." Like I could have stopped her.

"His malware and antivirus are so good, he's overconfident. Once I figured it out, I was able to exploit a weakness and slip past. Then I raided his passcodes and kicked the door wide open."

"Nice."

I let her go on for a bit, like I knew exactly what it all meant. I got the important gist. Let her have her fun.

"Yeah," she said, winding up. "I tricked his machine into backing itself up right onto my system and swept up after, leaving nothing more than a common, detectable phishing login attempt. Now if he looks, he'll think his super-duper protection staved off a raid on his castle."

"Why not leave no trace at all?"

"Usually I do just that, only I can tell that if this guy gets a hint something is going on, he's going to look. Remember, he might have other enemies. So, if he believes an attack occurred, why not let him see a failed attempt so he can rest easy?"

"Are you a hacker or a psychologist?"

She shrugged. "It's a multidisciplinary art."

"Are we on to something or not?"

"This guy is a class A scumbag. And he's pulling the same trick on at least three other people besides the old man that I can see."

"Ballsy. Can you prove it?" I said, knowing the answer very well.

"No, it's just a vague feeling I have. That's why I trekked all the way across town."

"Lay it on me, then."

"All right." She took a few pages from one of the folders. "This is a PDF of a document from the Penneys."

I skimmed all the legalese and saw the part about annual payments from the insurance company for fifty grand. Clarence and his wife had signed the bottom. "Looks like the agreement he described to us."

"That's it." She slid another document across the table. "Now take a look at this one."

I felt my eyes wanting to glaze over at more legal jargon, then spotted the words "lump sum" and flipped the page over. "Wait, what? Does this say a payout of *two million?*"

"It does. Check out the bottom."

I saw where she was going with this. As expected, there were signatures by the Penneys. I took the bottom sheet of the first agreement and compared the two. "I'll be damned." The signatures were similar. Similar, but I spotted distinct differences. "One of these is forged."

"Want to guess which one?" VP asked. "In the next folder, you'll see the bank and investment accounts, along with the balances."

"That's a lot of zeros."

"And those zeros rightfully belong to the Penneys and the others like them," VP said.

"This prick was hoarding the lump sums of the settlements, investing them and doling out pittances to the victims." I shook my head.

"Yup. And all the while, the poor victims had no idea that the companies settling weren't the hard-asses LeSuer made them out to be."

"The interest alone . . ." I marveled at the brass of this guy.

"The returns from the investments more than cover the cost of the payouts." VP nodded. "Not only that, but LeSuer hit them with a management fee along with his billable hours."

My eyes went back to the financial statements. "Do you think you could work your magic and 'reinvest' these funds in a more appropriate place?"

"That's the bad news. He's got layers of authentication on those accounts and even small amounts would be scrutinized. That goes double from his portfolio accounts."

"Well, I'm sure we could reason with the guy, and . . ." I couldn't get it out with a straight face. "Seriously, what else have you got?"

"Remember when you said Mr. Penney tried to take his suspicions to the authorities?"

"Yeah, the Disciplinary Board of Pennsylvania. He had the guy's card. A Mr. Mahoney, I think."

"That's him. I looked and it seems LeSuer and Mahoney know each other well. A deeper peek revealed that Mahoney serves on some boards where our boy has been rather generous."

"What a coincidence. Now, don't get snippy, but you can prove that?"

"Once you know what to look for, the picture is clear enough," she said. "But I get you. Just remember I didn't exactly get my evidence, you know, legally."

My mind was spinning with possibilities. "Don't worry about that. As long as you're sure of the information, I can work around that."

"How?"

"Not yet. I need to get with some people," I said. "I think it's time to cash in some favors. I might pick up a few before we're done."

"Ooh, so mysterious." She smiled at me.

"You're pretty sure LeSuer doesn't know he's been breached?"

"Like I said, if he looks, all he'll get is a report of a routine phishing attempt. I haven't moved anything, just copied data."

"Great. Keep watching him, but don't do anything else that could tip him off."

"Will do. We've got the guy cold on the forgeries. Just make certain that, no matter what, my name stays out of it, but yeah, I can get the info."

"Whatever you say, 'Source.'"

Chapter 8

Downtown Philadelphia, Bellevue Building

I tried without luck to stretch the neck of my dress shirt. The buttoned collar and striped silk tie felt like a noose around my neck. That, and despite the cool outdoor temperatures, I was roasting inside the suit jacket.

Sandy had helped me knot the tie. According to her, I looked great, but I tended to dress up for weddings and funerals and not much in between. The suit, nice as it was (another favor collected from a cash-crunched tailor) might as well have been a disguise; it felt so out of place on me.

That said, my suit was the inescapable camouflage-de-jour for today's meeting. The building, perhaps a half-dozen blocks from LeSuer's office, housed legal offices, including one occupied by one of the senior members of the Philadelphia prosecutor's office. This was where he worked when he was interested in more discretion than his taxpayer-funded digs around the corner could provide. Some of the place was still a posh hotel, and the dressy clothes made me feel less conspicuous in the ornate gold and marble lobby while I'd waited for the elevator.

Once inside the office, I took a seat in the waiting area. I was the only one there, not, I suspect, an accident.

"Mr. Logan?" the receptionist called to me. "Mr. Whitman will see you now." She held the door open.

"Kyle, great to see you." The tall, unnaturally tanned figure of Larry Whitman filled the door, and he shook my hand and clapped me on the back like we were old college roommates or something.

I'd only been here once before, and never to the man's official office. Just as well.

Whitman led me to a small conference room, empty save for a couple glasses of water that sat on coasters. "Have a seat."

I put my briefcase on the floor and sank into a luxuriantly padded leather swivel chair. Another little touch that reminded visitors of the money and power the place represented.

Whitman closed the door and held up a finger to ask for my silence. The buddy demeanor vanished with the click of the lock. He stepped over to a glass bar but instead of reaching for the amber tumbler to pour a drink, he pressed a few hidden switches and the room filled with a waterfall sound.

Besides making me wish I'd gone to the bathroom first, I knew he'd turned on the white noise to ensure our discussion remained private.

"Alone at last." Whitman took the seat next to mine and spoke in a low voice. "I agreed to meet you because, as you reminded me, I owe you one. No promises, but I'll help if I can. What do you need?"

I smiled. "The first part is easy. I need you to hear me out on an idea. That's it."

"Just listen, that's the favor? Must be a hell of an idea."

I could see his suspicion. Ryan had taught me well. We didn't throw around the word "favor" lightly. It was our currency, word, and bond.

I took out several folders. "You listen to my pitch and you can decide from there if you want to act on it. But if you do, when it's all over, you may owe me one again. Maybe even two."

"Fine opener," he said. "I'm all ears."

* * *

Downtown Philadelphia, three days later

None of us wanted to trek all the way out to Harrisburg where the main office for the Disciplinary Board was headquartered. Instead, we chose Philadelphia to pull our "intervention," where the mark worked his regular day job representing clients in another office building infested with law firms that fed off the activities in and around City Hall.

A little basic research revealed when Mahoney would be in the private office and Starving Steve videoed the pudgy guy on the way to his car. It was easy to tail him on his way out of the city, and we already knew where he lived.

Rollie sat next to me while I maintained a short distance through the evening rush hour traffic. I was in a nondescript Toyota on loan from one of my borrowers. I had a nice list of cars on tap when I wanted a bit more discretion.

"He should be turning soon if he's going for the Ben Franklin Bridge," Rollie said.

"Yup," I said. "Get on the horn to Bishop. He knows which vehicle?"

"He does."

Bishop, more of a colleague than a team member, had jumped at the chance for a little fieldwork. A corrupt Pennsylvania state trooper long relegated to the property room, he tipped off the Irish with inside info and sometimes did them favors. Nothing heavy, as far as I knew. He'd also helped Ryan line up a caper or two, including the fiasco I'd been dumb enough to work on. I got the sense he was bored.

"Good to go," Rollie said into the phone.

A minute later a Philadelphia Police SUV pulled in front of us and followed Mahoney's car. After a block, the lightbar exploded with strobes and flashes. The siren yipped, and at first, Mahoney signaled to pull out of the way. Bishop followed suit and parked right behind him. We pulled just ahead and left our car halfway on the sidewalk.

When Bishop got out of the SUV, I noticed he was wearing a city police uniform. Since he was still with the State Police, maybe technically he wasn't impersonating a cop, though I didn't think his commanding officer would see it that way. Whoever loaned him his duds must have been a hefty guy, as Bishop had packed on more than his fair share of "desk pounds" over the years.

He kept his hat low and approached the side of Mahoney's car like a seasoned traffic cop. While Mahoney was distracted and confused, Rollie and I pulled on fluorescent yellow safety vests with black "PENNDOT" stenciled on the back, put on yellow hardhats, and emerged from the car.

Mahoney's expression morphed from surprise to officious and indignant as he tried to school Bishop on just who he was dealing with. I couldn't make out the whole conversation but knew that Mahoney had been pulled over for a busted taillight.

That had been a nice touch by Steve. The boy showed real potential.

After he had returned to Mahoney with his driver's license and registration, Bishop invited him to step out of the car to see for himself.

Already turning a nice shade of red, Mahoney joined him at his back bumper.

"That must have just happened," he said.

"We pride ourselves on being observant," Bishop said.

Seeing his cue, Rollie stepped off the sidewalk and opened Mahoney's driver's side door. Giving me a tiny nod to let me know that the guy had left the car running, he announced, "Can't park here, sir."

Mahoney's head swiveled. "What, now? What are you—"

"That's a hazardous waste spill. I'll have to get that washed off for you, sir," Rollie said, and I stepped up to block Mahoney.

To the untrained eye, it looked like a simple water puddle that Mahoney had parked in.

"A what? Hey, get out of my car. Officer, he's taking it!"

Quick as a carjacker, Rollie had the guy's ride on the move and around the corner.

Bishop didn't act surprised. Instead, he addressed me. "I'm not done here. Where's he going?"

"The Salt Barn. Not far, we have cleaning supplies. You know it?"

"Yeah," Bishop said.

"What the hell is this?" Mahoney's neck jiggled as his head whipped back and forth between Bishop and the wet tracks where his car had been.

"Officer," I said, "can you follow him and we can all finish up there?"

"Get in, both of you," Bishop said. "You're lucky it's close; I get paid by the ticket." Dammit, if he made me laugh and blow this, I was going to be pissed.

"This is an outrage," Mahoney said. "I am a . . ." He proceeded to tell us what we already knew about his bona fides. At least he did it from inside the police SUV while we worked around traffic.

I tried to tell Mahoney about how we'd make sure his tires would be good as new but all he wanted to know were things like ID and badge numbers. He was way out of his comfort zone and trying to cling to a shred of authority. It was kind of cute.

We reached a place in southwest Philadelphia where we pulled into a lot leading to a large corrugated metal storage building. Winter was a long time away, and we had the place to ourselves. Rollie was already there, flinging mounds of rock salt at the bottoms of the tires of Mahoney's car.

"I've never seen anything like this," Mahoney sputtered.

"I've got good news, sir." Bishop turned around in his seat and handed over the license and reg card. "I think we can let this go with a verbal warning."

For the first time, I got a look at the nameplate on the uniform. "Fife."

Now I saw real fear on Mahoney's face. He wasn't dumb. "What do you people really want? I don't have much cash on me, but if you take me to an ATM and let me go, I can—"

Right on cue, a black SUV pulled into the lot.

"We aren't thieves, Mr. Mahoney," I said. "But we do know you've been taking payments to turn a blind eye to your responsibilities with the Disciplinary Board."

He blinked at me. "What are you talking about?"

"Since you asked." I took a notecard from my shirt pocket and began to read off names, dates and specific dollar amounts. He looked like he was going to pass out. When I finished, I looked up at him. "Are you going to tell me I picked all that out of the air?"

"What do you want?" He looked like a wilted dumpling.

"You need to talk to that man in the scary black SUV. We're helping him, and he wants to give you a shot at helping yourself." I pointed at the SUV and the door opened. Whitman sat stone-faced and gestured for Mahoney to get in.

* * *

"So now what?" Bishop drove Rollie and me back to our car.

"Mahoney made the smart call by getting in Whitman's vehicle," I said. "Right now, he's seeing concrete evidence that he took bribes to look the other way, just like I cited, only he'll see we have the actual bank accounts and everything."

"Wish I could see his face," Rollie said.

"Me too. I'm sure he's terribly confused, especially at how Whitman knows so much and in such detail."

"He'll think someone turned on him."

"I'm counting on it," I said. "Whitman doesn't want Mahoney, but you can bet if he doesn't roll over and give up LeSuer, Whitman will be happy to nail him to the wall."

"So, what's the game plan?" Bishop asked.

When we weren't working on a project together, we tended to stay out of each other's way. This time he'd stuck his neck out for us and come up big. I knew we needed to be quick because he had no good reason to be tooling around in a real Philly police vehicle.

"Mahoney deserves whatever he gets, but from a business perspective I couldn't care less what happens to him. We want the guy bribing him. LeSuer." I gave Bishop a brief recap of what LeSuer had done to Penney and other clients.

"I get it," Bishop said. "So, you're going to use Mahoney as a springboard for Whitman to get a search warrant on LeSuer. Nice."

"Who, me? I'm just a humble PennDot guy. But I can imagine that Whitman may be feeling a little more comfortable getting a warrant for a computer that he has every reason to expect will hold incriminating evidence."

"And once he has that evidence, a conviction would be a slam dunk."

"I should think so. A plea bargain is just as good, for our purposes."

"Very slick," Bishop said. "You're getting good at this."

"We'll see how it plays out." We'd reached our car. "You need any help returning your 'rental'?"

"Got it covered. It was fun," Bishop said. "Shall I send you a bill?"

"I'll put it on your account." I was about to follow Rollie out of the vehicle. "Hey, I just remembered something." I signaled Rollie to wait.

"What's up?"

I gave a fast rundown in broad terms what the Irish had asked me about. Bishop worked with them sometimes too, so this wasn't out of turn, and I had said that I'd put out feelers. Bishop was as tapped into the grapevine as I was. More so, in some areas.

"Have you heard anything?"

"I'd have to check with my city guys, but I haven't seen anything that jumps out," he said. "I'll ask around, subtle-like, but I haven't heard any special upticks in shots fired reports or cleaned crime scenes. I stay as far from that side of the Irish street as you do," he added, referring to the drug and more violent aspects of their business dealings.

"Yeah. You've known them longer, but I gotta think it takes a lot to scare the O'Briens."

Bishop nodded. "Never seen it. I'll get out from the property room and ask around. Whatever it might be could bite us, too, and I don't like surprises either."

CHAPTER 9

Old City, Philadelphia

I sat in Sandy's small office inside her new place. Late afternoon sun splashed across her desk. Today there were two assistants working, and I waited for Sandy to finish with another client.

Sandy gave me a hug and smooch once she was done. "Hi, sweetie." She closed the door and spoke in a soft voice. "Do you have news?"

I had to be extremely careful here. I trusted Sandy, but she already knew more than I might have preferred. All that time around lawyers and prosecutors had made me keenly aware of avoiding putting her in any legal jeopardy. So far all she'd done was introduce me to Mr. Penney, but we couldn't pretend that had been out of simple good manners.

"I suspect you'll have a more complete picture soon enough if you watch the news. I recommend Channel 6." I smiled. "But I can't say when for sure."

"You're mean. C'mon." She was joking. But not entirely.

"Let's just say a big ball has started rolling down the hill, but I can't be sure when it'll reach the bottom." I hoped she'd accept that.

"Still not fair." She understood, but didn't like it.

It had to be this way. It was all fun and games until a person landed in a prosecutor's metaphorical crosshairs. Or someone else's real ones.

"You're going to see Penney later?" I asked.

"Yup. You sure you don't want to stick around to talk to him yourself?"

"Can't. But tell him a lot is going on right now behind the scenes and he's going to hear something soon. In the meantime, please make sure he keeps his appointments with you, and"—I took out an envelope thick with cash—"give him this. Let him know that is to tide him over in case his payments are interrupted for any reason." I saw a shadow cross Sandy's face that hurt my heart. "Nothing like that. I promised you, didn't I?"

She took the cash and nodded. "Are you sure Clarence will accept it?"

"Tell him it's like a bridge loan, and the reason I'm offering it is that I'm that positive he won't need it soon." I realized I hardly knew the man. "But if he doesn't, you hang on to it in case he changes his mind."

"Nope. If he doesn't want it, I'll bring it to you and we'll have a nice dinner and you can tell me all about it."

"Okay, you win."

That seemed to satisfy her for the moment. At least I'd have time to come up with a sanitized version that would still protect her.

We stuck to mundane chatter the rest of my visit, which is fine with me. I was only too happy to put whatever chill had just passed between us in the rearview mirror. Maybe she was right though. At some point I'd either have to move on, which I didn't want to do, or give her a chance to be a bigger part of what I did. But that might chase her away.

* * *

On my way back to my truck one of my burners vibrated in my pocket. Left side, which meant it must be VP. "Hey, what's up?"

"Yo. I'm not sure. But I was bored and checking the feeds from your outside system."

"You got a hit?"

"No, the property is okay. It's just . . ." I could hear uncertainty in her voice.

"I trust your instincts." I stopped walking and cupped my good ear to make sure I could catch everything she said.

"There's this car parked across the street. A silver Hyundai with smoked windows. Nothing weird, but the driver hasn't gotten out. The engine is off, but whoever is in there is just sitting."

"You watched long enough to notice that? What else did it do?"

"Actually, I rolled the backup tape, and I can see the person park. The tailpipe stops smoking, but nobody gets out."

"Phone call?"

"Doubt it, and do you really think some rando is sitting there playing Words with Friends?"

"It's probably nothing," I said, but my gut said otherwise.

"Steve'll be here in ten minutes with a cam cap, to get the plate. Want me to call him off?" She'd been bothered enough to reach out to him.

"I'm sure it has nothing to do with me."

"That's not a 'yes,'" she pointed out.

"Tell him to go ahead. Roll by and get a plate number. That's all. No direct contact."

"Can do. Good practice, if nothing else. I'll run the tag and let you know if anything funky comes up." She hung up.

An outsider might think a resource like Bishop, being with the State Police, would be the one to run tags, but that was wrong. First, Bishop was cranky on a good day, and second, he'd point out that as a cop he needed to log in before using the database. A guy assigned to the property room outside the city might have a hard time explaining frequent tag searches. VP, on the other hand, had backdoors on the system and could sweep up after she made the request so the system wouldn't even record that the search had been made. Plus, she did that sort of thing for fun. If Bishop did it, I'd owe him and he'd never let me forget.

Just as I reached my truck, a burner phone on my right side buzzed. Sandy had been known to make utility belt jokes with all the gear I carried at times. "When it rains, it pours," I muttered and looked at the ID. It was Beet.

My brows knitted as I got in the truck and closed the door. He rarely called.

"Beet? What's up?"

"How did you know?"

Sometimes I forgot to slow down when speaking with him. "The caller ID. It's—"

"No, no, no. Remember you told me to keep an eye out?"

"Yeah. Did you see something?" His voice was strange. "What's wrong?"

"Not something. Someone. Milosh is back." Beet's voice quavered.

My head spun as if the parked truck had rolled into a ditch at high speed. "Milosh? Are you sure?"

"He was in a car near the front gate of the port. He rolled down the window and looked right at me."

Beet had his quirks but he'd never lie, and I knew he'd never forget the face of the goon who'd beat the hell out of him several times to collect a minor debt.

"Did he say anything? He's not still there, is he?" I debated warning Cliff.

"No, he just waved and then he threw a coffee mug at me and drove away."

"A mug?"

"Yeah, one of the old ones from Cream of the Cup. He missed, but I cleaned up the pieces when it hit the street and broke. You can still see the funny cow."

I could picture the old coffee shop's dark blue ceramic mug with the stoned cow décor. That Albanian prick had run the loansharking business out of there before we chased him out of town. Temporarily, it seemed.

All of a sudden, a lot of things made sense, but that raised even more questions.

"You're sure you're okay?"

"Yes. But . . ." Beet started to breathe faster.

"What?"

"You're not going to make me work for him again, are you?"

* * *

As soon as I made sure Beet would wait inside the port facility, I called Steve. I thought it would roll over to voice mail but he picked up.

"Is everything all right?" I asked him.

"Sure, why wouldn't it be?" He sounded surprised, which was a good sign.

"Where are you now?"

"On my way home from the drive-by. You'll have to give me a few minutes before I can upload the video to VP."

"You saw the silver car?"

"Saw it, taped it. They took off as soon as I showed up, even though I swear I hardly slowed down while I rolled by. Sorry, but I must have spooked them."

"Listen, be very careful going home. Make sure you aren't being tailed."

"Really? If I'd known it was going to be that hot, I would have made a different approach." I don't know if Steve intended it as a rebuke, but I heard one anyway.

"Sorry, I just got some breaking news not five minutes ago. I'll have to fill you in later. Just promise you'll be super careful getting home. We're dealing with multiple vehicles," I said as more questions than answers flooded my mind.

My next call was to VP, giving her the short version but making sure she understood to step up the monitoring and let me know if anything else strange popped up.

I called Rollie while I drove.

"You rang?" It didn't sound like anything was going wrong at his place.

"Guess who's back in town?"

"Your ex?"

"Much worse. Milosh. And I don't know how many of his Albanian pals."

"How do you know?" All levity had vanished from his voice.

I told him about Beet's encounter and the suspicious cars outside our places.

"That's a hell of a coincidence. And speaking of which . . ."

"I'm on my way to the bakery right now," I said in reference to the O'Briens' place.

"Want backup?" Rollie said.

"Thanks, but they might get jumpy if we show up in numbers. I don't have time to make an appointment."

"Be careful. Need me to let anyone else know?"

"VP knows," I said. "Call anyone else you think should hear."

"Okay. Want me to swing by Sandy's work?"

I didn't want to worry her, but at the same time, unlikely didn't mean impossible. "I'd really appreciate that, Rollie. Maybe low-key it though, huh?"

"Out of sight, out of mind," he said, "but never out of range."

CHAPTER 10

Fishtown, Heather Bakery

Despite the urgency, I forced myself to drive like an old lady the last block before the bakery. I even used my hazard flashers before I pulled into the "reserved" parking spot in front of the building.

I figured the familiar vehicle coupled with my familiar face would prevent me from getting shot, but some new people hanging around the corner had their hands on some hardware for certain. I got out and made sure my hands were in plain sight without looking like I was surrendering.

At the door, a big guy I didn't know blocked my way. "Where you think you're going?"

"I need to talk to them. If you don't know me, ask Red."

"Who's that?"

I could appreciate the guy's enthusiasm, but I didn't have time to play. I also couldn't shove him aside even if he wasn't packing.

"Hang on." Another big dude had emerged from a doorway. Him I recognized but couldn't come up with a name. "Might be okay, lemme check."

"Thanks. Tell them I'm—"

"I know who you are." He vanished inside.

* * *

Minutes later, the big guy who'd recognized me poked his head out the door. "He's good."

I noticed the place's windows had been soaped up, which made it impossible to see inside and even gloomier once I walked into the shop.

Red stepped into the room, his long, thin frame contrasting almost comically with all the wide-bodied hired muscle. Not that I was feeling a chuckle coming on. I saw more people in the shadows, and the back of my neck itched like it could sense the firepower in the darkness.

"Why are you here?" Red said. "Nobody sent for you." Not exactly welcoming, but at least he didn't look like he was about to kick me out.

"I know the rules. I wouldn't be here if it wasn't important. Tell them I may know who."

Red didn't budge, but I could see a question die on his lips when a second later a loud voice boomed from the shadows. "Why didn't you say so?" Charlie stepped forward, looking haggard and dangerous. "I got him." Gripping my arm, he waved Red away and yanked me toward the stairs.

Neither brother had ever met me down here before. Come to think of it, I don't think I'd ever seen either of them outside of their lair, though I knew they weren't hermits. We didn't exactly move in the same social circles.

I took the hint to keep my mouth shut until we got upstairs. Twice I needed to squeeze past well-armed hulks clogging the narrow hallway.

Charlie waved at the camera that looked down on the entrance to their suite of apartments. The locks buzzed open.

In better light, I saw the dark circles around Charlie's eyes. At first, I thought it was because he was drunk, but his eyes had a keen glint despite his exhausted demeanor.

William was inside waiting. I half-expected the usual pleasantries and offer of whiskey. Nope.

William wore a button-down shirt but no tie, and the lines around his eyes looked deeper than the last time I saw him. "Well? What have you heard?"

Those five words blew away the aura surrounding the Bros O'Brien always being two steps ahead of everyone.

"Albanians."

They stared at me. "Keep going," Charlie said.

"I never would have guessed until today," I said. "I know you remember Milosh. I wouldn't be working with you if not for him." I recapped Beet's sighting for them.

"You trust that kid?" Charlie asked.

"Want to see the shattered mug from the old shop that Milosh threw at him?" I asked. "He kicked the shit out of Beet a couple times, so, yeah,

I'd say he's sure. And another thing, the fact that Milosh used him to reveal that he's been sneaking around sends a powerful signal."

"Oh, I don't know," William said. "Chopping our couriers into pieces and stealing our merch is a fairly strong message in its own right, wouldn't you agree?" He hadn't raised his voice, but his words cut through the air.

"Nah." Charlie shook his head as if to clear it. "That mook didn't have the stones to do what's happening now."

"I know how it sounds at first," I said. The last thing I needed to do was piss them off right now, but they needed to hear me. "I'm with you: I figured with the show of force you came up with to drive him away before that we'd never see him again. But he and his people are Albanian. They run hot, and probably have long memories. What if he rounded up enough reinforcements to take another run at things?"

"Can't be him," Charlie said. "You forget, he came to us first and paid the franchise fee and everything. We checked him out."

William nodded. "We knew he was loosely connected to a New York Albanian group, but they wanted nothing to do with Philly or, we thought, with him."

"They're all some cousin or brother-in-law of somebody," Charlie said. "Half the time they're at each other's throats."

"He may have roughed up your friend," William said, "but you haven't seen what happened to our people."

"I agree, that doesn't sound like his style, even with that tank of a bodyguard. Maybe someone else is leading it? Between what I've been seeing and what your guys got dealt, that's a strange coincidence, don't you think?"

William nodded slowly. "I don't believe in coincidences," he allowed.

"Me neither," Charlie said.

I nodded. "I can be a slow learner, but today was too much. Why would he show himself to me?"

"He didn't," William pointed out. "He sent you a message, no doubt figuring you'd wind up here."

Charlie jumped up out of his worn green leather chair and lumbered to an adjacent office. I could see bluish light flicker across his shirt and face as he stared at a screen inside the room. Then I saw him pick up a phone. "Nothing?" A long pause. "You sure?" He ran his fingers through his hair with his free hand. "Tell everyone to be ready." His jaw clenched. "Then *more* ready, dammit!" Charlie shook his head and was about to say something else when the phone inside the room with us rang. He hurried back and snatched up the receiver. "What?"

William and I waited. Charlie cupped his hand over the mouthpiece and waved us over.

We all saw on the security monitor a small kid riding a bicycle in circles in the intersection. No cars, just a little guy looking terrified.

They both shot me a look, and I shrugged with my palms out. The kid looked to be no more than ten years old.

"Well, bring him over to the front," Charlie said into the phone. "See what he wants."

We watched the kid react to being called over, like he'd been waiting for it. Charlie switched camera feeds, and now we saw from inside the shop floor as the kid got off the bike and handed a note from his pocket to one of the guards.

"That's it? Just the paper?" Charlie paused. "Ask the kid who sent him." He scowled. "What do you mean he doesn't know?"

Another eternity while we waited.

"No, let him go, and don't read the thing to me, just bring it up." Charlie took a deep breath and turned to us. "The kid said some stranger showed him a picture of his mom and said if he didn't do this for him, he'd never see her again."

"Should we tail the kid?" William asked.

I pictured those goons running down the sidewalk and scaring the kid right into traffic. "I doubt he knows anything more. Besides, they would have thought of that."

It didn't take long for a guy to race upstairs with the note. When the door was closed again Willian motioned for me to sit.

The paper was folded and bore a wax seal to hold it closed. The other side said "O'Briens."

"Do you recognize the writing?" I asked.

"No," Charlie said.

William took it from Charlie and studied the seal. He held it up. A double eagle clutching arrows was embossed in the wax. It reminded me of the eagle on the United States seal. "I've seen this before," William said, handing it back to his brother. "I bet you have too. On a flag."

"Albania?" Charlie said.

"And they say *I'm* the smart one," William said. "So, let's see what's on their mind."

Charlie cracked the seal open, unfolded the paper, and squinted at it in the gloom. "It just says 'Parley?' and there's a phone number."

"No doubt to a burner phone," I said.

William opened a drawer and removed one from a stack of similar phones. "One good burn deserves another." He stood. "We'll take it from here, Kyle. Thank you, and I'm certain we will be in touch."

I couldn't leave quite yet. "Guys, I know the timing can't be an accident, but you don't think that I . . . ."

Charlie led me to the door, more like a friend than a bouncer, which I took as a good sign. "Milosh knew where we hang out already. He wouldn't need to follow you."

I hoped my face didn't betray my relief. "I still don't know why he picked me, and Beet, to make contact."

"Maybe he figured you wouldn't kill him on sight," Charlie said, and closed the door.

CHAPTER 11

Kyle's place, several days later

Whatever the O'Brien brothers worked out with the Albanians was their little secret. All I knew was that I wasn't part of it, thankfully. No more Milosh sightings, either, and Beet acted like he'd forgotten the other day when his old tormentor had appeared.

I was just as happy he'd been able to shake off the scare as I was to be left out of having to deal with the Albanians.

Better still, I'd gotten a call earlier in the day. It was on a burner phone, of course, and all I heard was a voice say, "Watch the 6:30 news on ABC tonight," and that was it. I'd recognized the voice, and it meant good news. I had a TV date tonight with Sandy.

She was bringing dinner with her, and I realized I better get cracking on cleaning up the place. I never let it look like a dump, but I knew the difference between bachelor tidy and girlfriend clean.

On one of my trips past the basement door I remembered to head down to the hidden bunker room with all the security equipment. I shut off the motion sensors, glad I'd thought of it now and not during dinner, when it might have been awkward to explain if Henry the cat cruised through the backyard and set off the buzzer. Sandy would expect a simple alarm, but VP's idea of secure might've drifted over to Sandy's notion of paranoid.

* * *

Sandy didn't need to knock, as I'd seen her coming up the steps. Good thing, too, as her arms were full of boxes, all bearing the logo of a local Italian place. "Good timing," she said as she stepped inside and kissed me.

I took the food and headed for the kitchen. "I sat at the window as soon as I hung up." I smiled. "Vesuvio's. Good call. What did you get?"

"Nothing fancy. I know you like the veal Parmesan, and I added salads and some of that great bread."

My mouth was already watering. Hardly news: the bathroom scale had already told me this morning that I liked to eat. "Perfect. What do I owe you?"

She waited for me to put the food on the counter and wrapped me up in a hug. "An explanation for the occasion, mystery man, and a bottle of wine to go with dinner."

"I saved a cat that climbed a tree and the local station got it all."

She punched me in the ribs.

I glanced at the clock. "Won't be long now. Let's eat. I think I have just the right wine."

I went downstairs to the corner of the basement I jokingly referred to as the wine cellar, and went to the box of better bottles, most of them coming from my guy Ross at the liquor store. Apparently, I'd always be stocked with good stuff as long as his sister was doing okay on the insurance-denied cancer meds I was able to get him.

I knew enough to grab a bottle of red. I glanced at the security closet as I hurried past. Closed like this, its door was all but invisible, a fun touch Rollie was particularly pleased with.

"A Petrus?" Sandy knew more about wine than I did.

"No good? I have other reds."

"I should have dressed up." She had on a simple yellow top over jeans.

"You look great."

"Where'd you get it? And don't tell me you bought it."

"Why? I didn't steal it." She knew I wasn't broke.

"Because this goes about a thousand bucks a bottle. At least. You'd remember."

I didn't bother to hide my surprise. Ross gave me great rare whiskey that I usually passed along to the O'Briens. That stuff was astronomically expensive, too, but so were the cancer meds. I'd figured the wines he's passed along were just decent extras. "You got me. Let's open it anyway. This is going to be a great night."

"All right, as long as you tell how you got it." She stared at me with a little smile that told me I might as well crack under questioning.

I nodded. "Let's get it open first," I said, and felt a weird relief. She knew some things around the edges, but lately I'd been tempted to open up more and more to her. So far, she hadn't run screaming into the night, but just because I had my own limits to this game didn't mean they weren't past her tolerances.

I took the opener out of a kitchen drawer. "Here goes nothing."

"Besides a grand." Sandy chuckled. "I hope it's not corked."

"You were expecting a twist top?"

She laughed. "You really are a beer guy. It means spoiled."

"I knew that," I said, fooling no one.

While we put out the food on the dining room table and let the wine breathe, I told Sandy about how Ross had come to me more than a year ago and practically begged me to fulfill Ryan's promise for meds. I'd thought the guy was some sort of junkie at first, but it was a pricey chemotherapy drug that had been working wonders for his special-needs sister until the insurance coverage stopped covering it for a cheaper (and ineffective) substitute.

"You remember when I told you how my mom needed medicine and got denied the same way?"

"When you were a kid," Sandy said.

"Yeah. Ryan fixed her up and wouldn't let us pay a dime for it. We weren't allowed to ask where he got it, but he promised it wasn't taking it away from someone who needed it."

"Did you believe him?"

The question stabbed into my heart. "Yeah. And in case you're wondering, I'm not either." It came out sharper than I intended.

"I didn't—"

I took her hand. "It's okay. You know it isn't legal, might as well hear the rest." I told her about Doc Crock and how he exploited his own network of underground medical contacts. Like me, he had his own limits and would have told me to cram it if it had been for narcotics.

Her face relaxed, like my words had blown away stray clouds of doubt.

"Let's eat," I said. "If that wine breathes any more, it's going to hyperventilate."

* * *

We ate, and the simple meal along with the crazy expensive wine was perfect. Sandy oohed and ahhed and punctuated sips of the red with words like "velvety" and "plums to die for." I wanted to say I agreed it was tasty, but I might have insulted the bottle.

As we finished up the food, I poured the last of the wine into her glass. "Enjoy, but I don't think I can do this every time."

Speaking of time, the news was about to start. I cleared the table and met her in the living room. Sandy patted the spot next to her on the couch. I enjoyed the feeling of her leaning against me.

We didn't have to wait long. Right after the opening, they jumped right in to the top story. They plastered a huge graphic across the screen with "Exclusive! Prominent Attorney Arrested!"

The shot switched to a blonde reporter standing outside a familiar-looking building. "Good evening, I'm Susan Rainsford. Today members of the city's Office of the District Attorney along with the city police served multiple arrest warrants following indictments to a prominent local attorney."

"No way," Sandy said.

"Shh. Just watch," I said.

The reporter voiced over footage of a man being marched in handcuffs out of the entrance of the building. The raincoat he'd put over his head, like a costly tarp, did nothing but make him look guilty.

"Self-proclaimed Tort King, Clark LeSuer, seen here being escorted from his lavish office in downtown Philadelphia, had no comment, but our source inside the DA's office tells me that he has been indicted on numerous counts of fraud."

After LeSuer was placed in the waiting police car, the news showed a full screen shot of a smug headshot of the man and his name splashed under the picture in huge letters.

"I'm told the fraud is in connection with several high-dollar settlements where LeSuer allegedly helped himself to most of the proceeds, leaving a fraction for the true victims," the reporter said. "Our source declined to identify those victims and asked us to respect their privacy."

Sandy stared at me. "You?"

"I'm not the source," I said.

"Dummy. You set this up?"

"Let's just say I helped shine some light on a cockroach that was already there."

"Unbelievable." She shook her head. "But do you think they'll really get him?"

"Oh, he's got. The only question is what he will do to save himself. I have a feeling he might be willing to try to make things right, and if he doesn't, the DA will be happy to twist his arm."

"Including for Mr. Penney?"

"*Especially* for Mr. Penney. And some others, I imagine. Those were sort of a bonus."

"How did you pull all that off?"

She looked into my eyes, and our faces were so close I could answer or kiss her. I chose both. When I'd finished with the latter, I said, "You can't tell Penney, or anyone."

"Okay."

Her pupils were wide, and I felt a burden lift off my shoulders as I explained how we ran our op, from the surveillance to the laptop hack and uncovering all the fraud.

"How did you sell that to the cops, and the DA?" She looked puzzled. It was a lot to take in at once.

"I know him. A little. Enough, I guess." I wanted to avoiding implicating him, at least in any concrete detail. Still, I explained how a tip could lead to a suspect, and information could roll uphill. "It's not all that different from the way they develop a traditional case. We're not attached to any official outfit, so in a way we're just 'concerned citizens.' But it's much better if someone *else* who was dirty, too, gave them the excuse to get the warrants. We already know the info they will find is solid."

She fell quiet for a time then, digesting all that I'd told her. It was hard to read her.

"You wanted to know more," I reminded her. "It can be a messy process, sometimes. Most times. I think Mr. Penney is going to be okay though."

She hugged me, and I could feel her heart pounding.

Had I said too much? Confirmed to her I was just a weird crook? Would she bolt for the door?

Sandy kissed me, took me by the hand, and led me upstairs.

* * *

Later, I listened to the sounds of the city shift their rhythms toward the later evening, when most of the neighborhood turned in for bed. Sandy's head was on my chest, and her breathing was deep and regular as she drifted off.

Honking car horns punctuated the growing stillness. Sandy stirred and found my hand and gave it a quick squeeze before her breathing settled down again.

Thump!

I opened my eyes and realized I'd started to fall asleep myself. I thought I heard something, but began to doubt myself.

Several hard pounds on the back door echoed downstairs, and both Sandy and I jumped.

"What the hell?" Sandy muttered.

I was already out of the bed, pulling on a pair of jeans. "Someone's at the door. Stay here. I'll see what it is." I started to wonder why the security system hadn't alerted, then remembered I'd shut all that off so it wouldn't unnerve Sandy.

"Is that a gun?" she asked. There was enough ambient light in the room from the window for her to see the pistol I'd retrieved.

"Don't worry," I said, "it's probably nothing," which I'm sure sounded convincing while holding a loaded .357.

Sandy was already out of bed and getting dressed.

"Stay behind me."

As I made my way to the upstairs hallway, I heard another set of thumps at the back door, but not as forceful. I left the lights off and padded down the steps in bare feet.

The old boards creaked under my weight. Stealth was never in the cards. I sped up and paused at the doorway to the kitchen. I covered the back door with my gun, and the door remained shut. Whoever it was had to be lot bigger than Henry the cat but was at least still on the outside of the door.

I listened and heard fabric rub against the door. The window in the upper part of the door revealed nothing but the night.

Sandy reached the foot of the stairs behind me. When I glanced back, I saw she had found a baseball bat. I gestured for her to stay clear and crossed the kitchen. The door had a couple locks, so whoever was there would hear me no matter how fast I turned them. "Who's there? I have a gun."

It all felt very low tech, considering all the gear VP had installed, but that ship had sailed for the sake of privacy tonight.

"Lemme in, Kyle."

I didn't recognize the voice, but at the same time it sounded familiar. I kept the gun in hand and used the other to work the locks. The knob was difficult to turn due to weight pressing against it. An instant later I saw why when the door popped open and a huge body fell inside and slumped to the floor.

"Cullen?" His eyes met mine. His face was bone white and covered with a sheen of sweat. He let a pistol fall from his loose grip, and when he slumped over onto his back it looked like he was wearing pants with different-colored legs. One tan and the other maroon. Cullen held a belt cinched around his upper thigh in a weak grip, and now I could see fresh blood ooze from under the leather.

"Fingers slipping," Cullen gasped. "Help."

The aluminum bat clanked onto the linoleum floor, and Sandy rushed forward. "Are you shot?"

Cullen glanced at me.

"She's okay. She used to be a paramedic." She'd told me it was how she put herself through school. I was amazed how fast her training kicked back in. She'd ask questions later.

Cullen nodded. "Hit through the leg, must've nicked an artery. It got worse on the drive here."

From where? I wondered, but no time for that now. "Sandy, there's some thin rope under the sink. You can cut a length with one of the kitchen knives."

She moved fast. "Pull that belt tighter, Kyle. We need an ambulance, fast."

"No ambulance!" Cullen grabbed my wrist like a vice, despite the blood loss.

"You're going to bleed out," Sandy said. In a matter of seconds, she handed a length of rope to me.

By now I'd been able to reach a pair of scissors in a nearby drawer. I snipped away his pant leg and saw the entry wound from the slug. I made sure to wrap the rope above the hole and damaged artery. Sandy held the belt while I worked, and between the two of us we were able to cinch the new makeshift tourniquet before releasing the belt.

"Okay, Cullen. I have another idea."

"Crocker." Cullen was ahead of me.

"Did you drive?"

He nodded.

"Out back?"

"Yeah, key's in it."

"C'mon. Sandy, you're going to meet the infamous Doc Crock."

I grabbed an old flannel work shirt and slipped on a beat-up pair of sneakers. This was a terrible idea, but as long Cullen was conscious, he'd die before risking a regular hospital.

Sandy and I were able to support the big man while he held the tourniquet in place. The car sat on the sidewalk at an angle almost against my backyard fence. Dark blood spatters dotted the sidewalk under the streetlights. Otherwise, the outside of the vehicle looked okay. No holes in the sheet metal or shattered windows. The driver's side seat looked like . . . well, like someone had been shot.

We eased Cullen into the back seat, and Sandy joined him to make sure the tourniquet held.

It wasn't a long drive to Doc Crock's in Lansdowne, but I wanted to make the most of the time while Cullen was conscious.

"What happened?" I asked.

Cullen shook his head and started to shiver. Not good.

Sandy must've thought the same thing. "Is there a blanket in the car?"

"No." Cullen's voice sounded weaker. "You trust her?"

"With my life." I cranked up the heat in the car despite the mild temperature outside. He was going into shock.

"Fuck it. Tell William." Cullen was almost panting. "They got Charlie."

"Charlie got killed?"

He shook his head in frustration. "No. Maybe. I'm not sure."

"Take your time," Sandy said. She checked his pulse while the other hand made sure the tourniquet remained tight. I could see her face in the mirror, and the way she pressed her lips together.

"Hard to think. We set up a meet. You know with who."

"Yeah." I figured he meant the Albanians.

"We were going to settle it right there, understand?" Cullen said. "Lots of our soldiers. Most of them."

"You didn't surprise them?"

"Like hell. Fuckin' ambushed us. Hit us so fast half our guys never had a chance." Cullen's voice hardened in anger. "Some of us collapsed in on Charlie, then Red took him down a hall and I covered. Got a couple of the bastards. That was when I was hit."

"How'd you get out?"

"After I nailed the ones near me the rest kind of disappeared, maybe to chase Charlie, I don't know, but by then he was either gone or they got him, so I slipped out the side." Cullen paused to catch his breath.

I ran a stale yellow light and prayed there weren't any cops watching. If we didn't get to Doc Crock's soon, he wasn't going to make it.

"Why'd you come to Kyle's place?" Sandy asked.

"Closer and probably safer. He ain't one of us."

I glanced in the mirror, and Sandy seemed pleased to hear that.

"Didn't think I'd make it all the way to Crocker," Cullen said. "Why can't I feel my foot?" His agitation was growing.

"It's okay," Sandy said. "It's asleep. No circulation. I don't dare let up now. But we're almost there, right?" She looked at me in the reflection, emphasizing the question.

"One more block." We were paralleling the Fernwood Cemetery in Lansdowne. "Hang in there, Cullen."

CHAPTER 12

Lansdowne, Pennsylvania, Doc Crock's place

I leaned on the intercom buzzer like it could power open the door. If a security camera could glare, this one would have.

"What the hell do you want?" Doc Crock wasn't paid for his bedside manner.

"Important client in the car," I said in a normal tone, then lowered my voice. "Blood loss and shock."

The intercom just clicked, and I took it as a good sign. We returned to the car and prepared to get Cullen out of the back seat. The neighbors here were rewarded for an uncurious nature, and there wasn't time for any fancy smuggling here.

The door opened a minute later, and Doc Crock stood before us where we stood with Cullen between us. His mouth dropped open for an instant at the sight of his patient. Crocker's tousled hair belied a competent field medic. He'd lost his medical license due to a drinking problem, but I was pleased to see his eyes were less bloodshot than usual.

Crocker glanced at Sandy and shot me a look, but he'd already realized the clock was ticking for Cullen. "Get him inside," he said. "All the way to the stretcher, then straight to the back room."

We got into what served as Crocker's waiting room, and there was a clean white stretcher resting on the dusty floor. Doc Crock checked Cullen's vitals while we lay the big man onto the stretcher.

"What've we got?"

Sandy spoke before I could. "GSW, through and through, but he said he thought it might've nicked the femoral, but not sure. Lots of blood loss, early signs of shock. He was awake just before we got here."

"You a nurse?" Crocker checked the tourniquet, felt Cullen's lower leg and shook his head. "Too cold."

"I was an EMT," Sandy said.

I was impressed, but Crocker swore. "My nurse will be down in a minute that we don't have to spare. You're going to have to assist until then." Nurse Cindy had stitched me back together in the past. I knew she lived there sometimes and was relieved to hear tonight was one of them.

"You'll have to tell me what to do," Sandy said. We were almost to the table.

"My specialty. Grab some gloves and hold that tourniquet. I need to find out what we're really dealing with." Sandy and I pulled on gloves. It seemed foolish at this point but at least Doc Crock was washing up. "You," he barked at me. "Get the morphine on the top shelf, a pack of syringes, and those alcohol wipes." He pointed. "Down there."

I opened a drawer and found the wipes. "Now come hold the tourniquet. Miss, you can handle an injection?"

"Of course, but . . ."

Doc finished his hands and gloved up while he dictated the proper dosage to Sandy.

Cullen groaned.

"Hang in there, big guy. It's just a bad dream," Doc Crock said. "Kyle, use those scissors and cut the rest of that pant leg off. Miss? There's an IV bag and lines over there and more in the fridge. Take some out, he's going to need them all, I'm sure."

I cut the blood-soaked fabric off Cullen's leg and tried hard not to touch the wound, which wasn't all that large. I flashed back to my time in the Sand Box and the conditions some of the medics worked under after an ambush. God only knew what sort of germs and grime got blasted into my leg in one attack.

I heard someone come down a staircase, and the door opened. I recognized the nurse. She also lost her license a long time ago to the same drinking habit that took Crocker's, but the zipper scar on my torso was a testament to her skill with a needle and silk.

"Unsterile! You shouldn't be in here," she greeted us.

"Too late for that, hon," Crocker said. "Got a bleeder, possible artery nick. Gown and gloves, we gotta get his volume up, pronto."

Nurse Cindy moved fast. While she scrubbed, Sandy hooked Cullen to the first IV and hung the saline bag on a metal pole.

"Good deal." Crocker kept his gloved hands in the air and stepped closer. "Nice job, Miss. I didn't get your name."

He smiled when he heard it. "Cindy meet Sandy. Sandy, Cindy."

"Hello," Sandy said.

Cindy grunted and had already taken out another bottle and syringe. "Lidocaine."

"Right there." Crocker pointed near the wound. "And there."

I was holding the tourniquet again.

At Crocker's direction, Sandy put an oxygen mask on Cullen.

"Moment of truth," Crocker said. "Kyle, you gonna pass out on me when he bleeds?"

This wasn't fun, for sure, but I'd seen my fair share of blood and guts. I shook my head.

"Slowly loosen it and be ready," he said. "I just need to see the leak so we can clamp and repair. Don't go too hard either. Easy does it." He looked at Cindy. "Hemostat ready?"

She already had it in her hand. "Got it."

"Okay, Kyle."

I allowed the twist on the rope to loosen and Cullen started to shiver. Blood soaked the white towel under his leg.

"I see it," Crocker dabbed a sterile sponge in the area, and the wound refilled as soon as he removed it. "Yeah, tighten again, real slow Kyle. Clamp." Crocker held out his hand and Cindy delivered the tool into his palm with an audible snap. "Gotcha, sucker. Loosen again, Kyle."

I did and my heart sank when the wound resumed bleeding, but Crocker seemed thrilled.

"That's more like it. Lucky sonofabitch." Crocker sponged the wound, and I realized that I had nearly loosened the tourniquet completely. "Femoral artery is okay," he said. "Femoral *vein* was what got nicked."

"Still bad, though?" Sure looked that way to me.

"Bad enough," he said. "The difference for our boy here is probably a gallon of the claret and a trip to the morgue instead of the best little underground sawbones in Lansdowne."

"Do you know what he is?" Nurse Cindy asked me.

The question took me off guard. I assumed Crocker knew about Cullen's line of work.

"What blood type, she means," Crocker said.

"Oh! No idea," I said. "I'm 'A' if that helps."

Nurse Cindy took one of the bloody sponges and removed a test kit.

"B-pos here," Sandy said.

"He's going to need more than that broth he's hooked up to," Crocker said.

"I wish I could cash in favors by the pint," I said.

Cindy's eyes crinkled like she was smiling under her mask. She waved a card back and forth to dry the dots of blood taken from the sponge.

"Winner, winner, chicken dinner," Crocker said. He looked at Sandy. "Young lady, care to roll up a sleeve?"

"Wait a minute," I said. "She doesn't have to—"

"It's fine," Sandy cut me off. "Go ahead, Cindy." Sandy held up a finger for a lance to confirm her blood type.

"Out to the waiting room, Kyle," Crocker said. "We can get by with just a unit. As soon as Sandy is done, I'll send her out and Cindy will make some calls to get some more B positive here."

* * *

Out in the waiting room I felt dizzy like it was me that had lost blood. The events of the night catching up, I guess. Now I remembered what Cullen told me, and I searched my pockets for the right burner phone.

Time to call William.

The phone rang enough times I expected it to roll over to voicemail. I glanced at the clock in the room. 3:30 a.m.

A click. "Yes?" William's voice.

I knew better than to say his name out loud. "I know it's late, but can we talk in person?" It was very difficult to be vague when I had to deliver specific news.

"Bad time," he said. Of course, he had no idea I knew anything.

"I'm at our doctor's, with a friend." I let that sink in for a moment. "The one who gives me a ride sometimes?"

70

"He's okay?"

"He's been better, but in good hands now."

"Twenty minutes." William hung up.

A few minutes later, Sandy came out looking steady enough on her feet. "Where are my cookies and juice?" She smiled. I hugged her, and we plopped down on the old couch. "You know how to show a girl a good time."

"I didn't mean to speak for you, but I just don't want to drag you into this business."

She pointed to the dried blood on her jeans. "Consider me dragged."

"Charlie O'Brien's brother William is on his way. He's kind of shy, so don't take it personally if he doesn't want to say much around you."

"Don't worry, I don't think I want to know him. This is enough for one day." She looked over at the clock. "Oh, it's the next day already."

We sat in silence for a while, and my jangled nerves settled down to a low hum.

Soon headlights washed over the front windows, and the sound of a car door slam preceded a ring of the front buzzer audible from somewhere in back.

I was just getting ready to open the door myself when Nurse Cindy marched past us to the door and opened the locks. William stepped inside, looking slovenly (for him) in an open-collared shirt and sport coat. He glanced in my direction before whispering to Cindy. "How is he?"

Cindy spoke so we all could hear. "The doc is finishing up now. He's sutured the vein and closed the wound. We still need to get his blood volume up and of course infection will be a concern, but barring that, he should be okay."

"Can he talk?" William asked.

Cindy shook her head. "He's zonked out and will be for a while. He could've bled out, and probably would have if these two didn't get him here as fast as they did."

I stood up and gestured to the corner of the room. Sandy asked Cindy about the bathroom and excused herself.

"Did he tell you anything?" William's usual poker-face was etched in worry lines. "And how did you get mixed up in this anyway?" The thought apparently just occurred to him.

"I guess my place was closer than Doc's, and he didn't think he'd make it on his own. Look at the inside of his car and our clothes and I think he was right."

"What else?"

"He wanted me to tell you he isn't sure what happened to Charlie, but that Red went with your brother to escape while he held off the attackers," I said. "He thinks he got two of them before he was hit." I couldn't help myself. "William, you didn't go. Why?"

Normally I'd be lucky to be just warned to mind my own business. Instead, William pinched the bridge of his nose and squeezed his eyes shut. "This was Charlie's show. He wanted to hit back, you know how he is, and I knew better than to talk him out of it. He thought we could end the trouble in one fell swoop. I'd hoped he was right."

"They must've figured the same thing."

William opened his eyes and his gaze drilled through me. "You think?"

My tired brain piped up. "Hey, did you come here alone? You weren't followed?" After what I'd heard about tonight, I didn't think the Albanians were too concerned about bystanders, if that's even what they would think of Sandy and me.

"We weren't followed. It's quite safe here." William's anger had evaporated. "We lost a lot of men tonight, most of our best soldiers."

"What about the police?"

He shook his head. "We picked a discreet meeting place, gunshots and all. I sent a cleanup crew."

He meant Shamrock Sanitation. When I was growing up, everyone knew if they showed up you got out of there and said nothing, unless you wanted to disappear next.

I didn't know how to ask this diplomatically. "Did they find, um, Charlie?"

"Those bastards have him." He looked at me.

"You're sure?"

"Red saw them knock Charlie out, and then they worked over Red before dumping him out on the street to deliver a message."

"What message?"

William hesitated out of instinct. "Unconditional surrender, or Charlie comes back in pieces."

CHAPTER 13

Doc Crock's

The questions tripped over themselves in my mind. "What do they mean by 'unconditional,' and is Red okay?"

William said, "He's fine, they wanted him able to remember what he was supposed to say, I suppose. And as to your first question, they want our group out of the area and out of business."

I looked at him, and the silence turned William's face red. "Those filthy, inbred mongrels will never run us off." He rubbed his hands until the pale skin matched his cheeks. "But while they have Charlie . . ."

I never thought I'd be in a spot to feel sorry for William O'Brien, a night full of firsts. "Listen, you know I can't help with muscle."

"Muscle can be replaced." William sounded casual, but the creases on his forehead said otherwise. "We need to find him before . . ."

Sandy came through the door across the room. I lowered my voice. "Let me see if I can find out any more from my end. I don't have much to work with, but they'd have to be operating somewhere in the area, wouldn't they?"

"I would think." He looked over at Sandy. "Young lady, I understand you saved my man's life tonight."

"Uh. You're welcome. It just worked out that way." She seemed at a loss for words. She'd never met either of the O'Briens, but their name (and reputation) preceded them throughout the city.

Doc Crock stepped into the room. "Why don't you two go home? Cindy has some more units of blood on the way. I'll chat with William, but I can tell you that our patient is going to be okay."

William leaned toward me. "Stay in touch, won't you?" His tone told me that he'd taken my offer as more than polite lip-service.

* * *

Since our clothes were stained with Cullen's blood, we borrowed some sweatpants but we needed a way home. We took a split-second to decide against taking Cullen's rolling crime scene of a car, and William's man was as much a bodyguard as a driver. He wouldn't be leaving his boss. We ended up grabbing an Uber a couple blocks away. The short walk by the graveyard across the street from Doc's was creepy but quiet.

* * *

Back at the house, Sandy turned to me. "We need to talk about tonight." She looked exhausted.

"How about after we both get some rest?"

"I need time to absorb everything," she began, "but this is way heavier than I imagined." I could see fatigue stir the words in her head as she fought to stay awake.

"Agreed. But you know I didn't see Cullen coming." I tried not to sound defensive. My brain was turning to mush as well.

"Right," she said. "But it all happened so fast."

"I know. But can we pick this up in a few hours? You were amazing, but we're both out of gas."

"That was old reflexes," she said around a yawn. "All right, I can't keep my eyes open."

"I'm not going anywhere, promise."

I tucked Sandy in and put on some old clothes I planned to burn later.

* * *

Despite how much I wanted to grab some sleep myself, I had work to do. I rinsed the sidewalk and scrubbed the floor and parts of the back steps where Cullen had collapsed until my eyes watered from the cleaner fumes. The sunrise tinged the sky pink, making it look like the cement by the back door was still stained, but as the light grew stronger, I could see that my hard work had paid off.

I stretched and contemplated a quick shower and crash for a few hours and decided instead to make some industrial strength coffee and settle for just the shower.

The hot water on my body and the steaming rocket fuel in my stomach made it possible to think again. I checked on Sandy, who remained sound asleep. That was good.

She'd been pulled far too deep into my world, not to mention all at once. Even so, she wouldn't know the depths of the danger tonight's developments represented. Much as I tried to keep my dealings with the Irish restricted to a low level and the rest of their business at arm's length, this escalation threatened us all.

Charlie's stunt that backfired so badly left the Irish outgunned and vulnerable. I was no expert but knew enough that even by organized crime standards, the Albanians had earned their reputation for violence. After their victory and VIP hostage in Charlie himself, William and the Philly Irish Mob crew in Fishtown were looking at getting wiped out.

As for me and my little group, we weren't part of the Irish Mob, but was that how the Albanians saw it? My overtired and now overcaffeinated brain tried to sort it out.

A year ago, the Irish muscle, Cullen included, intimidated Milosh and his men at the coffee shop when I told him that he was being pushed out of the small loans "franchise" to allow me to run it. Now I had to wonder if Milosh took that to mean that I was part of the Irish Mob rather than a freelancer. Would he care?

Sandy had stirred in the bed when I checked on her but didn't argue with my suggestion that she go back to sleep a bit longer. I did notice the row of burners on my dresser. Several were blinking, indicating messages from VP and Rollie.

I decided to call Rollie first, as the sun was up. I knew he would be as well.

"About time, kid," he said. "You must have been out late celebrating. Nice when a plan comes together, eh?"

At first, I had no idea what he was talking about, but then it hit me that the whole crazy night had started out watching the news about the LeSuer indictment and the prospects that Mr. Penney would see some restitution, or at least justice.

"Yeah, and we were, at first. Then everything went haywire."

"What's wrong?" Rollie's tone shifted at once.

I told him from the point Cullen came to the house. "So, now our friends are in a world of shit." I used the word "friends" more as a caution while on the phone, as Rollie had no love for them but did tolerate the current working relationship, most of all because he never worked directly with them.

"I'm not their biggest fan, but I wouldn't wish that fate on an enemy," Rollie said once I'd explained that Charlie was a "guest" of the Albanians.

"I told his brother we'd try, so are you around for a skull session here? I don't want to run through all my phone minutes."

"Of course. You'll reach VP?"

"My next call. And be careful on the way over, huh?"

Rollie acknowledged. I'd reset the alarm system and had a weapon handy on each floor.

VP sounded like I'd woken her up and told me so in no uncertain terms. She kept strange hours, so I might've gotten the same reaction in the middle of the day, depending on what she was working on.

I gave her the shorter version and asked her to come over as soon as she could.

"Yeah, I'll be there in about an hour. Got anything to eat?"

"Sure." Then I remembered Sandy was here. "Crap!" VP was extremely careful about who saw her in person while she was working in our group.

"I don't criticize your eating habits," she said. "Unless you meant actual crap."

"Sandy could still be here. Is that a problem?"

"Dude, we're not dating. If she's already a blood brother with the biggest Irish hitter in the Fishtown league, I guess it's okay if she sees me."

"I was just thinking of your secret identity." I sounded stupid.

"It's cool. You still think my name is VP." She laughed.

She had a point.

* * *

Sandy came downstairs in one of my bathrobes. She had to hike up the hem to prevent it from dragging on the floor. "I can't believe how late it is."

I kissed her and handed her a mug of coffee I'd made fresh and more normal strength. "How are you feeling?"

"I thought I'd had the strangest dream until I saw this on my arm." She pointed to the cotton ball still taped where she'd had the blood draw. "Do you think he's doing okay?"

"I'm sure. He's in good hands, believe it or not."

"I was impressed. I'm not going to switch my doctor, but he certainly got the job done last night."

"I'm so sorry you got caught up in all that." I felt as awkward as that sounded. "Sorry I was too."

Sandy peered at me over her steaming coffee mug. "I'm still trying to process everything that happened. The good and the bad."

I decided to let her go at her own pace.

"I can't lie," she said. "I know what is happening with Mr. Penney started with me sending him to you. I knew it wasn't just for advice. But I guess I didn't know what to expect."

"I kept you in the dark. Sometimes for good reason and sometimes just out of habit. Not proud how fast that habit took hold of me either."

Sandy gave a little smile. "I remember when you were helping me out when Barnaby Bones was extorting me at the old location. What was it you said? Something about how his luck was about to take a terrible turn?"

"I remember. Those Strawberry Mansion rowhouses we have? The first ones used to be his. He gave us a great deal before he blew town."

"Good luck for them. And me."

I took a deep breath. "That was the idea, and the houses kind of just happened. Mostly for the good. But it isn't always the way it works."

"But last night. Cullen. How does that just happen?"

I wanted to completely disavow what was going on with the Irish. But it wasn't that simple. "The Irish got themselves a war. It may not have been their idea to start it, but as we saw, they're in it and if what Cullen says is true, they may be on the verge of losing it."

"I get your cutting corners to do what's right. Maybe even more than that. And I think the touch of outlaw swagger is cool."

"Swagger?"

But she was serious. "Last night, that's *not* what I signed up for. I don't want to be in a war with anyone."

I took her hand, glad she didn't pull it back. "I don't want that either. Not for me and especially not for you. That's not what we're about. But remember when the Mr. Beautiful project got dumped in my lap? I had to see it through or the guys on the other side were going to take it, over my dead body."

"I remember hiding out of town, wondering what was going to happen to you and if I'd ever see you again."

"Sometimes the only way out is straight through the shitstorm."

"But why this time?"

"We're still figuring it out," I said. "I know Cullen, but not all that well. I guess he trusts me, all the same. We had to protect ourselves, and it's gotten rough a time or two. But I'd never dream of hiring Cullen, not like that."

"I believe you," she said, and I felt great relief hearing it.

"Last night Cullen told you one of the reasons he felt safer coming here was that I wasn't part of the Irish Mob," I said.

"That's right, he did. So why is all this trouble your problem?"

I recapped the way I'd worked with the Irish and Cullen specifically to intimidate Milosh and drive him out of town. "Nobody got hurt back then, but maybe some egos got bruised. Enough to get me lumped in with the Irish? I don't know, but the brain trust is coming over soon to figure out our options."

"So, you really think the Albanians would come after your group?"

"I can't be sure they won't. They don't use the same rule book, and we have to figure out things so we don't get caught by surprise."

Sandy covered her face and rubbed her eyes. "I need to think about this. It's like being in a car with no brakes."

"It's not my fight, but we still may be caught in the blast. Or to use your image, not my car, but I accepted a ride at the wrong time." I paused. "But that doesn't mean you have to take the ride with me."

"Are you sending me away again? Don't I get a say here? This is just a lot to take in. I hadn't expected to be interviewed for a position as a gun moll."

"Of course you get a say. I'm thinking of your safety and . . . a what?" Suddenly, all I could do was picture Sandy in a 1920's-style flapper dress toting a Tommy gun.

She smiled back. "Seriously, I just need to absorb the situation."

I needed to know where Sandy stood. "Do you think it would help if you sat in on our discussion? We all want to avoid violence, but the possibility is real."

"Anything is better than hunkering down in the dark. But are you sure they'll welcome an outsider?"

"VP said she's okay with it after what you experienced last night. That's high praise from her."

"I guess I'm honored then."

"Hon, I don't want to frighten you." Yes, I did. "But these guys are vicious enough to scare all of us. The Albanians may well see a chance to press ahead for total victory. Including our group. What's a few more bodies to them?"

"The last time I went into hiding, you almost got killed. And then I wasn't even involved." She held out her arm with the IV bandage. "I'm definitely involved this time. I pulled the thorn out of a lion's paw."

"You have no idea how right you are."

"All the more reason for me to hear you guys out on the options." Sandy's eyes showed fear, but her jaw set in a defiant line.

CHAPTER 14

Kyle's place

Rollie was prompt as always, and now we were waiting on VP before figuring out our next move. I'd explained to Sandy some of the security system VP had helped put in place. Funny, just the night before, I'd been all worried about it frightening her. Now barely a day later, I was hoping it would bring her some comfort. She needed to see what we were really about, not when we got dragged into someone else's conflict.

She still might bail, but at least it'd be an informed decision.

At any rate, all the cameras were up and running, and Rollie was showing Sandy the "bunker" in the basement that housed the equipment and monitors. There were also some armored plates concealed behind pine board.

"You don't think that's overkill?" Sandy seemed more amused than freaked out. I guess that was good.

"The idea," Rollie said, "is to avoid any 'kill' at all."

"We might as well show her how crazy you really are." I figured she ought to see everything. To this day, I still couldn't believe I'd let Rollie talk me into this next part.

"Says you." Rollie winked at Sandy. "This is some of my best work." Rollie brought Sandy into the cramped room and pointed to a rectangular throw rug by the back corner.

"You weave rugs?" Sandy said. "Very talented."

"Smart ass." Rollie pointed at the floor. "Look underneath."

Sandy did and revealed a concrete-colored rectangular area just smaller than the rug. "Is that . . . ?" She tapped the spot with her foot, and it made a hollow sound. "No way."

"Oh, yes too, way." Rollie seemed thrilled for the chance to show off his secret. "Lift it up."

"I swear, he wouldn't take no for an answer." I showed Sandy the spot where she could get a grip, and she was able to lever up the sturdy wood cover, which was hinged at the back end.

"What is it, a bomb shelter?" She looked down into the hole big enough for a regular-sized man, and I could see the first of the ladder rungs.

"Nope, and don't give Rollie any ideas," I said. "It's a back door to the rabbit den."

"Huh?"

Rollie pointed. "That ladder goes down ten feet and it opens up a bit, think of a shape like the bottom of a thermometer."

"What's that wire? A boobytrap?" Sandy said.

"That powers the motion-activated lights, but you could use it in a total blackout with a little practice."

"Use what?" She peered down into the darkness.

I explained. "At the bottom, Rollie installed a wide pipe that he turned into a small escape tunnel. It's too shallow to stand in, but there's a track on the bottom for a crawler like they use to work under cars. You just lay back and pull on a rope and away you go."

"You're joking." Sandy frowned. "To where?"

"It comes out under the tool shed against the back fence. There's a false door there to reach the sidewalk."

I could see she was trying to decide if we were pulling her leg.

"I thought people liked you guys," Sandy said. "Ever need to use it?"

"Not yet," I said. Rollie had made me practice, in the dark even, just to make sure. "And you see by all the cookies, you're usually right."

"But it only takes once to be wrong," Rollie said. "And I don't think the Albanians are baking right now."

The back yard alert buzzed, and we all looked at the monitor to see a hooded figure slip through the gate.

"The mysterious VP, I presume?" Sandy pointed to the monitor.

"The one and only." We filed out of the security room.

* * *

"Yo, kids. Anybody home?" I could hear VP's voice over the speaker in the bunker despite being halfway up the basement steps.

I waved at VP peering in through the glass panel at the back door. "Hey. C'mon in," I said. "We were just in the bunker." Sandy and Rollie entered the kitchen behind me.

VP fist-bumped Rollie and then shook Sandy's hand. "Heard a lot about you."

"Likewise." Sandy paused. "Actually, not all that much."

"Just the good stuff, I hope." VP pulled her hoodie back.

"Great setup in the basement," Sandy said.

"Not everyone gets the top security clearance." VP glanced at me. "You dig that we like to keep things discreet, right?" There was a slight edge to VP's voice.

"Absolutely. Not all my dates end with me drenched in a hitman's blood and donating a pint of my own to keep him alive. Do *you* dig?" Sandy showed her bandaged arm.

VP flashed her lopsided grin. "You bet. Speaking of dig, did you ride the Fishtown Subway?"

Sandy shook her head.

"Rollie made it look like there was a new sewer pipe going in when he broke out the backhoe. Pretty slick."

Rollie gave a modest shrug. "If I'd flunked out of sniper school, I might've made a decent tunnel rat."

We moved into the living room, and I tried to fill in all the gaps for where we were in all this. "So basically, we don't know how much we could get dragged into this, but the way the Albanians roll, I don't want to take any chances."

"Meaning what?" Rollie said. "I'm not looking to get drafted into someone else's war."

"That's fair, but after what happened last night, the Irish are back on their heels and the Albanians may be on the warpath for a knockout blow. If they view us as part of the other team, we are in just as much danger."

Rollie leaned forward in his chair. "Maybe we need to find a way to make it clear to them that this isn't our fight."

"Milosh didn't exactly leave a forwarding address. VP, anything you can do to find signs of where these guys could be operating from?"

Her face scrunched up. "I dunno. I doubt they are posting videos of their success on YouTube or gangster chat boards."

"Probably not, but it's still hard to move around without leaving some sort of footprint."

VP sounded like she was thinking it over while she spoke. "Yeah, it might help if you gave me a better starting point." She paused. "You never said where this shootout took place."

"William didn't tell me." I saw where she was going with this. "Are you thinking of hacking the camera feeds nearby?"

"Something like that. Maybe any building security cameras as well."

"William indicated it was isolated but never said how far away," I said. "Considering Cullen was afraid of bleeding out, it can't have been far. That might narrow it down to some of the more industrial areas. They would have fewer neighbors to overhear a gunfight."

Rollie spoke. "From what you know, it sounded pretty one-sided, but even so, the Albanians took some damage. Where might they take their survivors?"

Sandy nodded. "If they went to a regular hospital, especially with a gunshot or knife wound, that would require an automatic report to the police."

"True," VP said. "Maybe they have their own medics like Doc Crock."

"If they didn't bring one with them, where would they go to ask?" I said.

Sandy said, "You told me Crock lost his medical license. There must be a way to look up doctors in the community who also lost theirs. Maybe looking for some tax-free side-hustle cash?"

VP smirked. "I like how she thinks. I can def look into that."

"It's easy to get spread too thin here," I said. "William said he wanted reports. Let me talk to him and see if he'll pin down the location for us."

"Good deal," VP said.

"Meantime, everyone needs to be extra vigilant," Rollie said. "If you see anything weird, bug out and call me or Kyle. These goons play for keeps."

VP looked at Sandy. "I have a lot of homework to do. Can you help me monitor the security cameras so we don't get caught with our pants down?"

Sandy glanced at me and gave a little shrug. "Yeah, I can do that, if you'll show me how. Will you need me at your place?"

"Nah. I'm kinda private. Nothing personal, ask anyone."

"Kind of," I agreed.

"I didn't mean to overstep," Sandy said.

"It's all good," VP said. "Anyway, I can push the feeds to the bunker right here. You need me, just pick up the bat-phone."

* * *

Fishtown, inside the Blue Bomber, the next day

Despite her misgivings, Sandy had jumped right into her role as security guard, as she called it. She'd learned the ropes of the monitors like a pro. She'd already rescheduled her appointments at her physical therapy office, and the new hires were able to take up the slack for her in the meantime.

I hoped "meantime" would be a short-lived affair, but not as much as I wanted to avoid becoming short-lived personally. For now, Sandy seemed okay just keeping an eye out for trouble.

"Wait in the car, kid." Rollie left the engine running, and I could feel the rumbling V-8 through the floorboard. He'd been so annoyed that I hadn't brought a pistol when we left the house that he insisted on stopping by his place to make sure I was properly equipped.

I understood, but doubted if I got ambushed that I'd even get the chance to use it.

Rollie locked his front door and dropped a cloth-wrapped bundle into my lap. It was heavy enough that I knew what was inside.

"Thanks, I guess. But you know we get frisked at the bakery?" Of course, he did.

"Plenty can happen between here and there," Rollie said. "And I can wait for you and keep an eye out on the street."

"You win." I was plenty worried about security, but more about the house and Sandy in it than for me. I stuffed the wrapped gun in the glovebox while Rollie raced up some side streets and kept his gaze rotating between the road ahead and all the mirrors. "Do you think we should offer Sandy some trigger time at some point?"

"Only if she's interested," Rollie said. "You should worry more about how she's going to handle everything she already knows."

"Are you talking about her going to the cops?" I was surprised.

"Not to hurt us, no. But just make sure she understands that it wouldn't solve anything and could make things much worse for everyone."

"I think she knows." Still, I decided to mention it when I got the chance. Personally, I'd take my medicine if it came to that, but the circles we travelled in made such transgressions a life-or-death matter.

"I suspect she will figure it out. And she'll be fine in the bunker, you'll see." Rollie's calm made me feel better.

"I hope so. She told me her girls can cover her work for now."

"Good. She can focus." Rollie looked at me. "Don't worry so much. If you could learn how to run the monitors, it'll be a snap for her. She's smart, for one thing." He slowed the car.

"Great pep talk, Rollie."

He slowed down, and we approached the intersection for Heather Bakery. Right away I noticed two things. First, the men outside the place and on the corners looked nervous as hell. Second, there weren't nearly as many of them as before.

"They pulled some real babies off the bench, didn't they?" Rollie said, noting the fresh-faced "troops," and pulled up to the reserved parking spot at less than walking pace. I saw the entrance door crack open wide enough to allow someone to signal a guard. They knew Rollie's car.

"Think William will consider going underground?" Rollie asked.

"Doubt it. Perception is as important as reality. He doesn't want to show weakness."

Rollie rested his hands on his steering wheel like he'd been pulled over by a cop. "Whatever you do, don't spook the kiddies. They're liable to shoot themselves in the foot."

"Or me." I left Rollie to wait in the car.

The bakery door opened, and I saw Red inside waving me in.

* * *

The inside of the bakery was even darker with the windows nearly opaque to prevent outsiders from seeing inside. They'd abandoned all pretense of the baking ruse. There wasn't a cookie in sight.

"How ya doing, Red?" He had a black eye I hadn't noticed from the street.

"I never thought lucky would look so bad," he said. "Got a real lump on the back of my head, but I'm not seeing double anymore." His lanky frame looked wilted, more like a squiggle instead of an exclamation point. He nodded toward the stairs. "C'mon."

No frisk after all, but I supposed I was the last of their security concerns right now.

Up the stairs, Red spoke in a low voice. "Wish I could've done more. Bastards. Glad to hear about Cullen. Any new reports?"

"No news, but that's good, I guess. How's William?"

Red's pale skin blanched a shade I didn't think was possible. "He's waiting."

I didn't recognize the jumbo-sized guy who opened the door to let me inside. He seemed to know who I was and, more importantly, didn't look like he was about to start blasting away at the next sudden noise.

The place was dark, and the only light came from lamps and overheads. The only window I could see from the front of the place was blacked out like a flat in London during the Blitz. No doubt Rollie would have approved, as any snipers would just be guessing.

"Come in, Kyle," William rose from a thick-padded leather sofa. He looked like he hadn't slept since the last time I saw him.

"I'll get right to the point," I began, but William stopped me and pushed a small box sitting on an end table closer to me.

I felt my stomach drop, and I took off the lid. Nestled on snowy white cotton rested a severed pinkie finger. Even in the dim lighting, I could see tiny red hairs below one pale, freckled knuckle and pictured Charlie's ruddy face. "Oh, damn."

"It came in this morning. The note said we need to surrender and leave Philly." William held up the paper. "Look at the bottom."

It wasn't subtle. A cut-out newsprint of the number nine. "I see where they are going with that." Nine fingers to go.

"If you have any ideas, they better be fast ones." William's voice shook with anger. "He won't last long."

"You can help me." I asked him about the shootout location and gave him the outline of what we were thinking.

"Fine." William took out an old folded paper street map of the city and folded it to a corner of Fishtown. "You recognize the area?"

I did. Growing up, there wasn't an abandoned or even unguarded waterfront haunt I hadn't explored with my friends.

"They hit us like they had the building schematics," William said.

"You're probably right about that. And it means you can't underestimate them. But as far as where they might be hiding, that doesn't help. They may have been caught on cameras though. You don't know what they were driving?"

"I wasn't there, remember?" William said. "Cullen is doing better, but if he saw anything it's too early to get anything sensible out of him. Too many drugs, and we can't afford to chase hallucinations."

"Maybe Red?"

"I asked. He says not, and by the time they drove him to be dropped off, he was blindfolded. He thinks a van. Maybe."

I nodded. "Okay. As soon as we're done here, I'll have my researchers all over it."

"We think this group came out of New York," William said.

"Any chance your people up there might have heard something?"

William jumped like I'd just jabbed him with a pin. "*My* people?" He looked like he wanted to spit.

I thought he was done speaking, but his gaze snapped to the open box containing his brother's finger.

Nine.

"It may be that the New York family knows all about it," he said. "But it just so happens that they are more like the Swiss Mob, for all the good it does me."

"I don't understand."

"They're sitting this war out. So are the New York Albanians. As long as our side stays on the sidelines, the NY Albanians have promised not to escalate."

"And they agreed to that?"

"I asked for some temporary muscle, and they told me in no uncertain terms it wasn't happening," William seethed.

"And you think the Albanians aren't supplying their side?"

"What I think doesn't really matter now, does it?"

I took that in. "They're scared of the New Yorkers."

"Great minds think alike," William said. He replaced the cover on the small box. "Now that we're not under any illusions, you can see I'm in need of all the friends I can get."

I couldn't say I wasn't sympathetic, but at the same time, I wasn't eager to deepen my ties with a mobster. Then again, if they lost, what would Fishtown look like, run by the bloodthirsty Albanian gang? "Are you thinking of giving in to them?"

"You don't know us as well as I thought," William said. "I'm disappointed."

"I'm trying to look at your options." Which wasn't really true. "Hell, I'm trying to think of *my* options. I told you before, this kind of battle isn't my group's thing."

"Perhaps not, but your group may be the battle's thing," William pointed out.

CHAPTER 15

Kyle's place

After I left William to get the new info to VP, Rollie and I discussed potential escalation for our people.

"He's right, you know," he said. "I don't want a brawl with these goons, but we need a plan if they don't give us a choice."

"I'm open to suggestions."

"Of course, we'll defend ourselves, and if they think we're soft, that can help."

"And?"

Rollie blew out a breath in exasperation. "Kid, I don't know. If we knew where they were, we'd have a much better chance and a ready-made army, who isn't us, dying to get some payback."

"They're depleted right about now," I said.

"If we can get the right intel, we might just be the force multiplier that can make all the difference."

"Or we catch a break for once, and the Irish solve this themselves." Rollie shot me a puzzled look. "But let's try our best to put our thumb on the scale."

"Attaboy."

* * *

"Old lady Timmons walks that little terrier a lot, Jerry Guilder smokes too much, and Mrs. Burton hides her wine empties in other people's trash cans. Otherwise, nothing else to report, sir." Sandy gave me a half-assed salute before a hug and kiss.

"Thanks for holding the fort," I said. "It can be boring, I know."

"Right before it gets really exciting," Rollie added. "Want anything from upstairs?"

"A Coke," Sandy said, "unless you're making coffee."

"Done," Rollie said.

I told Sandy about the meeting with William. The little box.

"That's awful."

"That's the idea. He also told me where the shootout happened." I called up an area map on a tablet and pointed to the cluster of old buildings. "Makes sense that Cullen stopped here. We are right between there and Doc Crock's."

"Does VP know?"

I nodded. "I told her on the way. We're hoping to get a lucky hit, but we don't know what they were driving. We figure it had to be at least three vehicles, considering all the muscle they brought."

"Better than what we had before."

My Tom burner phone rang. He usually called on my regular cell when it was port-related business. "What's up?"

"Yo, mate!" his cheery voice piped over. "Nothing much here. Actually, bored stiff at the moment—"

"TMI," I said, cutting him off. There was a pause while it translated, then he laughed.

"Right. Anyway, I wanted to see how you were getting on with hassling that bloke LeSuer. Fancy needing any help for another go at him?"

That felt like a century ago. I realized he must not have heard the latest on the LeSuer front. I gave him the short version and a site or two where he could fill in the details from the news.

"Too great. So why don't you sound more chuffed?" Tom was nobody's fool. "Drop the other shoe."

"More like a whole closetful. Some old competition is in town and looking to take the bakery scene by storm. Their first bid was extremely aggressive, almost a hostile takeover." I didn't expect Tom to know exactly what I meant.

He got the gist that something awful had happened, and my coded mish-mash told him I couldn't spell it out on the phone. "Ah. You need some assistance with . . . competitive intelligence?"

I was surprised at my sense of relief. "It could be damaging to your reputation."

"You had me at hostile, mate. I'll be there in the morning. Have my brand of tea on hand, yeah?"

"Safe trip."

* * *

While Sandy took a break, I sat in the bunker and watched the feeds on the monitors. If her screentime vigil had lulled her into being comfortable with things, the news about Charlie's finger had restarted the wheels in her mind. I knew she had plenty to think about.

The monitors showed nothing happening around the house, but I could sit on the porch and figure that one out. I added feeds from the port and saw routine activity. I did check in with Cliff and everything seemed normal.

I called over to Doc Crock, who loved chatting on the phone even more than surprise visits in the middle of the night. "What?"

"How's our friend?" I didn't take the attitude personally.

"Ornery." Crock spoke in a low tone that said Cullen might not be far away. "Remind me if I ever have a wounded tiger to be sure to drop it off at your place."

"Sounds like he's on the mend."

"The tough guy bit isn't an act. I'm getting tired of explaining that he needs to let his incision settle or he's liable to spring a leak. And then guess who he'll blame?"

I laughed. "I thought you always got the last word at your place."

"That reminds me. He wants to talk to you." Doc's footsteps echoed over the phone. "It's him," I heard him say. "No, the other him."

A pause.

"You there?" Cullen's voice sounded strong.

"Hey big man, how are you feeling?"

"I'm okay. Ready to go, you know?"

"So I hear. But you can't do much if you have to go right back."

"You might be surprised," Cullen said. "Listen."

I didn't know if he was still drugged up. "Sure, the phone's not special or anything but I can hear you."

"I know." Cullen sounded lucid. Crock's assessment seemed spot on. "I want to thank you and . . . your lady for what you did." I think he knew her name so he was tracking enough not to say it over an open line.

"You're welcome. It was just luck that you were her type." That sounded stupid. The guy didn't have to be in front of me to make me nervous.

"Saved my life. I won't forget."

For some reason, having a stone-cold killer utter those words didn't bring me comfort. At the same time, I wouldn't want to be any of the Albanians if he ever caught up to them.

"I'll let her know. Just get better. Our friend will be glad to hear it."

I continued. "I saw him this morning." I thought he was going to say more. The pause told me Cullen knew the situation. No wonder he was so eager to get back on the street.

"Okay. Get some rest and when everything settles down, we'll get back to work on that card collection."

Cullen hung up.

* * *

After a few hours of dehydrating my eyeballs staring at the monitors showing cars going by the street and pedestrians strolling on the sidewalk, I knew I hadn't missed my calling.

Rollie poked his head in from time to time. "You're welcome to take a shift, you know," I said to him.

"Really? Wow, you should have said something earlier. And you all by your lonesome here." Rollie grinned. "How's the 'pattern recognition' business?"

"About as fun as being a paint-drying observation technician." I stood to get the blood moving in my legs. "Is Sandy awake yet?"

"Let her rest. If she needs something, I'll get it."

"When Tom gets here tomorrow, don't tell him you wouldn't take a shift."

"I never said I wouldn't take one." Rollie feigned a hurt tone. "Just not right now."

"And later?"

"Later is the now of the future." Rollie looked proud of himself.

"Deep. I don't know how VP does it. Do you think she made any progress?"

Rollie pointed to the row of burners arrayed on the desk. I jumped on the excuse and dialed her up.

VP skipped the pleasantries. "Please tell me you found some more clues."

"Cullen was no help on that front, sorry. So, no luck?"

"The closer I get to where it all went down, the harder it is to get good footage."

"Almost like they picked the spot to avoid uncomfortable recordings?"

"Ya think? I'm beginning to realize this may not be the best play. I'll switch to looking for unlicensed docs in the area."

"Fair enough. They could switch cars next time anyway."

"Yeah," VP said. "But for you guys, keep an eye out for clusters of vehicles."

"In the city, we call it traffic," I said. "Sorry. I hear you. Holler if you find anything."

"Always."

CHAPTER 16

Kyle's place, the next morning

Tom must have driven through the night because he arrived shortly after Rollie went home to take a nap and get some things done around this place. Rollie had taken pity on me when I told him I was going to stay up all night to guard the place.

We knew we couldn't keep this up, but at the same time, given how hard the Albanians had hit the Irish, we knew we couldn't afford to slack off.

By the time he'd parked his car and walked to the door, I'd tagged the vehicle on the monitor so VP would recognize it as a "friendly" and put on a pot of water for Tom's obligatory cup of tea.

"Five-star service, mate." Tom plopped down his suitcase and took a seat at the dining room table. "Ever fancy turning this into a quaint guest house?"

I pushed the steaming cup his way. "You're willing to pay me now?"

"Sweat equity for all debts, public and private." He sipped and gave an approving nod. "So. What's not for the tender ears of an open phone line? Oh, and great show on that bell-end LeSuer."

"Couldn't have done it without you," I said. "After I tell you everything else, you might not want to unpack."

"Get bent."

I gave him the edited and by now well-practiced version of events starting with Cullen going thump in the night and ending with all the latest on the Albanian escalation.

"I can't say you didn't warn me." Banter aside, it was clear I had his attention. "You know more about these chaps, but what I do know is you're right to be worried. They aren't much for avoiding collateral damage."

I told him the thin leads we were pursuing.

"Better than nothing," he said. "But remind me of the stakes when I'm dozing off at the screens."

Water surged up the pipes in the wall as the upstairs shower turned on.

Tom smiled. "I didn't realize you had company. Three's a crowd? Say no more, I'll go pester Rollie. I'm sure he has vacancies."

"There's guest bedrooms here, and Rollie will make you really sweat for your equity."

"Oh right, Señor Chore," Tom said. "Anyway, I'm glad she's okay after all that."

"Had some strange nights, that ranks right up there." One of my burners buzzed and danced on the wooden dining room table.

William.

I took the call. "It's me."

"Eight." His message was brief, but the pain in his voice was unmistakable.

"When?"

"This morning."

"Damn. Do you need to see me?" I asked.

"Not unless you have anything."

"Wish I had better news, but we're trying hard."

"You know how to reach me."

I thanked him and hung up.

Tom watched, letting me go first.

"They just sent over another finger."

"Bloody hell. Charlie O'Brien's?"

I nodded. "Eight left. That's the message, and I have to think they intend to do this every day until William gives up."

"Or they run out of pieces of Charlie," Tom said. "Poor bastard."

Sandy came down the stairs, and we both clammed up before Tom greeted her and I got my kiss.

"Doing okay?" I asked. "Want some breakfast?"

"Sure, I'll get it," she said. "I didn't mean to interrupt."

I was still getting used to letting her in on all our business, and in this case, it really wasn't "breakfast news."

After she'd had something, I let her know what had happened. Her paramedic training ensured she wasn't squeamish, but a strong stomach and worrying about it happening to yourself were different things.

"He can't take much more of this," she said. "Either they'll kill him, he'll slip into shock, or infection will run wild." She started toward the basement.

"She's right," Tom said. "They can't keep pruning him like a bloody tree."

"Yeah," I agreed. "Something has to break. Hon, are you sure you want the first shift?"

"You may have to move out, and I'm okay here."

She went downstairs and Tom finished up in the kitchen. I lifted his bag to take it up to the guest room. It was awfully heavy. "Jeez, what's in here?"

"Whatever you do, don't open it, mate. It's rigged."

I was pretty sure he was kidding, but I was going to let him unpack his own luggage anyhow.

* * *

With Tom upstairs and Sandy monitoring between our place, Rollie's house and now feeds from the port, I had a few minutes to myself. I sat at the small kitchen table and stared at a blank spot on the wall, letting my mind drift. There was a small grease spot the shape of Sicily just under one of the cabinets. I hadn't gotten around to repainting this part of the kitchen, so the mark was from high school days. One of the rare times Ryan let me come over after school, we tried to make popcorn, and it could have gone better. At least nobody was killed. Staring at that stain took me back to simpler days and often cleared my head.

I heard a voice downstairs. If not for leaving the door to the basement open, I might have missed it altogether. I peeked out the back door and saw nothing. I went to the top of the stairs. "Sandy? Everything okay?"

"Yeah, I think so. I forgot how to work the intercom," she said. "A blue car just pulled up front." She said something else I didn't catch.

"Just one?" I yelled.

"Yeah."

I took the pistol hidden in the tin breadbox in the kitchen and hurried down the hallway. The camera feeds would record everything, so if they took off, I'd see it in review.

By the time I got halfway down the hallway, I heard the buzzer indicating a person on the front of the property. If Sandy was calling out new information, I couldn't hear her anymore.

I hit the front parlor at a low crouch and chambered a round in the Beretta. Only then did I peer from the curtains.

Parked in front I saw a familiar car. There couldn't be two such blue bugs with gaudy Bentley grills.

Beet.

Before I dropped my guard all the way I realized it could have been a different driver and my stomach dropped at the idea of the little guy snatched up.

The doorbell rang and the alert silenced. I caught a glimpse of Tom's face at the top of the stairs but keeping his body in cover. I peeked out the door and felt all the air go out in a whoosh. Flipping on the safety and tucking the gun in the small of my back, I opened the door.

"Beet, I didn't expect you. You always call first."

His usual goofy grin was nowhere to be found, and I glanced behind him and tried to see past the smoked-out window tint in the car. No dice.

"Hi, Kyle. They said to come in person."

My heart skipped a beat. "They?"

"Can I come in?" It wasn't cold out, but he looked like he might start shivering in his Leonard Nimoy T-shirt.

"Of course." I looked upstairs to make sure Tom wasn't about to blow a hole in us by mistake.

Beet moved to the living room but remained on his feet. Usually, he took "make yourself at home" to heart and would plop into one of the overstuffed chairs.

"You came alone, right?"

I wanted to take the question back as soon as it left my mouth. Typically, that was a roundabout way of asking if someone was wired, but Beet was more into literal communication. "I drove myself," he said. "I don't think that guy could fit in my car."

Wasn't such a bad question after all. "What guy?"

Beet smiled and it might've passed as sincere if I didn't know him. "Nobody. Just kidding. Hi, Ms. Sandy!"

"Hi, Beet," Sandy said. "Did you need anything?"

"No, thanks, but it was great to see you." Usually he'd ask for a snack. Instead, he was all business. He shifted on his feet, a classic Beet tell that he had important information to share. It always reminded me of a little kid who needed to use the bathroom.

"I'll be upstairs if you need me," she said.

"Let's go to the kitchen. We can talk in private."

"Are you sure? I saw another car out front." Beet was whispering now. "I thought maybe they came here first."

We walked to the kitchen, and I explained that Tom was in town with a rental car. "All right, Beet, spill. Who is 'they,' and what happened?"

"Milosh again." Beet sank into a metal chair, and his hands were shaking.

No fresh bruises or cuts on his face. "All right. You saw him? Where? Outside the port?" Maybe we missed it and it would be recorded on one of the security feeds.

"He saw me. He and the guard, the guy you call Tank. They were at my house." Beet buried his face in his hands. "*In* my house. Waiting for me."

"Did they . . .?" Blood heated my face.

"Not this time. But they said they would if I didn't give you this." He took out an envelope.

It was sealed and had my initials on it: KL.

I gave Beet's shoulder a squeeze to let him know it was okay. As usual, Beet himself was part of the message. *We know where he lives.*

I tore open the envelope to see what the rest of it was.

Meet me at my old office. 10 a.m. tomorrow. Alone. You will be safe.

CHAPTER 17

Kyle's place

I tried to ignore the grumbling at the "All-Hands-on-Deck" message because I knew we didn't have much time, and our other leads weren't panning out.

As usual, Rollie arrived first (besides those of us who were already at the house), and VP was last. She had the farthest to travel, though she kept her exact location secret, something that made sense after what happened to Beet. I'd sent him to the port and told him not to go home. I figured he'd be safe there, at least until this latest development was finished.

"It's a trap, of course." Rollie flipped the note onto the dining room table. "'Come alone'? Really?"

"So, where's this office?" VP said. "Maybe your Irish buddies would like to know."

"It has to be the alley behind his old coffee shop, Cream of the Cup. That's what he used to call it when we used to exchange pleasantries and threats."

"Figures," Rollie said. "Terrible sightlines." He was thinking like a sniper.

"And plenty of privacy," I said.

"So that's out, then?" Tom said.

"Hold on." I held up my hand. "Sure, it could be a trap, but why would he bother? He knows where I live. Rollie too."

"Maybe he don't want a fair fight," Rollie said.

"Neither do I." I smiled. "But I prefer the scales tilted the other way."

"Right," said Tom.

"Look," I said, "I don't think he went to the trouble of the invite simply to kill me. He's got something on his mind."

"Why not a longer note?" VP asked.

"Notes can get intercepted," Tom said.

"VP," I said, "did you get any further on your search?"

Her head dipped down. Usually this was her cue to dazzle us with her hacking prowess. "Yo, these bums are too analog, you know?"

"Not sure," I said. "You mean not much of a digital footprint?"

"Neanderthal level. On the medical front, I found some doctor dudes who got their hands slapped, a few who got suspended. Usually, it was prescription drug crap. But there's too many of them to stake out, and nobody is taking out Craigslist ads saying, 'Will stitch you up for cheap. No questions asked.'" Her voice cracked in frustration.

"If you can't find them online, nobody can," I said. "So, that's why I'm going to meet him."

"Alone?" Sandy asked.

I shrugged. "That's what the note demands."

Sandy looked at me with a skeptical squint. "Just like that?"

"Not quite. I have an idea."

* * *

Fishtown, the next morning

I was glad I allowed plenty of time to find a parking spot. The extra driving-around time let me scope out the area around the coffee shop. Since we'd run Milosh and his crew out of the place more than a year ago, it was under new ownership. I didn't think they'd appreciate if I barged through the shop and went to the alley via the back door. It would have to be the scenic route. I didn't see any surly characters watching me, but that didn't mean they weren't.

Over in the Sand Box, I learned to trust my gut if danger was close. Strangely, despite my nerves, I didn't get that creepy feeling. Maybe that meant Milosh was coming as a friend. Sure, that was it.

Around the corner, the entrance to the alley beckoned. I could see the big dumpsters right by the back of the café.

"At alley," I whispered.

The deep-concealed Bluetooth earpiece crackled, and VP's voice came through like she was next to me. "Clean signal," she said.

"Going in."

I walked to the dumpster by the back door for Cream of the Cup. No sign of Milosh or his hulking bodyguard. A rat scurried along the wall, but he didn't count. I half expected Milosh to pop out of one of the garbage cans but more likely it'd be out the back door itself.

I checked the time and at a couple minutes after ten began to wonder if I'd been stood up.

Just then I heard the trill of a cell phone, and for an instant, I was certain it was the trigger for a bomb. A moment later, I knew it was just a phone but my legs got shaky as I pulled my mind from a roadside in Iraq that day the IED took out my truck and nearly me with it.

The phone rang again, and I snapped back to the present. It wasn't my phone. Had someone dropped one? The sound came from around the side of one of the dumpsters. I stepped around and realized the phone was taped to the underside of one of the metal boxes where a trash truck's forklift could pick it up.

"Cell. He's playing games," I whispered and tore the tape off and hit the button to answer. "What are you doing?"

Milosh's Eastern European-accented voice was unmistakable. "I thought you'd know where to come. You are alone?"

"Aren't you watching me from somewhere?"

"Maybe I am, maybe not."

"You think it will rain today? How's the Eagles defense look this year? Pat's or Geno's cheesesteaks?"

"Huh?"

"And I just love what you've done with the alley," I growled into the phone. "Enough crap, why am I here?"

"You were there to find the phone. Next, you have some errands around town to run so I can make sure you are really alone."

"You gotta be kidding."

"We need to talk face-to-face. Now, or things will get out of control. Go to the skatepark at Tenton and Hazzard. You know it?"

I repeated the intersection so VP would have it right away. "I know it. Not much of a boarder myself."

"You'll see a red fire hydrant. A playing card will be taped to the bottom. Tell me the number and suit so I'll know you're there."

"That it?" I said.

"No. Leave the call connected."

"What if it drops?"

"I'll know you're lying. I tested it."

"Whatever. If it's such a great phone, then just call right back. You picked the stupid game, don't get pissy with me if it doesn't work."

"Get going."

* * *

I kept my mouth shut and VP didn't say much to me beyond, "Quarterback calling the audible," in my earpiece.

Traffic wasn't too bad. The tiny skateboard park was usually buzzing with kids practicing tricks or trying to see which bone they could break next. Sometimes it was hard to tell the difference. At any rate, this time of day there were only a few diehard daredevils.

I drove slowly over the cobblestone street, the car alignment center's friend, trying to minimize the staccato vibrations. On the plus side, I did find a parking spot, a nonstarter on a weekend.

The red hydrant was hard to miss, and right behind a trash bag leaning against it I saw the taped playing card.

"Got it," I said into the phone.

"What is it?" Milosh said.

"Jack of Hearts. Come out, come out, wherever you are."

"The park at Aramingo and Lehigh," Milosh said.

"Where? That's a big place." I named it again for VP. He was sticking to the neighborhood. He had to be close.

"Near the corner at the mural for the policemen. There's another card at the bottom."

"How's the cell service?" I hoped my sarcasm came through the cheap phone.

"Let's find out."

* * *

At the next park, a more sprawling complex, for the neighborhood anyway, with a baseball field and basketball court along with other playgrounds and a small pool. Lots of open space. Rollie would have approved, if he'd had the time to set up.

Near the corner, a mural for two fallen police officers faced the street. At the bottom of the paint, I saw the telltale electrician's tape. I reached down and peeled it off. "Two of clubs." I listened, but the traffic noise was pretty bad. I cupped my hand over my ear with the phone. "You there? Two of clubs."

"Very good." The voice came from behind me.

Milosh stepped off the unused basketball court next to the wall, with his neat, trimmed beard and wire-rimmed glasses looking as much like a baller as I had a skater.

I held up the phone. "We're done with this?"

He held out his hand, but I dropped the phone to the concrete and stomped on it with my work boot.

Milosh shrugged. "Would you like to pee on it as well? We don't have much time."

"I already figured out you aren't here to kill me." Even so, I kept an eye out for his bodyguard, the Tank.

"No. Not me. But you need to listen carefully, because your safety and that of your friends are not guaranteed."

"It's your dime." I saw the confusion on his face. "You got me out here. Let's have it."

"My cousins do not know we are speaking," he said.

That threw me. "You're going behind their back?"

"If they found out, we would both be dead men." Milosh was sweating. "You have to get William to reconsider."

I had to play this carefully. "Even if I thought that was a good idea, why would you want that, especially if your cousins don't?"

"Sometimes they only think about the short term. Like you, I take the longer view."

I wasn't sure what he meant by that but decided to play along. "Go ahead."

"The Irish are weak, and my cousins know it. But if they continue with the war, they may sacrifice the greatest prize."

"And you propose what to preserve it? C'mon, what do you want me to do?"

"If they destroy the Irish, are you saying you'd really run the port for them instead? Willingly?"

The port. Holy crap, it made sense! They thought the Irish ran the port through me, that the Irish were financing it. *That* was the prize.

"Let me guess, if you save this deal, then you want me to work for you. Managing your prize?"

"What is it you Americans say?" Milosh smiled. "The devil you know?"

"So, you want me to convince William to do what? I mean, *exactly* what?"

Milosh closed his eyes like he was trying to force himself to slow down. "The only way he can save his brother, himself, and the rest of you is if they agree to go quietly. That leaves my cousins the territory to run and me with the port."

"They do understand that without my cooperation they can't just walk in and take over the port, the permits, and all that?"

"*I* realize it. They have less value for the port and are close to abandoning the best part of their operation."

"That's too bad for you."

"Are you trying to ignore what that means?" Milosh glared at me. "It's worse for you and the O'Briens. They will simply decide to wipe you all out and run things in their usual style."

"How do you intend to convince them of the value of the port?"

"I wouldn't have been allowed to return to Philadelphia in the first place if they didn't think the port was attractive. However, only I see that isn't a bonus, it is the future. Wars attract all the wrong kind of attention, wouldn't you agree?"

Not *allowed* to return? Interesting detail. "I'd agree. And you're perceptive about the value of the port. But it has to be managed very carefully, the official scrutiny is on another level."

"I'm sure. But those obstacles can be overcome, can't they?"

I smiled. "So far, so good." He really thought it was the Irish, running a scam through the port. He had no idea about Ali and his family financing the place as a legitimate operation.

"Leave convincing my cousins to me," he said. "Their blood is high, but they can see reason. We fight for our lives as well. We can't go back to

New York." Milosh smiled back, and was that relief I saw? I think it was. "First, I need you to promise to do your part. Between us, I may be willing to cut the Irish in on a percentage of the port profits for their concession."

"You also need me to agree to keep operating under new management."

"Of course. But if you and I fail, they will never rest until they have killed you all. Be aware that while I know where some of you and your friends live, they don't. Not yet."

There it was.

"If I agree, you need to help me," I said.

Milosh practically salivated. "Yes?"

"The best leverage you have is Charlie O'Brien. But only while he lives. If I'm going to have any shot at convincing William, I have to know that they haven't already killed him."

"He is alive, I can assure you."

I didn't have to fake my laugh. "You're going to have to do better than that. Errand time for you. I need to speak to Charlie, within the hour, or there's no deal. Not negotiable." I gave Milosh a burner number.

Time stretched out and blood whooshed in my ears.

"Agreed."

CHAPTER 18

Fishtown, Aramingo Square Park

I leaned against the wall with murals and watched Milosh cross the street. "He's getting into a black Camry," I said.

Milosh turned immediately and drove northeast up Aramingo. I lost sight as soon as the car went under a railroad underpass.

VP's voice crackled in my earpiece. "T's got him. Heads up for your ride."

Just then I saw a small scooter mixed in the traffic. It had saddlebags with some logo I couldn't make out, and the rider appeared to be a small guy wearing a fully blacked-out helmet. The scooter banked to the right, following Milosh's car.

A second later, a white van with tinted windows and GreenTurf Landscaping stenciled on the side pulled up and the side door slid open. "Get in, boss." VP leaned forward with an outstretched arm.

I hopped in and Starving Steve took a second to say hello before mashing the gas hard enough to send me sprawling as the van rocketed across several lanes of traffic to follow up Aramingo. VP had several laptops open and anchored to a custom rig so they wouldn't fly all over the place. She'd ridden with Steve before.

"Welcome to the Scooby Van," Steve said. "Mobile Command, at your service."

"Think he took the bait?" VP said.

"We'll find out soon," I said.

We hung back. I could see Tom on the scooter more often than the Camry. Tom was careful not to get too close, and I wasn't worried. He'd played this sort of cat-and-mouse since he was a kid. About half a mile up the street, Tom's voice cut in on the monitor. "Target's pulling into the shopping center on the right. I'm going past in case he made me."

"What's this?" I said.

The Camry pulled into a spot outside a department store.

"Maybe he's meeting someone?" VP said.

Milosh got out of the car and looked around. I was glad we'd pulled over a hundred yards away and the van blended in with other vehicles parked along the busy road.

Milosh began walking toward the store entrance.

"Out of clean underwear?" VP suggested.

"Something's wrong." I told Tom over the radio what happened.

"I'll orbit," he said. "Keep me posted."

VP popped an earpiece in and a transmitter, then pulled up her hoodie and yanked the sliding door open.

"What are you doing?" I asked.

"Going shopping, what's it look like?" She started walking fast toward the same entrance. Milosh was already inside.

This wasn't in the playbook, but neither was our target turning into a pedestrian.

Now we heard VP on the radio. I had to assume Tom was on the same frequency. "Dude, we can't lose this guy now. He's up to something."

"Probably including waiting inside the entrance to grab you as an insurance policy."

"I don't think he made us, but he's still being super careful. Almost to the door, going dark for now."

"At least Milosh doesn't know her," I said, as much to reassure myself as Steve, who sat and drummed his fingers on the steering wheel.

After a couple minutes that felt like hours, we heard VP. She was whispering. "He circled the men's department. Went right by me while I was trying on sunglasses. A little pucker factor for me then, not gonna lie. He's moving toward the back of the store."

"Is he near the bathrooms? Changing rooms? Going for a costume switch?" My mind raced.

"I'm not sure, he's . . . damn!"

"What?"

"Pick me up in front. Fast."

"WHAT?"

VP was breathing harder, I assumed she must be running.

"Steve," I said, "get to the front of the store. Just don't crash."

I was about to ask if he had a gun when VP broke in. "He went through an 'employees only' door."

Now Tom cut in. "He's going out the back, cheeky bastard. I'll be there in thirty seconds."

"Don't get too close."

"Do you give Rollie shooting tips too?" Tom said.

Cocky SOB.

Steve snaked the van around shoppers and carts, and we saw VP emerge just before we got there. I opened the door and she dove in.

"Let's move from here in case he comes back out the front," I said.

Steve drove near to the exit to the street. I could still see the entrance through the tinted back windows.

Tom said, "Right. I'm loitering by a pizza shop. Got a good view of the back of the place."

I clicked the microphone. "Nothing out the front."

"There's our boy," Tom said. "Popped out like a Jack-in-the-box."

"Where's he going?" I said.

"He's waving."

"At you?" A shot of fear zinged through my chest.

"Don't think so. Couldn't be." I hated the doubt in Tom's voice. "Ah. Not me. Here comes a silver Chevy with some huge bastard at the wheel."

"Which direction?"

"Right, sorry. Heading east. I'm hanging back and flowing."

"Get ready. He's with his bodyguard."

"Got you," Tom said. His voice was all business.

I glanced at a map. "Steve, stay on Aramingo. Fast. Let's get ahead of them. Take the second right."

The van roared up the street, and he weaved around slower traffic, earning some horns and digital salutes, but no accidents.

"They are going straight," Tom reported.

Not for long. The street ended at an intersection, and I had no idea which way they were headed. The van tires moaned in protest at the turn as Steve put the big vehicle through its paces.

"We're turning ahead of you, looking good?" I said to Tom.

"I have you in sight. You're about half a block ahead."

I stared through the van's darkened rear windows. "I see him." Milosh was talking to Tank, who held the steering wheel like a toy. Tom puttered along well behind.

"Almost, Steve." I loved the way he slowed down, pointed out the window, sped up and slowed again, like he was looking for a particular address. Milosh and Tank caught up to us, and I was glad of the dark windows.

Steve almost stopped and angled the van just enough so that it would be difficult to pass on the narrow street.

"Now." I braced myself, as did VP.

Tank blasted the horn and Steve got off the brake and hit the gas. The moment the silver car also accelerated, Steve slammed on the brakes.

The nose of the Chevy dipped under heavy braking, but they'd been caught by surprise and the car hit the rear with a metallic thump. I saw the car's hood dent.

Steve hit his flashers and leapt out of the van. "Shit! Aw man, I'm so sorry! I was lost."

Tank waved at Steve to clear a path. I moved closer to the open window on the driver's side.

"Move that piece of shit out of the way." Tank's English had improved.

Steve stood by the car's side and fumbled with a wallet. "I have insurance."

While both men were now screaming at Steve to move the van, Tom pulled up behind them in the scooter. He ducked down, just for a second, while Steve tried to force Tank to take his insurance card. Tank was fully distracted. Steve tried to match the two men's volume by shouting that it was all his fault.

Tom pressed the nasally little horn on his scooter and putted around the two vehicles and up the street.

Steve stopped waving his card at the big Albanian, and I could hear him clear as day, "I'll call the police. The accident report will be official. I screwed up!"

"No police!" Tank shouted and shoved Steve with one arm.

Steve went flying and staggered backward until he tripped over the curb and landed on his butt. He seemed okay.

Tank put the damaged but drivable car into reverse and pulled about twenty feet back to a cross street, where he sped away.

Steve was already on his feet.

"You're good?" I asked as soon as he was back in the van.

"Scraped one palm, not bad." He pulled forward. "But Kyle?"

"Yeah?"

"I call 'Not it' for fighting that guy if it ever comes to it."

"You're a smart man." I smiled. I'd been manhandled by the beast and wasn't interested in a rematch. "Great job."

I glanced over at VP, who was hunched over one of the laptops, lost in concentration.

"Bitchin!" She turned to me and gave me a huge crooked grin. "Strong, steady signal."

I let out a huge breath. "You guys are the best. Tom, I don't care what anybody says about you, you're a stud."

"How would you know, mate?" Tom shot back. "Great news. Going to circle back for a slice of that pie."

"Eat it fast, the hard part's coming up."

"Too right," Tom said.

* * *

Philadelphia, in the van

"Take it easy, Steve," I said. "We don't need to see him."

"Gotcha." Steve called over his shoulder to VP: "How far?"

"Chill. The tracker's GPS. We just want to be able to see where they land." She looked at me. "Bluetooth ones need to be a lot closer, like two hundred feet, tops."

I was still learning. "Okay. When they do stop—and it can't be too far, I'm sure of it—we just want the lay of the land."

VP returned to staring at her laptop. "Doubling back and onto Route 676. I think they are heading into Jersey."

We were just across the river. I thought about toll booths and other revenue-collecting cameras. "We legal?"

Steve was already looking for a spot to pull over. "Nope. I didn't want to give those goons anything to work with in case they aren't all knuckle-draggers." He glanced at VP, telling me the fake tags were his idea. "I have the legit ones here. Give me a second."

While he was outside fixing the plate and tearing off the logo to reveal what I was told was a pest control company, VP said without looking up from the screen, "I think he's a keeper."

Steve was the most recent person in our inner circle.

"He did well today," I agreed. "You're thinking for strategy as well?"

Steve was her find and was as much a part of her network as he was mine. Still, we had be extremely careful who got to know our secrets, as we usually operated outside the legal lines.

"Maybe," she said. "Let's see this play out."

Steve popped open the door and tossed in the lawn care sign he'd removed. "How we doing?"

"Steady on 676," VP said. "Over the river."

"And through the slums, and not to grandmother's house, I'll bet," I said.

We rolled along, and VP called out an exit that put us in scenic Camden. We passed by Rutgers Law School.

A few minutes later, VP stared at the dot. "Pretty long for a red light. Slow down, Steve. Yeah, I think we got it."

We drove under a set of railroad tracks and past an old cemetery.

She pointed. "There's the building, the rough place on the corner."

Rough was an understatement. The place looked like it had survived some near misses by a bombing run, and the old brick-strewn field across the street had been the target of direct hits.

VP held up her phone, taking video as we went by. Parked in front of the dilapidated but intact one-story structure, we all saw the silver car. An old Dodge SUV sat next to it.

"I didn't see anyone in the car," I said. "We were what, five minutes behind them?"

"Four and a half," Steve said. "Want me to park?"

I patted my pockets for phones and located the one I had for Milosh to call. "Yeah, just keep your distance. We need to know for sure. Does it look like their main hideout?"

"Not my field, dude," VP said. "Not too many cars, unless they're all out on the warpath."

"Good point."

Steve raised his hand like he was a kid in school. I just gave him a look. "Well," he said, "if it was me, I wouldn't want a guy like Charlie O'Brien knowing where we holed up. Not if I was going to let him live."

"Go on."

"This place looks plenty private but also disposable, know what I mean?"

"Interesting. I agree."

VP peered through binoculars. "Oh, snap!"

"What snap?" I said.

She handed me the glasses and began to tug an aluminum case out from under one of the seats. "Check it. Boarded-up windows, but look at the top corners of the building."

"Nice catch," I said. "One camera, two camera, and here's another one lower down to watch the front door. I'll assume they have the back covered."

"No need to assume." VP pointed to a small camera drone nestled in cut-out foam lining the opened case at her feet.

I shook my head. "Not worth the risk. If they somehow see it, Charlie is as good as dead."

"So, we just chill for now?" she said.

"Shouldn't be too long. Milosh was in a hurry. If Charlie really is in there, we should know soon."

While we waited, Tom checked in that he and Rollie were back at the house. Sandy had been watching the feeds and so far, all quiet.

We all jumped when the phone rang. Milosh.

"Yeah?" I answered. Everyone else knew to be quiet.

"You know who this is."

"Long time no talk." Sweat rolled into my eyes.

"We have a deal. Don't get clever, just do your part."

"Let me talk to him. I'll ask him something only he would know, or the deal's off."

"Fine. We will listen as well."

After a long pause, I heard first gagging and spitting, then some very Charlie-like cursing. Then Milosh's voice. "Talk."

"Who's this?" His voice sounded rougher and at the same time weaker, but I recognized it right away.

"Charlie? It's Kyle. Are you okay?"

"Fuck no, I'm not okay," he said. "Where's William?"

"Not here, but I'll let him will know you're"—I was going to say okay—"still alive."

Charlie growled, "Don't give these cocksuckers a damn thing, you hear me?"

Milosh came on the line. "Are you satisfied?"

"It's him. Look, I'll speak to William right away, but he's not an easy man to persuade."

"We all have our problems." I could hear Milosh's footsteps crunching on what sounded like broken glass. When he spoke again, I assumed Charlie wouldn't be able to hear me. "The clock is ticking. My cousins won't hesitate to send the next message, and the next, until he's out of parts to remove. Understand?"

"You're all butchers."

"Then pay the butcher's bill." He hung up.

CHAPTER 19

Kyle's place

Since everyone was already at the house, we were able to hit the ground running, so to speak. We all huddled around the dining room table. VP had cobbled together an overhead satellite picture of the building courtesy of Google Maps, and we all tried to fill in details that we just saw from the ground.

"Is that image close to current?" Rollie asked.

"Pretty much," I said. "The windows are covered, but the doors look the same."

VP pointed. "Cameras here, here, and here, and on the door."

One of VP's laptops was on a side table. She glanced at it, and I saw the tracker on the silver car hadn't moved.

"Milosh is still there, looks like."

"Wish we knew how many others were inside," Rollie said.

"Only one other vehicle, so it shouldn't be too many," I said. "Charlie will have a guard or two on him. I was thinking whoever is chopping pieces off him must come in to do the work. They still want him alive."

"For now." Rollie shook his head. "If you'd told me I'd feel sorry for an O'Brien . . . Ah, hell. They're not the worst, and if those animals are going to replace them . . ."

"If they let us live," I added.

"Speaking of O'Briens, what are you going to tell William?"

We knew we didn't have much time, and collaborating with other groups wasn't our style. "Nothing, for now. A few more hours won't hurt. Anyone here think telling him anything before we move will help?"

"Oh, sure," Rollie said. "We point William and Cullen that way and they'll charge in and get everyone, including us, killed. No thanks."

I couldn't have said it any better.

"Tom, you and Rollie have the most experience." I knew Tom had worked scouting for an extraction team once or twice over in Iraq.

"Only a little," he said. "But we came up with something while you were on the way over."

Rollie scrolled through some of the footage we'd recorded. "Those trees by the overpass. Thick enough for an old fart like me?"

I saw where he was going. "Yup."

"Right. Here's what I was thinking," Tom began.

* * *

Camden, NJ, two hours later

I shuffled down the street, pausing to hike up my baggy pants. The puddle Sandy insisted I sit in had left one side still damp after the ride over the bridge. She said it was worth it, but then again, she didn't have to wear the soggy getup.

Once in sight of the building, I paused at a trash can and began to paw through the contents. There was half of a hot dog that smeared mustard on my sleeve. Something near the bottom that must have festered for days made my stomach clench so I held my breath. I extracted a couple bottles and an aluminum can and stashed them in a plastic bag. Peeking up the street, I finally saw a short figure staggering in my direction. He looked like he hadn't changed clothes in a month. We both wore greasy baseball caps pulled low on our heads. He had the 76ers while I favored the Flyers.

He adjusted his cap, which was my signal to abandon my treasure trove of recyclables and proceed toward him on the sidewalk in front of the building.

While there was car traffic on the main road around the corner, we had this side street to ourselves. This rundown section of town kept the tourists to a minimum. The same SUV was still parked in front, and we'd confirmed that Milosh's car had left the scene.

"Where's my stuff?" I slurred at Tom as he approached, looking like he was trying to turn invisible and slide by me. We were right in the sightline of the camera trained on the front door.

"Hey!" I said. "I'm talking to you." I put my hand on Tom's shoulder.

"Get off me! Help! Rape! I don't have your stuff." Tom tried to wriggle free, and I spun him around and slammed him into the side of the SUV. He slapped the side and absorbed the shove like a Mexican backyard wrestler. The force was enough to set off the car alarm.

Over the din of the honking alarm horn, I heard an impact on the camera. I glanced at it and saw a neat hole in the side, and a moment later another hit and the camera wept shards of glass.

Tom punched me in the chest and slapped the side of my head, being careful not to knock off my cap. I hoisted him up and slammed him down on the SUV's hood.

Soon after, the front door swung open. Tom and I pretended not to hear while we cursed each other over some stolen prize.

"Get the fuck out of here!" We turned to gape at him. A heavyset guy with black hair and a five-o'clock shadow. He had an aluminum baseball bat, and his dark eyes were red-rimmed with fury.

"He took my money!" I yelled.

The guy was in no mood to play referee, and as I'd hoped, decided to yank us off his car before he bashed our heads in. We both hit the ground in a heap, and as we rolled off each other, the guy raised the bat to clobber someone.

When we were separated, both of us drew pistols. The long suppressors screwed on the end of the barrel told the guy he wasn't dealing with winos after all.

"Bat down. Hands up. Da?" I knew the prick wasn't Russian but hoped it would insult him.

He was faster on the uptake than I expected. He lowered the bat, but he looked like he was thinking way too much. I spotted the butt of a pistol in his waistband.

So did Tom. "Ah, ah." Tom rose fluidly to his feet, pressed the suppressor into the guy's chest, and grabbed the gun with the other hand. I picked up the bat. We spun the guy around, and I used the bat lengthwise to buckle his knees while Tom zip-tied his arms behind his back. We pushed him over, and Tom taped his mouth while I zipped his feet together.

"Good speed, mate. Now get down." Tom crouched near the door on the hinge side. I squatted by the back bumper of the SUV, making sure to stay in the blind spots for the other cameras.

Not two seconds later, the door slammed open like it had been kicked. It might have hit Tom, but I didn't have time to worry about that. I knew the first thing in the next guard's vision would be his buddy all trussed up and unable to speak.

"Jak?" I heard the guard call out to his partner over the din of the still-honking car alarm.

Then he cried out in pain. I risked a look and found him clutching his knee. He was holding a gun in his other hand and scanning for a target. A moment later, he collapsed just outside the door when his other knee took a round. This time the impact happened between horn honks. There was a hiss, way too close to my head, then a smacking sound and the guy was down. But not out. He still held the pistol, barely, and his expression told me all I needed to know about getting kneecapped.

Avoid it.

Tom stepped out from behind the door in a flash and stomped on the guy's gun arm. It didn't take much. Tom scooped up the weapon, and I dragged him next to his buddy. We zipped his arms and ignored his legs. Crawling would be agony, let alone walking. Tom prepared the tape, but first I leaned in close to the guy. "How many more?"

He answered, but it was likely Albanian and probably involved taboo relations with our mothers. "Okay, no doctor." Tom got the last word and taped his mouth shut.

I searched the men while Tom covered me. I found the key fob for the SUV and silenced the alarm. Still no other guard, but that didn't mean that there wasn't one.

"We can't wait forever," I said. "Even if they're the only ones here they might have made a call."

"We'll have to chance going in now," Tom said.

I agreed and we went inside with Tom taking the lead. I was right behind him, and we'd already worked out that he would crouch so I could fire over him if necessary. Neither of us were special operators by any means, but we'd been in some tough situations before and tried not to trip over each other.

Just inside the doorway we both froze and listened. Nothing. Seeing pieces of glass on the floor of a hallway, I pictured Milosh walking on them when he called me. "I think he's down here."

There was a door with a slit glass window in it. It was heavier, not just a flimsy, hollow interior door. I tried my best to tiptoe around the noisy glass pieces and moved ahead of Tom. When we'd pause, it was still quiet.

Tom hung back and watched out for a surprise from behind us.

I reached the door and peered through the glass. It was filthy but someone had recently rubbed a clean spot presumably to use as a look-out. I half expected a face to appear, but when none did, I looked through it. I saw a desk with a bunch of old TVs in a row. One was snowed out, and the others looked like camera feeds.

I scanned the rest of the room through the grimy peephole, and my heart jumped when I saw the back of a big guy in a chair. I didn't need to see the face to know that the red hair belonged to Charlie. That, and the person was strapped into the chair and struggling.

If he was trying to escape, there weren't any men in that room. "Got him," I hissed at Tom. "Check the men out front."

I got a good grip on my pistol and tried the door. Unlocked.

I opened it and swept the muzzle around the room. It was clear. Charlie was in a large area with a closed tall metal garage door designed for truck deliveries. His left hand looked like dirty white bandages over a catcher's mitt. At the other end of the room, I could see a wooden butcher's block and crimson stains. The whole room stank of urine, sweat, and rubbing alcohol.

"Charlie!" I hissed.

He stopped struggling and started trying to turn around. His head whipped back and forth, and all I could hear were muffled sounds around the gag in his mouth.

I tucked the gun in its holster and stood in front of him. He looked confused and for an instant I was worried he might be delirious, then I remembered the disguise. I took off the hat and whispered. "It's Kyle."

Instant recognition. Good.

"We got two of them out front. Are there more?"

He began to shake his head, then he shrugged. He wasn't sure.

"One sec." I ran over to the camera feed screens and saw a pile of cigarette butts ground out next to a chair. It was a sloppy setup, but best of all, no sign of a recorder. I yanked the power to the whole thing and returned to Charlie.

"Don't move." I flicked open a small, sharp pocket knife. I cut his gag off and then freed his hands and legs.

His face was flushed, out of rage or possible infection. Maybe both. "Think you can walk?"

"Help me up and I'll know," he said. "Is William here?"

"No." He slung his good arm over my shoulder, and I lifted him to his feet. He shuffled a bit, and after a few steps, he appeared to be able to move. "We had to move fast. We still need to get out of here."

His balance wasn't so hot, so we made do with him leaning on me. I drew the gun and kept it in one hand as we made our way down the hallway. We paused at the entrance, and I saw Tom, who had corralled the two guards, prone next to the SUV.

Tom spoke in a menacing whisper. "Right, the next one of you mugs tries to inchworm to the street gets me backing this thing over your legs. Now face down and shut up."

The one who'd been shot had clearly been having some trouble with the shut-up part, as Tom had stuffed one of his socks in his mouth.

"Stay here," I said to Charlie. Despite the brutal treatment he'd received, I was glad to see him gaining mobility. He spotted the guards and perked up even more.

I stepped closer to the street. With no need to worry about the cameras, I gave two thumbs-up to Rollie, concealed in the trees half a block away, his signal to radio for our ride. From this distance, he was invisible, and the suppressed .22 wouldn't have even bothered the nearby pigeons.

I heard a faint, whirring hum and glanced over the top of the building. Sure enough, a tiny drone hovered, and as soon as I noticed it, it waggled in the air. I waved back.

"Ride's coming." I met Tom's gaze and pantomimed closing my eyes with my palm.

He nodded and used wide tape to act as makeshift blindfolds.

"Wait," Charlie said before Tom taped the first guard, who hadn't been shot. He climbed down several cement steps from the front entrance to the driveway. "Flip him over."

I took another look at Charlie's hand and nodded to Tom, who understood.

Charlie waved the wrapped paw to get the man's attention, then braced one hand on the SUV for balance and kicked the guy hard in the ribs. Once, twice. He'd drawn his foot back for a third kick when the van pulled into sight up the block.

"We have to go, Charlie." I helped him toward the sidewalk but not before he stepped on the other guy's wounded knee.

"No," Charlie said. "Gimmie that gat. They have to go."

"No time," I said. "This is my party right now." He wasn't used to taking instructions, but he allowed himself to be moved along.

The van pulled alongside and the door slid open. Tom had covered the guard's eyes just before the van arrived.

VP was shrouded in her hoodie and staring down at her smartphone nestled in a drone controller. "Yo, I think company is coming."

"I was afraid of that. Step up, Charlie." Rollie was already in the van, and he reached out to take Charlie's good hand and help him inside. "It's okay. You know me." He'd pulled off a camo-style ski mask.

VP kept her head down, focused on her present task. "Yup, just in time. There's a van pulling up to the entrance. Should get interesting. Steve, rights and lefts for the next couple blocks, then pull over so I can recover the bird."

"You got it," he said.

"You put those guys down?" Charlie knew Rollie.

Rollie gestured to a case. "Suppressed Ruger .22 with subsonic ammo."

"Yer shittin' me."

"Discourages the bad guys and won't wake the neighbors."

"I got another way to discourage them," Charlie said, cradling his wounded hand, "and the neighbors know better than to speak out of turn."

I think this was well shy of the outpouring of gratitude he'd expected, so Rollie shot back, "Yeah? How's that working for you?"

Charlie inflated to respond, then just as quickly deflated and slumped in his seat. This was a sight I imagined few if anybody had ever seen, but getting slowly dismembered wasn't part of his program. He began to shiver.

"Tom, you got a blanket?" I asked.

"Sure, here you go. Have some water." Charlie shook his head, but then took the bottle and gulped half of it down.

"Got a chaser for the chaser?" Charlie said to me.

I smiled and fished out the glass pint flask I'd packed on a hunch. "Not collector grade," I said, "but it'll have to do for now."

Charlie took it and took a deep pull of the whiskey. His eyes watered. "Thank you." He looked around. "All of you." He saluted us with the flask and had another draught. He lowered the bottle to his lap, and it bumped the wounded hand. He winced. "Christ, that hurts."

At a traffic light, VP, who'd moved into the front seat, lowered the window. "Don't move, Steve. Easy, easy . . . got it." She'd landed the small drone on the roof, grabbed it, and brought it inside the van.

Okay. I called up front, "Steve, RTB." That meant stopping off at my place, a necessary pause. "VP, can you get Sandy and let her know we're good and to stay alert.

"Got it," she said.

"What the hell is going on?" Charlie said. "Aren't you taking me home?"

"Soon. Dropping these guys off first. We just kicked the hornet's nest." Rollie met my gaze. "We're going to Doc Crock. William can meet us there."

"Call William now," Charlie said.

I wasn't sure that was a good idea, but what would I say if I was in the same position?

"All right," I said. "Everyone clear? Steve, stay there too. Rollie is in charge of security."

"Best listen if you like your knees," Tom said, and Rollie punched him in the arm.

"A phone." Charlie held out his hand.

"I'll get him on the line."

Now he gripped my arm and squeezed my forearm hard enough to leave a bruise. "Make sure he's alone."

"Why?"

"Just do it," in his best not-going-to-ask-again voice.

CHAPTER 20

Kyle's place

When we reached the house, Charlie decided to wait until everyone had gotten out of the van and then he made me wait outside.

Rollie and Tom hung back while everyone else went inside. So far, the street was quiet. I thought it was still a little fast for the Albanians to organize a response. I had expected my phone to go crazy, but it occurred to me that Milosh might not have been in the Albanian van pulling up right after we left.

Rollie spoke up. "Mind if I help myself to something a little more potent than a .22?"

"Mi shotgun, su shotgun," I said. The house felt like a sitting duck. I swallowed. "Think it was a mistake to leave those two back there?"

"We could have taken them with, but that's too many moving parts. And I don't kill just for convenience."

"Yeah. But if those guys get another shot at us?"

Rollie got a spooky, distant look in his eyes. "When we have a choice, we choose. When we don't . . ." He looked at and through me at the same time.

There it was. Simple. Brutal.

"Tom." I waited until he got close and kept my voice low. "I need you to go back to Ohio."

"Mate, don't you need as many people here as possible?"

"You're reading my mind, but not like you think." I recapped what Milosh had said about the port being a major goal for the Albanians. "Ali's investment is very much at risk. If those people get their hands on it, we'll lose everything, not just our sorry butts but his whole operation there."

"If I catch your drift, are you sure you want me to ask Ali that?"

"The Irish are about tapped for manpower, and the Albanians are ready to pounce. The Irish need to be able to show strength. If they can, maybe we back them down. Ali's people are real warriors, not goons."

We'd both seen Ali's people in action, and they were tough, brave, and absolutely loyal.

"Right. I'll leave straightaway." Tom pointed at Rollie. "Don't start anything without me, yeah?"

Charlie pounded on the van door. "Ambulance driver, let's go."

Rollie smiled. "You left that bottle in there didn't you?"

* * *

I grabbed my phone as I climbed into the driver's seat.

"What are you doing?" Charlie asked.

"Calling Doc so he can be ready."

"Just go. William is taking care of it."

I wanted to argue that William didn't understand the extent of his brother's injuries, but of course he did. The Albanians had been sending them to him a piece at a time.

"So, you were able to get a hold of him, then?" Leading Questions 101.

"Kyle, we got big problems."

"Are there any other kind?"

"We have a mole."

It hit me as a surprise, but when I thought about it, a rat on the inside made sense. The Irish had walked into a perfect ambush when they'd thought they were the ones to set the trap.

"Who?"

"In a minute." Charlie held the bottle, and I saw he'd put a big dent in the pint. "How the hell did you find me?"

Fair question, especially since he was thinking about traitors. I explained about Milosh and the Albanian's mistaken assumption that the Irish really ran the port.

"So," I said, "Milosh is worried enough about losing his big reason for involvement that he would risk his neck trying to get my cooperation."

"You screwed him good with that tracker." Charlie let out a loud laugh.

123

That hadn't been my intention, exactly, but I suppose that was true. "I screwed myself and my people as well. Even if I convinced Milosh now that you guys aren't in on the port, this rescue adventure seals the deal."

"Welcome to the party," Charlie said. "That was a slick number. I'll give you that."

"Yeah, well now we have big problems together."

"William told me how bad we got hit. A lot of good men," Charlie said. "Glad to hear about Cullen."

I wasn't going to use the word "good" to describe a bunch of hired killers, but felt it would be rude to interrupt.

"He also said that was you guys too," he went on. "Means a lot."

"He came to us." But maybe now wasn't time for the "Aw shucks" bit. "Charlie?"

"What?"

"We need to trust each other if we're going to make it through this alive. Who's the mole?"

Old habits clamped his mouth shut. New realities pried it open. "The night of the sit-down ambush, we had our guys in position. We were all set. Hell, we called the location, so why wouldn't we be?"

"The mole?"

"They had a way in that we thought was covered, so by the time I heard the first shots, the bastards were already in behind most of our guys." Charlie took a small sip from the bottle, and I didn't see a point to saying anything. I'd make sure Crock knew before he shot him up with drugs.

"I wasn't carrying; we were all frisked. I'd have shot them on the spot." Charlie laughed. "Those two cousins weren't either, but when their guys busted into the room, one of their boys tossed each of them a gat."

"But you weren't shot."

"Obviously. Cullen and Red pulled me out of there down a bailout corridor. Cullen covered our retreat. I heard screams so I'm guessing he didn't miss."

"He thinks he got two of them. That's when he got tagged himself," I said. "Hey, who are the cousins? I only know Milosh."

"They head up this branch of the Albanian crew. Named Besmir and Mergim. Big mothers. If they'd looked like Milosh, I could have smashed their heads together and ended it."

"Okay, so then what?"

"Red and I kept moving, Cullen was further back, blasting away. Red ran to the last room leading to the alley and our car. Only as soon as he got to the room he was clipped from behind. I ran in to help, but there was another one who cracked me in the skull and down I went."

That didn't sound right from what I'd heard, but I let him go on.

"I couldn't have been out long, just enough for them to pull a bag over my head." Charlie smiled a little. "I guess I have a hard head. But I decided to play possum."

"You were awake when they took you?"

"Damn right I was. I heard an accented voice say, 'He's out.'" Charlie grimaced. "Then, clear as day, a very familiar voice say, 'You sure?'"

"Oh shit."

"Yeah. The Albanian said, 'Now get out of here and make sure they know he's still alive.' The other voice said, 'I know what to do.'"

"Red?"

"Ungrateful son-of-a-bitch." Charlie stared at his bandaged hand. "He's gonna find out what this felt like and so, so, much more." He spoke softly, and it gave me chills.

"Let's get you fixed up first." My mind raced, and I forced myself to pay attention to the rest of the drive.

* * *

Lansdowne, Doc Crock's

Crocker and Nurse Cindy were waiting for us, as was William, who was inside. I couldn't see the driver of the car that brought William.

Crocker let the brothers reunite briefly, then gave William the eye, and Nurse Cindy had no compunction about hustling Charlie into the back area.

"Doc," I called out. I was half surprised he actually listened and came over.

I let him know about the whiskey. He nodded. "Okay, good. I'll just give him a leather strap to bite down on," he deadpanned. "It's fine. He already told me he only wants local shots. I'm going to check the wounds and clean them, maybe re-suture the incisions. Then my big worry, just like for your friend"—I presumed he meant Cullen—"is infection. He gets to be here a couple days while we hit him with the IV antibiotics."

"Thanks, Doc."

When he left to work on Charlie, William approached. "Kyle."

Then the brains behind the Fishtown Irish Mob wrapped me in a bear hug.

"I didn't think he was going to come back," he said. "We owe you. Big."

"Like I told your brother, don't keep me in the dark. We need to work together. These guys are animals, but they aren't stupid."

"Agreed. On all points."

I made sure we were alone. Doc and Cindy had plenty to do with Charlie. "Charlie told me what he heard, and who said it." Alone or not, I didn't want to say Red's name out loud.

"That stays between us," William said.

I felt a surge of relief. "So, he doesn't know Charlie was really awake?"

"Correct."

"Can you make sure he stays in the dark?"

William gave me a little smile. "Did you just ask if I can keep a secret?"

I filled him in on my conversation with Milosh. "So, while we're in a stronger position with Charlie freed, they're going to come at you, and me, with everything they have, to finish it off."

"I always figured you were the key to it all." William was being sarcastic, but he saw the larger point about the port.

"I think current events have overtaken that scenario," I said. "Especially with their inside source sharing intel on how hard you were hit the first time."

The last remark stung, I knew, because it was true. "And you want that leak in place?" he asked.

"First, there's nothing you can do now about the manpower problem. They already know."

"I suppose they do," William said.

"But with their source still in place and feeling safe . . ." I began.

William smiled. "We have a trusted way to feed them crap."

"Exactly. And now I'm going to give you some good news."

"Be still my heart."

"You may have a shot to be way stronger than they realize."

He frowned. "Riddles now?"

I leaned in. "Sorry. I'm lining up some top-tier fighters. These guys are veterans and have access to all the gear needed to knock out the Albanians, especially if we can recapture the surprise."

William pursed his lips and struggled to be polite. He wasn't comfortable when he couldn't control the conversation. "With all due respect and humble gratitude, Kyle, since when did you become an arms dealer? You're a soft-hearted loan shark and favor-monger."

"Since never. And, for the record, I'm a lousy loan shark, but you better hope a great favor-trader," I said. "Even so, my patron will do whatever it takes to protect his interest in this port. He's invested millions, and it's enough for you to know his people were battle-tested before they got here."

"My soldiers—"

"You throw that term around," I broke in, "but face it; they're killers, not soldiers. I'm talking about the real thing."

His face hardened and jaw clenched. He spoke through gritted teeth. "You think you're the only one who knows war fighters? There's some boys in Belfast who've seen the match to anything your Sand Box refugees have."

"Then why haven't you called them?" I wasn't trying to embarrass him, but this was important. "These men are loyal to the death to their boss."

"And to you?" William asked. But I could see new possibilities sprouting in his mind and a glint of hope in his eyes.

"Not me. To their mission, and to the guy who brought them into the country. And he is used to fighting for what belongs to him."

"Tell me more about him," William said.

I had to be careful here. "The same rules go now as when I told you about my arrangement for the port. He stresses the silent in silent partnership."

"That's all well and good. But you want me to bet my entire organization and our lives on your say-so?"

"Gee, when you say it that way." The joke fell flat. "I get it. Tell you what. When they get to town, and they understand the urgency, will you meet with them?"

William shrugged. "Get us that far and we'll see about the rest."

"Fair enough. But just in case, once Charlie is stable, can you two stay somewhere else, rather than give the Albanians a fixed target?"

Now William's face fell, just for a moment, but in the instant the mask slipped I saw the bone-deep weariness. "We can't."

"I understand, but if you came up with a good reason, maybe?"

"We can't afford to show any weakness. Especially now with Charlie back." He raked his fingers through his hair. "We're close to losing people out of fear alone. If we hide, how do you think the rest of our crew will react?"

"I see the dilemma."

"We need a win."

"Let me get out of here and find out how soon for the cavalry. Okay?"

William just turned away to go wait for word on his brother.

CHAPTER 21

Outside Doc Crock's

It was just getting dark as I sat in the van and called over to the house, where VP told me all was quiet. Milosh's silver car, the one we'd stuck the tracker on, was still driving around New Jersey. If we could get a fix on where the Albanians' other hideout, that would be a game changer.

I told VP that if she and Steve wanted to try to follow the silver car, from a safe distance but still in range of the tracker, that it might be worth the effort. If they could find the hideout, we might get a chance to move on them before they had a chance to relocate.

That left Rollie with Sandy until I could get back to the house.

By now all the Albanians knew Charlie was in the wind. I hoped it might make them a little more amenable to negotiations. At least we'd shown them that the Irish weren't as helpless as they'd figured them to be. One thing for sure: they were now more pissed off than ever.

I was thinking we all could use some food in case we had to hunker down for a while, but I'd barely put the van in gear when the phone rang and it was Rollie. "What's up?"

"Sorry, didn't mean to scare you. Still all clear." Rollie spoke quickly. "Kid, I was thinking we could get some supplies."

"Great minds. I'm going to swing by WaWa for some food and drink. Any requests?"

"Um. A hoagie with a side of thirty-round mags stuffed with hollow points?" Rollie lowered his voice. "Don't want to scare the lady, but if something goes down, we may need a bit more firepower."

"Oh, *that* kind of supplies. You've got a point." I cancelled my turn signal. "I'll go later. I'm coming straight home. Should be there in less than half an hour."

"I can be to my place and back with gear in half that."

"Can you take Sandy with you?"

"Will do."

I relaxed, knowing she was in good hands. I wanted to remind him to lock the place up tight, but of course he would.

The phone rang again two minutes later. I pulled over because I was starting to juggle too many phones. This one was Sandy. "Hey."

"Kyle, Rollie just left," she began.

"What? You were supposed to go with him."

"Look, the longer we waited, the bigger the risk. But if we both went, who's to say we wouldn't come back to someone waiting to jump us?"

I hadn't thought of that. "I'm ten, twelve minutes out."

"I'm going to go tuck myself into the bunker. And Rollie will be back in a few minutes." She sounded unsure, but they were probably right. Maybe this was the best play.

"Lock everything and watch those monitors."

"Drive safe."

* * *

Traffic thickened as I tried to hurry back to Fishtown. Every red light blocked my progress. A few minutes later the phone rang again. I was all set to chew out Rollie when I saw it was Sandy again.

"Kyle?"

"What's up?"

"Could be nothing, but right after I got to the monitors, I saw a car that went around the block. Then right away I saw it again." She didn't sound panicked at all, but definitely concerned.

A chill swept through me. "What kind of car?"

"A gray sedan. Blacked out windows . . . shit, there it goes again."

"Is Rollie back yet?"

"Not yet. Want me to call him?"

"Sit tight. Does that board to your left show a row of red lights?"

"Yeah."

"Okay, you know all the outside doors are locked. I'll call Rollie and VP."

I felt a little better and tried not to drive like a lunatic.

"Now what?" she said.

"Is that car still moving?"

"Hang on. I'm still getting used to the controls here. It's coming around to the front."

"On second thought, can you call Rollie? Just to be safe. He's gotta be right around the corner."

"It still could be nothing. I was just thinking staring at these screens was boring. Wish it was, now."

I thought of telling her where the shotgun was, but I remembered she hadn't learned to shoot yet. Not the easiest thing to teach over the phone. "He won't mind."

"Damn. That's three times. All right, I'm calling. Hold on." She put the phone down and picked up a second. I couldn't tell how that was going between the muffled sound and road noises.

Three interminable blocks later she came back on the line. "You there?"

"Yeah, did you get him?"

"I left a message, just asked him to call, nothing specific. That's how you do it, right?"

"He should have answered." So much for feeling better. My foot pressed harder on the gas, and I nearly rear-ended a car in front of the van. "Keep trying and I'll call VP."

I put Sandy on speaker and mute from my end and took out another burner.

VP picked right up. "Yo."

"You still out in Jersey?"

"Yeah. What's up?"

I gave her the short version.

"That doesn't sound good. Our target is still driving around, never landing. Starting to feel like a wild goose chase."

"Son of a bitch decoyed us! Can you two get to your place and back up Sandy on the monitors?"

"Want us back at your house?"

"Your place is closer. Anyway, I'm on my way and Rollie is coming back heavy," meaning well-armed.

"Be careful."

Then I heard Sandy. "Uh, Kyle? That car stopped circling. It's pulling up."

I took the phone off mute. "Where?"

"Right in front of the house."

"Lock the door to the bunker." I passed the SUV in front of me and received headlight flashes and horn honks.

"The Hulk just got out of the car," Sandy said. "Should I call the cops?"

"I'll be there before them." I ignored every traffic light. If any cops lit after me, I'd lead them right to the house. She'd just described Milosh's bodyguard, Tank.

VP called and I hit the button from the burner on the passenger seat. "I got the laptop patched in," she said. "We'll be at my place pretty soon."

To Sandy: "Rollie?" I asked.

"Not yet." Sandy was trying to stay cool. "Hulk's on the front porch. Looks like he's peering into the windows."

"I see him," VP said. "Ask Sandy to turn on the interior cameras. The panel directly behind her." I did.

A while back, VP finally won a long argument about putting hidden cameras inside the house to remote-monitor when I wasn't around. I'd insisted that they couldn't be enabled unless a master board in the bunker permitted it. Also, not in my bedroom, and I could always disconnect them altogether. Today I was awfully glad she'd convinced me.

"He's off the porch," Sandy said. "Kyle?"

"Almost there." The tiny streets didn't allow for much passing, but somehow, I was still alone after breaking every traffic rule in the book.

"Got him going around the back," VP said.

"Hit the lights," I said.

"Done." VP had lit the backyard with floodlights.

"He didn't even react," Sandy said. "Coming for the back door now."

"Oh crap," VP said, and Sandy let out a small shriek. "He's kicking down the door."

As a human battering ram, he was built for the job. "Did it hold?" The door was reinforced, but it still looked like a door, not a bank safe. I was in Fishtown now. "Two minutes."

"Barely," VP said. "The frame looks jacked."

"Sandy, go off speaker and cut all the other sound. If he gets in, don't let him hear you down there."

"What does he want?"

"Probably Charlie," I guessed. "He's not going to be taking our word for anything. Stay away from him, no matter what."

"He's in," VP said.

Would he search upstairs or down first? I couldn't take the chance. "Sandy, get out of there now. Keep the bunker locked. Remember the subway?"

"Yes."

"I'll pick you up," I said.

Just then, another phone rang. I could either reach it or steer around a phone pole. I could see it was the phone for Rollie. I was almost to the house.

I got to the phone before it went to voicemail. "Rollie?"

"Murphy's law, I was in the bathroom, left the phone in the kitchen and—"

"Tank's in the house, looking for Charlie, but Sandy is in there."

"On it." Rollie hung up. But I doubted he'd make it in time.

I felt like I could have run the remaining distance faster, but I'm sure it was nerves. I already knew there wasn't a gun in the van. I thought I remembered a wrench. No matter what, I intended to keep between Tank and Sandy, and if all I could do was slow him down while he beat me to a pulp until Rollie arrived, so be it.

I pulled up the last street that led to the back on my place. Still a few blocks away, I wanted to hit the sidewalk in time for when Sandy emerged from the hidden door through the fence. She wasn't there yet.

Out of nowhere, a kid on a bike zipped between some parked cars, and I jammed the brakes with both feet. His eyes went cartoon-saucer wide, and he put on a burst of speed to dodge the bumper by inches. When he was clear he recovered his wits enough to scream curses at me.

At least it meant he was okay.

VP cut in. "Big dude is in the basement. Crap, he's going straight for the bunker."

The entry door was disguised, but if he'd figured out it was there at all, then he'd know where to spend his energy. I prayed Sandy had been able to access the tunnel.

"Hey, beef-head!" VP called out, and I realized she was yelling at Tank over the intercom. "You try coming upstairs, and I'll blow your head off. I already called the cops."

I didn't know if that was going to work, but it was a good try. Every second counted.

"No sale," VP said. "Jeez, he just hit that door like a horse."

"Is she still in there?"

"The room's clear." Relief washed over me when I heard the words. "But the rug is pulled up."

"As long as she made it." I had to stomp the brakes again for another car pulling out of a parking spot. The old lady inside crawled up the street like she was trying to remember which pedal to use. I recognized the car. A neighbor, Mrs. Whitaker. I doubt she'd understand if I rammed her out of the way.

But c'mon lady, GO!

"Scratch another door," VP said. "He's in the bunker. I shut all the screens off first."

"The floor?"

"Damn, he only looks dumb. He's pulling the cover off and shining a flashlight down."

"Is he talking?" The old bat turned finally. I punched the gas.

"He's climbing down and . . . Ha!"

"What?"

"He doesn't fit! He can't follow her down the ladder." VP was cracking up with nervous laughter. "Maybe he'll get stuck."

Now I could see the sidewalk up ahead but still no sign of Sandy. She shouldn't have had any trouble running the crawler down the passage.

"No such luck, he's hauling ass to the back door," VP said. Not laughing now.

I spotted the fence boards swing out and saw Sandy crawl through the opening and stand up.

"I see her!" I honked the horn. She turned.

"Look out!" VP yelled.

Between us, the locked back gate to my yard shook. I saw two hands grip the top of the gate and, incredibly, Tank hauled himself up and over it, sticking the landing.

"Did you *see* that?" VP sounded like some sort of sportscaster.

Sandy sure did. She took off running for the corner away from both Tank and me. She could run faster than me, but that wasn't saying much with my bad knee. Luckily, I was still behind the wheel.

Tank charged after her. All of his speed appeared to be generated through brute force, but he was gaining and she'd need all of her head start. I was close behind.

Just as Tank reached for the back of her shirt, Sandy cut around the corner of the street that ran in the front of the house and left him grabbing air. His momentum carried him past the turn, and he almost overshot the sidewalk before he could change direction.

I had to brake almost to a stop to avoid doing the same thing in the van, which might've rolled over otherwise. As soon as I got the nose of the van around the corner, I swerved around the first parked car and squeezed right up on the sidewalk.

Not two car lengths ahead, Tank pivoted to face me. He glared at me through the windshield and I floored the gas. Tank gambled and ran straight at the van, charging for a gap between two houses. If he'd just double-checked his slide rule, he'd have known he wasn't going to make it. I both heard and felt a satisfying thump when the right front of the van caught him, just a glancing blow, but enough to spin him around and take him off his feet. I swerved back astride the sidewalk before I took out the front of my own house, then eased the van up to Sandy.

"Get in!"

I didn't have to ask her twice. She climbed up and pulled the door shut. I noticed she had a small can of pepper spray clenched in her fist.

Most of the way up the block, the way ahead was blocked by a phone pole. I was scanning for an opening in the line of parked cars big enough to let us back on the street when Sandy piped up.

"He's up," she reported, staring at the side mirror. She slapped the lock down. "He's limping, but still coming."

"This guy's a pain in the ass. Turn him down if he shows up to your place for therapy."

Sandy laughed a little too hard at that one, but it was good to see the tension break, if just for a moment. Luckily, an alley gave me chance to return to the street, and half a block later we were even travelling in the correct direction in this webwork of one-way streets.

I picked up the phone with VP on the line. "Got her in the van. Call Rollie and tell him to get back to his place. They might come there, and we want to be ready this time."

"You think he'd follow us there?" Sandy slumped back in the seat.

I'd relaxed a bit once VP confirmed that Rollie was turning the Blue Bomber around and would probably beat us back to his place. "I hope not. We have to assume they know where he lives, but at this point, I don't know what they have to gain other than just a straight-out attack, which doesn't make sense. Charlie is free, I don't think they know about Doc Crock, and Rollie and I will make them sorry if they take a run at his place."

"I could use a little of that boredom right about now." She was still breathing hard but not like when she got in the van.

"You were incredible. You got through the subway like a pro." I smiled.

She gave a nervous grin back. "That was easy, not like I was going to get lost. The scary part was hearing that guy stomp on the floor to find the tunnel."

"He almost got stuck in the ladder tube," I told her. "He couldn't fit, so he had to go out the back door through the yard."

"And he's Milosh's guy? You know him?"

"I've run into him before, when it was just Milosh at the coffee shop doing the loans for the Irish."

"Must've made some barista." Sandy stifled a giggle. She was wired, and who could blame her?

"That's a picture. But I figure he was the one who worked Beet over to get me to go along with his plan."

"Poor Beet."

"Yeah. He didn't understand, and these meatheads only have one answer to everything. I wasn't thrilled to deal with the Irish, but that moment when we kicked them out of town made it all worth it."

Sandy studied me as we approached Rollie's. VP had already told me to go around to the back and stash the van in Rollie's garage. "And one thing led to another . . .?"

I nodded. "And another and another and here we are," I said. "Ain't it funny?"

"And terrifying and, not gonna lie, exciting too." She smiled.

"Something to break up the monotony of shipping, I guess."

"And that's what they want so bad?"

"Milosh thinks it's the expansion chance of their dreams."

"Could he be right?" she asked.

I thought about the money Ali invested and what I'd paid him to service the loan, not to mention the bulk of his furniture business flowing through it. He took real pride in his transition into a legitimate businessman in the States. Becoming a prime target for a DEA bust was never in the cards. Even if Milosh had wanted to try something so stupid, I'd die before allowing it to happen.

"I think"—I wanted to be careful not to reveal too much—"that Milosh is going to be shocked how wrong he is."

CHAPTER 22

Fishtown, Rollie's place

Moments after we'd pulled in to the backyard area at Rollie's place, I heard the distinct rumble of the Blue Bomber behind us. Rollie hit a remote and the garage opened for me. I pulled into the garage, and Rollie parked right outside. He got out of the car.

"Everybody okay?"

I nodded. "He didn't follow you?" Rollie pulled his untucked shirt over the butt of a .45 and retrieved a blanket from the trunk of the car, which he used to wrap up a long gun, probably a shotgun. He handed the bundle to me. "Take it. The neighbors think I'm strange enough as it is." He gestured for Sandy to head to the back door.

Inside, he rushed to the front of the house. The door looked intact, always a good sign.

I unwrapped the pump shotgun and confirmed the safety was on and one shell in the chamber.

"Good idea to keep the van out of sight," I said. "It might be time to get Steve an upgrade."

"Yeah?" Rollie was lowering the shades and studying the street. I followed him room to room.

"I clipped him with the van, not as hard as I'd have liked, but it left a dent, in the van at least. I don't think anyone saw me do it or take off."

"Hit and run? I'm shocked at such lawless behavior." Rollie appeared satisfied that a home invasion wasn't imminent.

"Yeah, well, I don't think he's the type to press charges, but I'm certain he's the kind of guy who holds grudges."

"We're hip deep in the grudge-zone all around. Those mutts who were guarding Charlie will be itching for some payback."

"That includes me too, huh?" Sandy asked.

"I don't know if he knows who you are, but if you stick around bums like us, yeah, probably," Rollie said. "But don't go anywhere just yet. I have some food in the fridge, if you don't mind leftovers." He moved toward the kitchen.

"I'll get it," she said. "You shouldn't leave your post."

"Kyle gets a turn, seeing how he pissed the guy off and everything," Rollie said. "Any beer you find is all yours," he called after her.

I watched the street and, as the adrenaline subsided, felt the fatigue roll in. While the minutes ticked by, I decided I didn't think that Tank would come lumbering down the street like some sort of indestructible monster out of a horror flick.

That was the good news.

The bad news was that this nightmare was no movie, and we'd gotten ourselves smack-dab in the middle of a full-blown mafia war.

* * *

Rollie's place, the next morning

We'd decided to stay at Rollie's because it seemed safer. My back door and the one to the bunker were trashed. We could clear the place tomorrow. VP checked in that the house looked clear and was pissed that she hadn't caught me hitting Tank with the van on camera. I was okay that my crime wasn't on video. The way I saw it, it was self-defense, but I wouldn't want to try to make that case in court.

None of us got very much sleep, but we'd tried to take turns. Rollie cheated and took extra shifts. I would have felt bad taking advantage of a guy his age, except it was clear he was enjoying himself.

Sandy wasn't in the bed next to me when I next came to. The light filtering through the shade made me wonder what time it was. After 8:00 a.m. The smell of Rollie's coffee hit my nose.

A few minutes later I found him and Sandy at his kitchen table. Rollie was finishing a plate of eggs and scribbling on a napkin.

"See? I'll weld the frame here and here, then the rebar bolts will have something to grab onto, you know?" I could see he wasn't even waiting for Sandy to reply.

She glanced up and gave me a little smirk that was as good as the coffee I'd just poured. I looked at the napkin and saw that Rollie was designing replacement doors for the ones Tank had ruined.

"Hey," Rollie said. "Hope you got enough rest. I'm going to need some young hands for this. Oh, and your truck."

"Fort Fishtown?"

He pretended to look insulted and waved the napkin. "This is just for now. Wait until you see what I have for later. A tornado will be able to roar through Fishtown, and I know one place will still be standing."

"Sounds like slight overkill."

"Yeah, and your hardware superstore locks and toothpick frames really stopped that goon, didn't they?"

"Touché."

"I know this will look like crap, but when we get through all this, I'll do it up nice and stylish, okay?"

"Curtains on a vault door?" I said.

"Ye of little faith." Rollie stood and stretched his back. "Sandy, check out the couch in the living room at the front of the house."

I followed out of curiosity.

"Okay." Rollie pointed at the wall next to the end of the couch. The walls in the room were painted a soft, rose red. "Knock on it."

She did. "Ow. What is that?"

Rollie grinned. "It's not plaster."

I rapped on the painted surface. Like hitting stone or . . . "Is that steel?"

"Inch-thick steel road plate, my man. It was a bitch getting it in there, but you're covered a foot past the couch on either end." Rollie beamed. "And don't it look pretty?"

I shook my head. "Well, hon, looks like we're hiring Apocalypse Interiors for our remodel."

I heard a trilling from upstairs. One of my phones. "I swear I work for those damn things." I lumbered up the stairs.

The neat row of burner phone arrayed on the top of the dresser was disturbed by one in the middle trying to walk across the surface as it shrieked and buzzed.

It was Tom. That was fast, he'd only reached Ohio last night. "Hey," I answered.

"Hey back, mate. Easy run yesterday, but I didn't want to keep you waiting."

"You work fast," I said.

"No, no. Our patron is out of town."

"When will he be back? Did you call him?"

"A couple days, and you know how he likes interruptions."

"I didn't mean with a shopping list."

"Too bloody right. I just wanted you to know we have to wait until he returns. How are things there, if I can ask?"

I knew he meant if I was able to be specific. I felt disappointment about not getting a fast response from Ali, but that was stupid. We wanted Ali to bail us out with men and material, no small request. I couldn't expect him to have been waiting with troops like a SWAT team. And like Tom reminded me, we damn sure weren't going to ask him for that sort of thing over a call.

"We're rather busy. Some of the new neighbors decided to pay a social call."

"Oh?" I heard the concern in his voice.

"We just missed them, darn the luck, but I'm certain we'll get another chance soon. We've been talking about a welcoming party. If you can help, don't hesitate to let me know." Subtle as a brick, but I figured I'd made my point without totally incriminating myself.

* * *

Kyle's place, two days later

The last couple days had passed in a blur of blisters, curses, and aching muscles. While we "rested up," the Irish were about as relaxed, healing physically but seething all the while. Charlie especially, in both regards. William said, so far, they hadn't heard anything from the Albanians. It felt like a military cease fire where all either side was doing was reloading.

Rollie hadn't been joking about fortifying my place. The back door was now solid and looked like painted wood, but was reinforced metal like a garage entry door. On the inside, he'd added another steel frame with three crossbars using rebar. It was ugly as hell, even ridiculous-looking, but I had to admit it would probably be easier to try to go through one of the walls than the door itself.

The front door received similar treatment, but the real fun was the bunker, which wasn't a bit disguised after we'd somehow dragged hundreds of pounds of road plate to affix to the outside of the room. We didn't have time to try to rebuild the whole room on the inside. Rollie promised a redesign in the future.

For the subway, he built a sturdy hatch that opened to the shed from the tunnel side but would keep anyone from accessing it from the shed so we wouldn't have to worry about someone sneaking in from that direction. I know that vulnerability had been bothering him for a while. The way he'd had all the right parts handy, I think he'd been waiting for an excuse.

As exhausting as the work was, at least it helped pass the time. The port was running its regular business and other than Beet being allowed to crash there to avoid his home, things were normal enough. Now that I knew the Albanians wanted the place intact, I figured they would leave it alone both to avoid attracting attention and not to damage their prize.

I'd called Tom once and he'd said Ali was returning sometime today. Then he insisted I wait to hear from him. He knew Ali from back in Iraq, and I decided the best approach was to let him handle it. It wasn't the most relaxing, but probably the smarter way to go.

We were almost done for the day, and I was looking forward to a beer. Sandy and I were in matching painter's coveralls trying our best to make the bunker armor look a little less like a tank fell through the kitchen floor into the basement.

We stepped back to see if we missed a spot. "Yeah, right here." Sandy dabbed a white dot onto the end of my nose.

"I'm a clown? I amuse you?" This was my Joe Pesci, from *Goodfellas*.

She pulled me in close. "Yup," and planted a kiss on my lips.

"Now you've got a spot on your cheek."

"Maybe we should go . . . clean up."

That beer could wait.

* * *

Kyle's place, later

The shower was fun and afterward even more so, and as we lay beside each other, Sandy chuckled.

"That bad, huh?" I said.

She punched me in the ribs. "Dummy. I was just thinking, what if you ever wanted to sell the place?"

"What about it?"

"How would you describe all those home improvement projects?"

She had a good point. "'As is'?"

I loved the sound of her laugh.

"Seriously, I hadn't really thought about it. I didn't exactly plan on owning the place to begin with, but now that you mention it, that might be tricky."

"I wouldn't want to have to fill in that tunnel," Sandy said.

The once-dormant hustler side of my brain began to flex its muscles. "I suppose the best thing would be to do a quiet sale to a 'sympathetic party' and then knock it down and have the new builders, also friends, sort out the tunnel in a new foundation."

She propped herself up on an elbow. "You've already thought about it."

But I hadn't. I never used to think ahead. "Nope. This just came to me now."

"No way."

"I swear." But it was weird how fast some of these ideas popped into my head these days. Was it Ryan's ghost taking possession? Maybe not, but was my hustle-brain developing a subconscious?

"Not bad."

* * *

Sandy and I cobbled together a supper of beer and leftovers, which suited us both just fine. No texts or calls from VP, who I think even managed to get some much-needed rest as well. Tom was the only person I wished had called, but it could wait until morning. Dragging steel around all day had me ready to turn in early.

Sandy went up, and I set all the alarms and triple-checked the locks. Fort Fishtown was secure.

While she was in the bathroom getting ready for bed, I scooped up my collection of burners and carried them into a guest room.

Before I could switch on the light, one of them vibrated and squirmed in my arms like a fish out of water. I deposited the lot of them onto the bed and flipped the overhead. One phone trilled again.

Milosh.

"You can't be serious," I said into the phone. I was already moving toward the nearest weapon but wanted to wait before scaring Sandy.

"Do you have any idea what you've done?"

"On a phone? Why don't you refresh my memory?"

"You are going to get me killed," Milosh said.

"If you and Tank show up at my place again, you'll get yourself killed. I'm done playing games."

"You screwed me! You followed me after we had a deal."

"What deal? I heard you out, and now you butchers can't torture your guest anymore." It was so difficult to remember phone rules in the heat of a conversation.

"You've left us with nothing. They'll never want to work with you now."

"I'm satisfied with the current arrangement. I'm sure there's other work you can do for them." Like I cared.

"You don't understand. I'm out too."

"Really? And that's why you attacked my home?"

"What did you expect? We were desperate. And he was only looking for you know who."

"Yeah, well Mr. You Know Who is probably going to return the favor."

"Tell him to get in line." I could hear a hint of panic in Milosh's voice.

"What's that supposed to mean?"

"You tell me what it means when you screw up and get called into a meeting with your bosses and your bodyguard calls in sick?"

"Oh, come on! I didn't hit him that hard. He stood up and everything." Then I realized he wasn't talking about the bump with the van. "Oh, shit!"

"I am a dead man."

"Sucks to be you." It just slipped out.

"And you as well. After me, they will target you and your whole clan. You will be wiped out, and everyone close to you will suffer, like our guest. Think about that."

I already was and the thought of them touching Sandy, let alone all my friends who never bargained for this mess, set my pulse pounding.

I took a deep breath. Rage could wait. "Then why are you calling and spoiling the surprise?"

"We may be able to prevent that from happening. If we work together."

"You have to be shitting me."

"Listen and decide for yourself if it is shit." Milosh sounded more composed. "Can we meet?"

"Hard pass." But what the hell *was* he thinking? "Screw the phone rules. What are you talking about?"

"If you insist," Milosh said. "But you will have to trust me."

"I don't."

Now I heard Milosh take the deep breath. "Fine. Do you at least believe that I do not wish to die here in this filthy city?"

"Yeah, I buy that."

"Progress. I have a solution that will allow everyone to win." He paused. "Let me rephrase. My cousins must win. They *will* win, but my idea allows you and even your Irish friends to survive."

"It's your dime. Let's hear it." No harm in listening. Maybe I'd learn something.

"The Irish surrender. For real this time."

"That's it?"

"That's not enough? The Irish agree to a ceasefire, and they abandon their interests in Fishtown and the rest of Philadelphia."

"And the port?"

"Perhaps it wasn't meant to be. They may allow you to operate, for a price. Much like you took the loan business from me, you would give them a cut."

"Is that right?"

"I would leap on that if I were you. They don't see the potential that I did in the port, but I can't go near them again."

"So why are you even telling me this—and, I have to ask, what do you care?" He was sticking around town for something.

"I can hear in your voice that you do not believe me."

"Why should I? I spent all day fixing what Tank broke trying to trash my place."

"Tank? Ah, I understand. He was following my orders, but no more. He works for my cousins now."

"That's cold."

"It's a cold world. Now to my point. I have information. I will give it to you in exchange for a promise from the Irish to leave me alone and to share what is coming so I can leave town."

"Share? Of what?"

"Listen to me. My cousins know how weak the Irish are."

My gut clenched. I focused on not reacting. "Of course. They were there that night."

"No. More. Much more. They know The Irish in New York won't help. And that they are almost out of soldiers. They also know their people are getting scared and are about to quit."

"How would you know about things like that?" Would he say?

"So that you know I am on the square? No, on the level. I can say this much: My cousins have a spy in the organization."

"What? Who?" *Don't oversell it, Kyle.*

"When we have a deal. But understand, they know every move before the Irish make it."

"That explains how they got destroyed at the last meeting."

"Correct," Milosh said.

"Okay, I believe you. Now tell me why they wouldn't simply finish the job."

"I told you before, my cousins and I were outcasts. The New York Albanian families were frustrated, and this move to Philadelphia allowed them to be rid of us, without violence among our families."

"Makes sense, I guess."

"They wanted us to succeed, not just to unload us but for the ongoing tribute," he said. "In order to give us a chance, they ran interference with the New York Irish Mob,"

"I remember. Both sides from New York would stay out of it, or else."

"Yes. But the agreement is extremely fragile. If the New York Irish see my cousins as savages who insist on a massacre, the treaty could shatter. The New York families do not want a war with them."

Plausible.

"Let's say I accept your version," I said. "Why would the Irish agree to just run away? They've always fought for everything they have."

"I understand. This is why I contacted you. You know this started when they lost several large shipments?"

"And the couriers," I added.

"I can't help that." Milosh's tone said that he wouldn't have bothered if he could have. "But you need to explain to the O'Briens that the merchandise has not been lost."

"What do you mean?" And though it was a good practice to avoid naming things like meth specifically on the phone, we were talking about pure poison, though with an undeniable street value.

"My cousins held on to the product as a bargaining chip. Now they are prepared to offer it as a, how do you say, consolation prize?" Milosh said. "And that, my friend, is what is in it for me. I need a portion of the product."

"How big a piece?"

"Not large. Merely enough to seed my relocation. A city far from either of you. Away from the East Coast."

"I see. So, if I get you, the Irish agree and all the stolen merchandise will be returned in exchange for rolling over to your cousins?"

"My English must be improving. You understand perfectly."

My mind was racing. "But if you are on the outs with your cousins, how do you know the offer is legit?"

"It's been part of the plan all along," he said. "I've seen the stuff myself."

"Where are they keeping it?" Worth a shot.

Milosh chuckled. "This needs to end peacefully. Inviting a desperate attack won't do."

He'd all but said the stolen drugs were being held at their hideout. It helped explain why he hadn't tried to make a move himself, since they wanted him dead already.

"I had to ask." I tried to keep my tone light. "This is a lot to digest. Let me see what I can do to persuade them. I want this to end peacefully as much as you do." But what I wanted and what would happen were not the same.

Milosh said goodbye.

I looked up and Sandy was there with worry lines creasing her face.

"It's okay," I said as much to myself as her. "I'll be right up and fill you in. I need to make a quick call."

That call was one to the O'Briens. I set a meeting with them, only this time they were coming here, and it went without saying that Red would not know about it.

When I went to bed, I gave Sandy the condensed version. I left out the part about the drugs. If the Albanians knew what we'd learned, it would tell them that Milosh was dealing with the other side. The dumber they thought we were, the better.

I'd been considering not telling the O'Briens either, but that wasn't part of our new policy. It was their business, much as I hated that part of it, and certainly it was their concern.

I had to remind myself that these particular drugs were a side issue. The more pressing issue was life or death. And the drug market was one of the big reasons the Albanians wanted the territory in the first place.

CHAPTER 23

Kyle's place, the next day

Charlie and William agreed to come over, another first in this strange time. Rollie and VP volunteered to help with external security. Sandy would work the monitors from the bunker. That the O'Briens went along with all of that told me two things. First, our credibility had risen considerably with the latest ventures and rescues. Second, the Irish were every bit as depleted as we'd thought.

It had taken all my willpower not to call Tom. He had his own way of operating, so when he said leave him alone, he meant it.

Starving Steve was up the street in a new van. We'd decided the old one was too hot. We were fairly sure nobody had called in a hit-and-run in response to the Tank incident, but it wasn't worth tempting fate, especially not parked so close to the "scene of the crime."

I radioed Rollie, who sat in the back of the van watching the street though one-way glass. He was behind his rifle, which perched atop a tripod for comfort and stability.

"In position," he said.

"How's the view?"

"Clear lanes. Ready with a light touch if needed. Haymaker in reserve."

I still felt goofy using shorthand and code words, but I saw the value. Rollie had the little suppressed .22 ready to discourage interference in case Milosh was playing games and setting up an ambush. The "Haymaker" referred to Rollie's high-powered rifle, if it turned into an all-out attack. I prayed it wouldn't because those rounds would go as far as I could see and farther, including through bad guys and into neighbors' homes. Not ideal.

"Eye in the sky, on standby." VP's voice came into my earpiece. She'd joined Sandy and was operating from the bunker as well. She was running a drone that was currently perched atop my chimney. The O'Briens preferred meetings as lean as possible, but they were aware my people would be around.

A phone rang. It was William. "We're two blocks away." He hung up. We'd already been briefed on their car. It was a big, old station wagon with dark windows. The key was to make sure that two jumpy sides didn't have any accidents.

I let everyone know about their imminent arrival.

"Birdie is up," VP said. I pictured a watchful dragonfly circling the property, scanning for threats closing in.

"Driveway clear," Rollie said.

"Grass is green." Sandy stifled a laugh. She was worse at the code-words than me, but it meant the backyard was safe.

A tense minute later, VP cut in. "Yo, I got 'em. One blacked-out family truckster in sight."

"Anything tied to the bumper?" I meant another car tailing them.

"Nope. Nothing to spoil those classic lines."

"Eyes on," Rollie said. "No fans seen from here."

I stepped onto the porch and watched the wagon come down the street. The hazards flashed on and the vehicle pulled up to the walkway by the street. The driver's side door opened.

It was weird, but when Cullen emerged to open the back door, I actually felt glad to see him. He helped the O'Briens out of the wagon, but his gaze never stopped darting up and down the street. That was okay. Nobody from our side was going to do anything to startle the guy.

They moved as a group toward the porch. I kept a lookout and listened to my earpiece.

"Thanks for coming, guys. Right inside." Time for chitchat later. I followed Cullen back to the car.

"How are you feeling?"

Cullen's head was on a swivel. "Fine. Thirsty more and a little tired. Mostly pissed off."

"Sounds about right. You know where to go to wait around back?"

"Yeah."

"I know you'll be looking out, but we have the block covered. Anyone comes, you'll know, fast."

"Thanks." Cullen ducked into the big wagon.

* * *

Inside the house, the O'Briens had already taken seats at the dining room table.

"I appreciate the house call," I said. I'd put out a pitcher of ice water and a set of glasses. No whiskey, as I wanted to make sure we were all thinking clearly. I hoped it was early in the day, even for them.

William got right down to business. "What did you hear?"

I gave the rundown on what Milosh had told me, including the tip about the insider.

"Do you believe him?" Charlie said. He looked like a different person than the one we rescued just days ago. His mutilated hand was still heavily bandaged, but his overall color was back to its ruddy norm, and he seemed rested. The calm before another storm, I suspected.

I took my time before answering. "I can't say I know him half-well enough to be able to read him perfectly. That said, I buy that he was scared."

"That's all well and good," Williams said, "but what about the rest?"

"Could he be pushing a trap? Of course. But even if he's lying about the purpose, some of the other information pans out. He also stressed they knew how depleted your muscle was from the first attack."

"That could be a good guess," Charlie said.

"True, but it is also exactly the sort of thing Red would know."

Charlie's face contorted with rage. "That cocksucker."

I nodded. "He's going to help us, he just doesn't know it."

William raised a hand. "We're getting ahead of ourselves. You said they expect us to surrender all that we've built and that they will return the product they stole?"

"Right," I said, "in order to avoid going overboard and antagonizing the New York families."

Charlie glowered. "Nice to think we'd have to get killed before they'd step in."

"That's not an option." William looked at his brother. "Agreed?"

Charlie glanced around as if to raise a glass. "On our mother's grave."

Now that I heard it from the men themselves, it clarified the situation.

"Well," I said, "that simplifies our next steps. Not that it makes things any easier, but we know we need to set that meeting."

William cocked his head. "You're sure about that?"

I nodded. "The way I see it, whether Milosh is lying or telling the truth about wanting you to go along with a surrender, it is clear he wants to see you go to the meeting."

"But his own people want to kill him. Supposedly," Charlie said.

"Yeah. And that, too, could be crap. On the other hand, tailing him to the hideout had to have pissed them off." Charlie grinned at that. "If those cousins decline a sit-down, we'll know he was lying about them wanting to make a deal."

"Sounds familiar," William said.

"Doesn't it? But this time they are the ones who will get skunked by the inside leak." William gave a little smile to show he saw where I was going.

"Tell me how this doesn't end the same way?" Charlie asked. "I don't have as much 'other hand' as you two." The red flush creeping up his neck told me how much pent-up fury was behind his flippant comment.

"All right, son," William said. "I see how you want to bait the trap. Clever enough. But I haven't seen any answers here for how we'd spring it. Our firepower shortage, however temporary, is all too real at the moment."

"I think I have that covered."

"The silent partner?" Charlie gave me a close-lipped smirk. "Saved by the terrorists?"

"One man's terrorist is another man's freedom-fighter, as the old saying goes," William said to Charlie.

I felt compelled to defend Ali and his men. "They're neither. Their experience is closer to trained mercenaries. I imagine they fought their share of real terrorists over the years, not to mention elements of the Republican Guard in Iraq."

"Where will they hide their tank?" Charlie asked.

"If you think you can handle them alone, be my guest," I said, my temper flaring. "But meeting or not, they're coming for you. And I'll do what's necessary to protect my own people."

William put a hand on Charlie's arm to avoid an escalation and spoke to me. "Don't misunderstand. We welcome any help as long as we can trust it. Remember, we are the ones in the crosshairs."

Charlie let his shoulders sag. "You've seen these men work? First hand?"

That was fair. "Only once, and just some of them. They were professional and brave. Also, discreet." Both brothers understood what that meant.

"What, exactly, are we talking about here?" Charlie asked. "Numbers, hardware, like that?"

"I don't know. Not specifically." Not generally, either, but this was a delicate point in our conversation. "I should have an answer very soon, and I know they could be here fast, like a day."

William nodded. "We won't set anything up until we have concrete information about these forces. I'm sure you understand."

"I know *you* wouldn't go in and just drop your pants," Charlie said.

"And make them jealous? That would be rude," I said. "Seriously, we will need to plan around the specific assets we get. Rollie has a lifetime of experience working with large forces and all the way down to no forces. He'll make them count." I saw that resonated.

William raised a finger. "For the sake of discussion, let's set aside the backup issue. What were you thinking with regard to our Judas?"

"Set the meeting with the Albanians. I wouldn't say it was to surrender, but more that ongoing war will hurt both sides and it's better for business to settle things. Keep your head up. Pretend you have cards left to play, but have Charlie work with Red to explore new places to set up shop, like he expects you guys to be vacating Philly."

Charlie smiled. "That rat'll leak faster than a text message."

"Yup." I grinned.

"And if they fall for the story, they will think we're bluffing, and they can break us once and for all," William said.

"Or they will accept your terms and offer the merchandise after all, but I frankly doubt it," I said.

"I frankly don't give a shit," Charlie said. "They need to pay for what they did." He held up his hand. "All of it."

CHAPTER 24

Kyle's place, an hour later

We'd ended the meeting with the O'Briens on a high note, if that was the right term for planning to sandbag a bunch of killers. Knowing the Albanians had the same intentions for us made the prospect easier to stomach. But only a little.

Once they'd left out the back way, I called a huddle and everyone stopped the surveillance and returned to the house. VP and Sandy came upstairs and Rollie and Steve came inside.

"Great job, gang."

I headed toward the kitchen to dig up some snacks for everyone. I heard a phone ring and was about to rush to my current burner collection but I saw Sandy answer her own phone.

I was about to turn back to munchie duty when I heard the tone in her voice.

"What? Slow down," Sandy said. "Okay. Keep them locked and we'll be right there."

We all stopped what we were doing.

"That was Jessica."

"One of the ladies covering for Sandy at the rehab center," I shared with the group. "What happened?"

"She's not sure. Some guys started hanging around the front and saying things to the clients on their way in."

"What kind of things?" I asked.

"Stuff like, 'Where's Kyle?'"

I felt my stomach drop. "Okay, what did they do?"

"Jess asked them to leave. She said they were big guys. White, and they had accents."

"Damnit. We all know what kind of accent." I took Sandy's hand and felt her fingers tremble. "Did they go inside?"

Sandy shook her head. "No, they said it was nice to meet Jessica, they read her name off her tag, and they promised they would be back."

"Did she call the police?" Rollie asked.

"She threatened to, but she said they were just scary. She wasn't even sure they were technically trespassing." Sandy gripped my hand hard. "She locked the place up and told Leslie not to come in today. We're cancelling everyone for at least a week." Sandy paused. "And she's still in there. She's scared to go outside."

"I can't blame her," I said. "This is my fault. I have to go get her."

"I keep telling you," Rollie said. "It might not be your fault, but it's still our problem."

"I'm sorry," I said to Sandy. "They're going to keep coming at all of us until the Irish fold."

Sandy absorbed the thought. "Then they are in danger because of me."

* * *

Old City, Philadelphia

It may have been getting tiresome rolling around town in what amounted to a low-key motorcade, but it was better than the alternative, one of us getting captured like Charlie, or even killed. Sandy and I were in my truck. I had a loaded pistol on me, and Sandy looked more relieved than nervous by the fact. I'm not sure if that was a good thing, but I was still impressed how well she was taking the crazy developments.

VP, Steve, and Rollie rode in the van, which kept a discreet distance. I knew she had her drones in the van in case we needed to scope out a wider area.

In this part of town, like much of the old neighborhoods, the streets were narrow and crowded. Our plan was to let Jessica know when we were there, and she'd be able to come out safely. Rollie and VP would have our backs.

This way, if the Albanians were really gone, we could get Jessica home with little additional drama. If they weren't, we'd look like an easy target and Rollie, Steve, and VP could intervene with surprise on their side.

Sandy called and told Jessica to go out the front and lock up as normal. Later, we'd add a "Closed for Renovations" sign. Maybe the Albanians would leave the place alone after that. A short-term answer, but if these bastards ended up here for the long term, we'd all be closed for renovations.

I pulled up in front. I knew Jessica would recognize my truck. A moment later a young lady with dirty blonde hair stepped out and gazed up and down the street. She waved, and after she locked the door, she worked her way to the passenger door. Sandy moved to the middle of the bench seat to make room.

"Hey, Jess, you okay?" Sandy asked.

"Yeah. You didn't have to come over just to get me." She gave a nervous laugh. "I could have slept on the floor."

"Sandy told me what happened," I said. "I'm sorry. It has nothing to do with your place, or you guys."

"Who were they?"

I wanted to tread lightly here. "A group of idiots from out of town who are having a problem with some people I know. Somehow the idiots think I really work for the other people and that bothering me will get them what they want."

True, as far as it went.

"Do you think they'll come back?" The quaver in her voice told me she sure did.

"Hopefully they will get frustrated and give up." I saw how that take wasn't exactly winning her over. "But, Sandy and I thought that, just to be safe . . ."

"We're going to close up for a week, more if necessary," Sandy said. "But you and Leslie will still get paid." Sandy looked at me and I nodded. The least I could do.

But I felt bad for the clients. I knew their work really helped those people. Then it hit me.

"If I can get some of the equipment out, you know, portable stuff, would you be able to do your therapy?" I asked both ladies.

Sandy thought about it. "Yeah, for quite a few of them."

"But where would we see them?" Jessica asked. "I take the bus to work."

"If I could arrange for pick-up and drop-off for you and Leslie," I said, "could you go to clients and still help them?"

Sandy's smile lit the truck up.

"Yeah, I'm sure we could," Jessica said. "You'd really do that? That'll be quite an Uber bill."

"I can do better than that. I have a guy who works for me at the port, and he also helps me with some of my side gigs. He can take you guys around."

Sandy laughed. "You mean Beet?"

I nodded.

"You'll love him," Sandy assured Jessica. "He's a character but super nice, and I'm sure he'd be very happy knowing he was doing good. I'll make a list of what we need, and, Jess, you and Leslie can call the clients."

"Sure. Kyle, is that the guy with the crazy car Sandy told me about?"

"The goofy Beetle, yes, hence the name," I said. "I can send him out with a spare car from the port though. No need to confuse your clients." Also, no need to wave a flag at the Albanians with a car that stood out worse than a 1970's pimpmobile. Milosh certainly knew the car well. I didn't want to test if he'd shared that detail prior to being excommunicated (if he really had been).

Jessica looked much more cheerful as I followed her directions and we headed home. No news from any phones was good news as far as our silent escorts in the van were concerned.

I enjoyed the pleasant vibe in the truck for the rest of the ride. Such moments were in short supply lately, and the contrast highlighted what a cloud the Albanian situation had cast over our lives.

"I'll email the contact list and schedule." Sandy told Jessica when she got out of the truck at her place.

I got one quick glimpse of Steve and the van. I'd gotten good at spotting trouble, and Steve had done an excellent job of hanging back and blending in.

"She's inside. We can go." Sandy blew out a long breath. "So, they know who I am."

"I'm sorry, but apparently they do."

"And just like that, I get to be leverage in some weird organized crime war," she said, her voice rising.

"I wish that weren't true. It's a horrible, helpless feeling I wouldn't wish on anyone."

She paused.

"Look," I said. "I understand you want out of it and I can't blame you. Please realize that at least for the moment you can't stick around and be safe, even if you disavow me and everything we do."

"Is that what you want?" She stared at me.

"No. Of course not. But most of all, I want you to be safe. I hate that being close to me puts you or anyone else in danger," I said. "Just like I wish none of my group was associated with the Irish. But it isn't so simple."

Now Sandy stared straight ahead. "It *is* simple. One thing led to another . . ."

"Which led to another," I finished. "But it's not too late for you to get out of town."

"Yeah, it is." I heard steel in her voice beneath the fear. "It was when they showed up and bothered my girls. Probably sooner."

I wanted to argue, but she spoke the truth.

"It does feel horrible, but I'm not helpless." She looked at me. "I'm in."

"Really?"

"Whatever you need me to do to help. I won't leave my girls at risk or ditch you guys," she said. "Plus, it's better than looking over my shoulder."

"Less boring, maybe," I said, trying to lighten the mood because I couldn't find the words to convey how proud I was of her courage.

She leaned into me and gave me the best kiss of my life before moving back over on the seat. "Why didn't you tell me your idea about the house calls?"

"I just thought of it now. You think it'll work?" It felt right to speak about more mundane tasks now.

"I don't see why not." Sandy seemed as relieved as me. "Except for the ones who need the more specialized weight machines or the hot tubs, but we can get by without those for a little while. Even in those cases there are still stretches and resistance work to keep the gains we've made from disappearing." It was great to hear her explore the possibilities.

"My good idea for the week," I joked. But despite how happy I was to have Sandy stay in the picture, the other side of that equation loomed large. I still didn't have any brilliant insights to avoid bloodshed.

The trill of a phone broke into my thoughts. It was the one for the trailing van. I handed it to Sandy, who thumbed it on and put it on speaker. VP's voice filled the truck's cab.

"Yo, we got a blip of movement in the backyard."

"What do you mean a blip?" I said.

"Just that. A quick movement detected, then it was gone."

"A cat or squirrel?"

"I don't think so. It should filter out critters now."

"Cameras?"

"Bringing them up now. Uh-oh."

"What?" It was hard to focus on the road while trying to picture what was happening.

"Someone just opened the trick door on the shed," VP said. "We don't have that angle on camera."

My foot dropped hard onto the gas, and I got a honk while a passed a slower car. We weren't far away, but the tight streets made fast responses a torture.

"Glad you're here with me," I whispered to Sandy.

"Me too." I'm certain she was reliving Tank's visit, just like I was.

"So, who's paranoid for adding that hatch now?" Rollie yelled in the background.

"Any more movement?" I was wondering if this was another fishing expedition or an all-out attack.

"Nothing in the yard," VP said. "Now I wish I'd stuck a camera inside the shed."

"Okay, Steve, we're in a race to the house," I said. "But we don't go in until we're both there."

* * *

The rest of the way to the place was maddening, with double-parked cars slowing us down, but we still made decent time. VP monitored for new movement or additional breaches of door. So far, nothing.

We parked in front of the house. It was strange, but the neighbors gave the two places right out front a wide berth. I'd never asked for the courtesy, but after a couple years of small and sometimes not-so-small favors for many people living up and down the block, it was a nice bonus.

Rollie came out of the van, and I half-expected him to deploy rifle in hand. Thankfully he was being more discreet. I had my own pistol holstered and covered under my shirt.

Even so, we wasted no time getting to the front porch. I stuffed my earpiece in and VP came online while she remained in the van to try to track progress from the laptop.

"Hatch open," she said. "Company is coming to the basement."

Steve stayed in the van. Frontline tactical work wasn't his role right now. Rollie and I could move in tight spaces and not trip over each other. Mostly, I let him do the work as I was still a truck driver at heart.

"They didn't waste any time coming back, did they?" Rollie said. We took positions covering the door to the basement. Both of us had our pistols out.

"Bunker door still closed," VP said. "Oh, cute. Whoever it is just fired up the monitors."

"I thought that wouldn't work," I said, moving to the door to the basement. If the intruder was still in the bunker, then he was contained. Best not to give him full run of the basement.

"Without the passcode they get a stale recording of video feed," VP said. "Don't worry, they won't see us out front. Or you guys."

"That's our cue," Rollie said. He could hear her as well over his own receiver.

I went first before Rollie could take point. My house, my risk.

I moved as fast as I could without sounding like a tap-dancing elephant. Rollie was a ghost by comparison. In seconds, we were positioned to cover the only way out of the bunker.

Rollie whispered to me, "Kid, whatever you do, don't shoot the steel. Rounds will bounce right back at us."

Good to know.

"VP, can you see in there?" We did have a camera in the bunker ever since the tunnel went in.

"The light will come on in the unit," she warned.

"Go on."

"I don't . . . crap," she said. "The lens is covered."

I rushed forward and Rollie moved behind me, covering while making sure he wouldn't hit me. Then we had to wait.

When locked from inside, the whole room was designed to frustrate threats on the outside. Mission accomplished. I was definitely feeling frustrated.

"Here he comes." The door opened a crack, enough for VP to have detected.

Finally.

Whoever it was wouldn't get a chance to change his mind: I tucked the gun in its holster and ran up and yanked the door wide open with all my strength. Rollie saw the move and adjusted himself.

Initial resistance gave way to a surprised yelp and a small-framed person fell out of the room face-down onto the floor.

Rollie's gun was at the guy's head before mine was back in my hand.

Rollie flipped him over and spit out a curse. "You got a death wish or something?"

Tom stared up at the huge muzzle of the .45. "Surprise?"

Rollie looked reluctant to withdraw the weapon. But he did. "What the hell is wrong with you? You can't use a phone, or the damn front door?"

"I didn't want to be seen." Tom looked shaken. His face beaded with sweat. "All right if I get up?"

"We're a little on high alert." I held up a hand while I relayed to VP what was happening.

I switched off the headset for now. They'd be in the house in a moment.

"How did you get through the hatch?" Rollie asked. "That lock was supposed to be pick-resistant."

"It was. That took me longer than I expected."

"Never mind that," I said. "Why the drama, Tom? You could have called, you know. Or were you planning on bringing the cavalry through here as well?"

Considering the danger of being shot by mistake had passed, Tom's color, pale ashes, hadn't improved.

"I did bring them," he said in a small voice.

I glanced back into the bunker. Empty. I pulled off the sock he'd put over the camera. "Where?"

"I am the cavalry, mate. As much as you're going to get."

CHAPTER 25

Kyle's place

I tried to process what Tom had just said. "What do you mean, you're it?"

Tom stared at his feet. "No point sugarcoating it, mate. Ali said I'm all the help you're going to get for this situation."

"Whoa. You couldn't have explained what we're up against? What's at stake? What he has to lose?"

"I'm sorry, but you're wrong." Tom's voice sounded like it was going to break.

"What exactly did he say?" Rollie's dark eyes were intense and focused on Tom, and he waited for Tom to meet his gaze.

"Right." Tom swallowed. "Remember, this is him speaking." He paused again.

"C'mon, Tom, out with it," I said.

"He doesn't want to lose the port. He knows exactly how much he's spent setting it all up. He appreciates what you have done here."

"You said no sugarcoating."

"But he said it's time to earn your keep. Deal with the threat, or he will allow the port to fail. He said he has too much to lose on everything else than to get caught up in a mob war and being sent to jail or worse."

"He's scared of the Albanians?" I couldn't believe it.

"Not scared. He did what was needed over in Iraq. I understand this." Tom spoke in a slow and deliberate voice. "So should you."

I didn't understand. Fury built in my chest. "And now he's too good to get into the trenches?"

"He's a businessman first. He's fought to get where he is, and now sees that the risks outweigh the rewards," Tom said. "For what it's worth, he said he is rooting for you."

"It isn't worth shit!" I didn't care if my voice carried upstairs where the rest of the group waited. "You might as well go back and tell him that. None of us is safe."

"You'll notice I'm here. They have phones in Ohio; I could have called."

My anger deflated like a punctured tire. "I'm sorry. I should be yelling at myself."

"Maybe you were." Tom accepted my hand for a shake. "I tried to change his mind. By the end, I think he was close to having some of his cousins mash me into a paste."

"I can't believe how stupid I've been. I was sure he'd pull our nuts out of the fire."

"Thanks for not shooting the messenger." Tom turned to Rollie. "So, how much trouble are we in, really?"

"Almost more than we can handle," Rollie said.

Unless he had some great idea, all I could figure was that we were fucked.

* * *

Rollie and Tom went upstairs ahead of me. I needed a minute.

When I ascended the steps, my mind felt disconnected from my body. People who counted on me were waiting to hear our next move.

Everyone was in the living room, where there was enough space for the whole group. Steve had come in with VP and Sandy, who had gone to the van until we signaled the all-clear.

VP was explaining to Tom how she spoofed what he saw on the monitors.

"Brilliant! You'll have to teach me how to do that." Tom grinned like everything was right in the world.

"Right after you show me how you picked the lock on the hatch," VP said.

"Deal."

"Uh, guys." It wasn't exactly 'Four score and seven years ago' for an opener, but I didn't know what the hell to say at this point.

I had the floor anyway.

"Tom's dramatic entrance aside . . ." I began.

"I prefer 'discreet.'" Tom's levity chafed my nerves.

"Tom came with the bad news that we can't expect help from Ali, the guy with the ability to raise a force of people with enough muscle to resist the Albanians, if not scare them off."

That punchbowl turd drew silence for several long seconds.

VP held up her hand like a kid in class. "It's getting real, I understand. I know we help the Irish and stuff, lately a lot, but isn't this a 'their problem' thing?"

A good question and an even better one after this last disappointment. "Fair enough. Let's think it through and put all the knowns on the table. The least I can do."

I hated making it sound like I kept secrets from people I trusted, but it was a secretive world we'd built. "What if we abandon the Irish? We're involved in some things together, but last I checked, none of us were made members of their family. It's never been who we are." That felt better to say out loud.

I explained how the Albanians knew the current weakness of the Irish forces, and their choice of surrender or death. "So, if the Irish get wiped out, or even just quit, that leaves the Albanians in charge of the territory. As far as they are concerned, that includes our operation."

"Bull crap," VP said. "They don't know about me, not specifically, and hell, they can't know half the stuff we do. Most of it they wouldn't be interested in, anyway."

I looked at Sandy. "They have a way of finding things out when they want leverage, as our field trip to Old City just now shows. But you might be right about the other activities. However, they aren't going to give up on the port."

"That's nothing to do with the Irish," Tom said. "But at this point, they may not care. They know Kyle, and one way or another they are going to make him work for them."

"They see it as a chance to smuggle drugs by the ton." I shook my head. "And I never would. But I can't say it couldn't succeed for a while. Even that might be enough for them."

"The port would close," Tom said.

"Sure, and if I tipped off every Fed and prosecutor on the East Coast as to what was happening, we might see some arrests that stuck."

"But their whole family?" Rollie asked.

"No. Not a chance, and I'm a dead man. And the port is shut down regardless."

"How many people work there now?" Sandy asked.

"Over a hundred. And they haven't done anything wrong. I keep all port business and what we do in the community separate." I rubbed the back of my neck where the muscles were turning into marbles. "I'm sure they'd all appreciate getting job references from a guy accused of being a major drug trafficker." I paused. "Or if I got labelled a snitch, then I'd never live long enough to recommend anyone."

VP spoke up. "Wasn't it problems with their drug trafficking that got our Irish friends into trouble in the first place? Is that what we're supposed to be defending?"

"Yeah." What else could I say? "It was. But you know as well as anyone we have nothing to do with that part of their business."

"And the Albanians aren't trying to stomp out the drug trade, just the competition," Rollie added. "If anything, they want to make it worse."

"Probably," VP said, "but isn't there a way to get the Albanians to understand the difference between us and the Irish?"

Sandy spoke. "That hulk with a crewcut who chased me out of the house the other night didn't come across as much of a conversationalist."

I shook my head. "If there was a time for that, which I doubt, I think we burned that bridge when we rescued Charlie." And the thought of leaving him, or anyone, to that mutilating fate just didn't fly.

The room got quiet. It felt like we were in a maze where every path led us right back to the Minotaur.

"If we leave the Irish to the wolves," Tom said, "do you think the O'Briens will take the hint and quit?"

"Nope." Rollie and I spoke simultaneously.

"So, they get wiped out?" Tom said.

"The O'Briens personally, for sure. Some of their crew might bail, but as a 'going concern,' this branch of the Irish Mob will be replaced."

"And if we stay out of it, does that buy us protection?" Tom said.

"Only if I play ball and involve the port, and I'm not sure even then," I said. "If I refuse, then they take me out. If I'm lucky."

"Lucky?" Sandy said.

"If I'm *not* lucky, they'll start with everyone they think is close to me to try to force me to comply," I said. "Unless you all leave town. For good."

"Is that what you want, mate?" Tom said. "Captain goes down with the ship—or shipyard, if you prefer?"

I shook my head. "I'm not trying to be a martyr, damn it. But if that's the only way to keep the rest of you safe, maybe that's what I deserve for getting cocky."

Sandy had tears, and Tom and VP looked like they were going to burst. Steve looked shocked, and Rollie's face could have been carved out of granite.

"Don't we all get a vote here?" Sandy said.

"Sure, but I wish I knew what we were voting on." I smiled.

"The Irish will get wiped out in a war," Tom said, "and we are lumped in with the Irish. The ace up our sleeve just flopped to the floor. I think what we just voted is that we aren't going to turn you into a human sacrifice."

"If I go to the cops, at any level, I have no proof beforehand—and probably not after, either, the way both sides are able to cover their tracks. For sure, word will get out that I tried to turn them in."

"Is that so terrible?" Steve asked. "I mean, assuming you get away from them?"

"Witness protection? Like that?" I said. "The Irish would have to go after us just to show they aren't also snitches. Of course, the Albanians would as well, and if the info happened to step on any Italian, Mexican, or any other group's toes, add them to the mix." I shook my head. "I found a way to rewrite some of the rule book, but not all of it."

"Why not a fresh start somewhere else?" Sandy asked.

"VP, how long do you think it would take you to figure out where I was?" I asked. "Including some inside access from sources on the payroll."

VP chewed her lower lip. "A week? With inside access, maybe an hour?"

"I'm the only one handcuffed to this ride. The rest of you have a chance, but not here." I looked at Sandy while I spoke. "Make no mistake, the Albanians will not think twice about using any of you to get to me." Then I glanced at the floor. "And it would work."

"I'm not going anywhere." Sandy hugged me.

"Me either." VP made me settle for a fist bump.

"I like you owing me favors," Tom said. "I'm in, mate."

"You'd make me give back that new van if I bailed, wouldn't you?" Steve asked. "I'm in."

"I think I voted when I kneecapped their guard." Rollie stepped forward. "Folks, we're on what the great Chinese general Sun Tzu called 'Desperate Ground.' We can't run away from the fight and keep our current lives. The enemy is stronger, and in a mood to wipe us out, along with all resistance."

"Good talk," Tom said. "I feel better already. What do you propose?"

"We fight to win," Rollie said. "Whatever it takes. Like our lives depend on it."

"We know the true situation," I said. "Thanks to me, the Irish don't fully understand that we are the only cavalry coming to save them."

"They have some people left?" Sandy said.

"Not many, and most aren't fighters. They have Cullen, themselves, and a few more. We need to make sure they know what's up so they can call in every favor they have to try to improve our odds."

CHAPTER 26

Kyle's place, two hours later

I'd begun to worry the house was becoming too much of a fixed target. On the other hand, for now it was also the most easily defended. Tank's visit aside, the Albanians must have been holding off making a direct move on me in hopes of securing the port with my cooperation.

We couldn't risk our next conversation with the O'Briens being overheard, so we called them back to the house. Of course, they were annoyed at a second visit in one day, so I made sure to arouse their curiosity.

Hopefully they wouldn't try to kill me on the spot.

* * *

"This feels familiar," William said, taking a seat next to Charlie. "Would it be too much to ask for a fresh glass?"

As before, Cullen was by the backyard in his car, and my people were scanning the surrounding block. All except Rollie, who joined me at the table.

I brought them soft drinks and sat across the table. "I have news and I wish it was good."

"How bad?" Charlie set his jaw and balled up his right hand into a fist.

"Bad enough that I invited you back here to ask you to rethink your position."

"Which position was that?" Charlie snapped.

"Cutting a deal with the Albanians." Before Charlie could go off at that suggestion, I gave them the bad news. "I'm sorry," I said when I'd finished. "I was sure my benefactor in Ohio would protect his own investment."

"As long as you're sorry, that fixes everything," Charlie said.

"Charlie." William put a hand on his brother's arm.

"Now he expects us to head for the hills? That might work for him, but we can't—"

"We're staying with you," I said. "And fighting."

This caught both of them off guard.

William spoke. "The two of you?"

"My whole team. We are all in the same boat."

"You forgot to mention that the boat is the *Titanic*," Charlie said. "You promised us an army."

That was enough for Rollie. "Did you miss the part about us risking our lives for you people? Again? And since we're being honest, I'm not your biggest fan. But for him," he hooked a thumb my way, "I'll go to the wall for all of you."

Something about the way Charlie phrased, "promised us an army" resonated with me.

"You're handy in a fight, no question," Charlie conceded. "But the Albanians are bringing a war. How many rounds will your rifle hold?"

"Sometimes it's not how many, but who," Rollie said.

William leaned forward. "So, you have a plan, then? You should know I don't think the Albanians are going to wait much longer. They reached out just this afternoon."

"What did they say?" I asked. The back of my mind was buzzing so fast I couldn't keep up with my own thoughts.

"That we need to meet," Charlie said.

"Does Red know anything yet?" It was like my brain was sending thoughts directly to my mouth and I was just along for the ride.

"No," William said. "We were waiting for you, remember?"

"You're sure?" I asked. "It's really important."

"Then we're *really* sure." Charlie was losing his patience.

"What's on your mind, Kyle?" William said.

"You know heavy hitters, back in Ireland?"

"What do you mean?"

"Belfast boys, old-school soldiers who saw the elephant." They were staring at me. "Guys who were IRA during the Troubles. Ones who made their bones against the British Army."

Charlie looked ready to slug me with his good hand. "We know lots of people. They know us, and none of them crave publicity."

"Of course not. But they would be willing to repay some old favors, wouldn't they?"

"Are you deaf? We never said anything about them owing us anything." Charlie was about to come over the table at me. William, on the other hand, was rapt.

"Actually, I *am* mostly deaf in my left ear from an IED." I caught William's gaze and hoped he'd keep his brother from killing me for a few minutes longer. "I was sure you said some of their leaders owe your family and would be happy to square their tab with an overseas operation."

"If we held markers like that, don't you think we would have already . . ." Then Charlie began to get it.

The lamp had lit faster for William, whose lips spread into a real smile.

"I certainly *do* think so." My brain was still racing, but my conscious thought process was catching up now. "I think these soldiers would be on the way, and they might even be so hard-core that they would be on some terror watch lists preventing them from legally entering this country."

Charlie wasn't sure where I was going, but I could see I had them both hooked now.

"Unless, of course," I said, "you knew a way, somehow, to smuggle them across the Atlantic, maybe destined for a small private port on the East Coast."

"Great idea," Charlie said. "But one small problem . . ."

I pressed on. "One could imagine how hard a crew like that could hit an organized group if they had the element of surprise. Heck, a scary bunch to mess with in a straight-up fight." I looked again at William. "But to succeed, such an operation would require absolute secrecy."

Now Rollie began to grin.

"William," I said. "If you were on the other side and managed to learn of such a devious plan, what do you suppose you might do?"

William jumped out of his seat, grabbed my shoulders and I thought for a second he might kiss me. "I'd hit them first. With everything I had."

"So, we'd want to hope they never would learn precisely where the mercenaries were going to hole up after their long journey?"

"That would be terrible, wouldn't it?" Charlie said, fully onboard now. "Good thing we don't have any secrecy issues."

Rollie did a slow clap. "Our own FUSAG. Kid, that's brilliant."

"Our what?" Charlie asked.

"First United States Army Group. The name for a phantom army supposedly commanded by General Patton in World War II before the D-Day Invasion. Inflatable tanks, fake radio traffic, and leaked information for spies to find. The deception helped spread the German defenses and keep them guessing about the real invasion spot in Normandy."

William nodded. "I remember now. We're fresh out of model tanks, but I think we can generate some rumors that ought to pique the interest of our opponents."

I saw in their eyes a glint of hope, but we still had a long way to go. "We're only going to get one shot at this," I said. "Our bait has to be irresistible, but at the same time, believable."

"A moment with my brother, if you don't mind," William said.

* * *

When Rollie and I returned from checking with everyone else and confirming that the coast was still clear, William and Charlie still leaned into each other, speed-whispering. I imagined that they worked this way often, making sure conversations remained private.

They pulled away and regarded us for a moment before Charlie said, "We think we know why Red decided to betray us."

"He doesn't know that, I hope?" I said.

Charlie's face scrunched up, and he didn't dignify it with a response.

"Red was recently passed over for promotion. Not to delve into our family business, but we weren't prepared to trust him with more responsibility."

"Not so dumb after all, eh?" Charlie said and folded his arms. His bandage looked like a half-mowed catcher's mitt.

"Despite Red's assertions that he accepted our decision," William said, "it appears he has decided to, shall we say, test the free-agent waters."

"We think we need to give him another chance. An important job, to show he's ready to step up." Charlie grinned like a shark.

I smiled back. "That's good. What've you got?"

"If we understood you correctly," Charlie said, "we've already made arrangements for, let's call them the Irish Foreign Legion, to enter the country past some bribed customs agents to arrive in 'our' port."

I nodded. "Exactly. They think the place is a smuggler's dream already; let's run with it. A shipping container wouldn't be the most comfortable way to travel, but they are large enough."

"I've travelled in worse," Rollie said, "and if you knew for certain that nobody would look inside, you could fit one out to be cushy enough. And they could bring a lot of firepower with them."

"All the better to tempt an early pre-emptive strike," William said.

"Definitely," I said. "Now, if we were bringing this Irish Foreign Legion into our facility next to the main port, we'd have to use one of our regular containers that had cleared customs."

"What exactly do you do with the containers once they are at your facility?" William asked. They'd never been all that curious about our routine operation, as it had nothing to do with them.

"Well, typically we'll track a shipment of furniture coming from Ali's contacts around the Middle East. Once the container comes off the ship at the Port of Philadelphia, we have to wait for it to clear customs."

"Sounds like it would be hard to defeat for real," Charlie said.

"The system works pretty well, but it isn't impossible. You won't be surprised to hear that our boxes get inspected more often, considering where they originate. Another reason we don't mess around."

"And if the Albanians figure this out?"

"I assume they have looked into it. I'm sure Milosh has. He's not stupid. But the system has flaws."

"People?" William said. Like my side gigs, they were experts in exploiting human weakness.

"You got it. Like I said, we don't take advantage, but that isn't to say we couldn't, and we know people who could probably be persuaded to make a few key errors."

"Good enough. But for our purposes, that won't be necessary?"

"Right. As long as they believe we've done it, we can handle a legitimate container and move it to my facility. Usually, we'll load the contents onto trucks bound for Ohio and Ali's warehouses."

William thought about it and then leaned in to Charlie and whispered so I couldn't hear anything, even when I turned my good ear toward them.

"Do you always unload the containers?" William asked.

"Usually, because it's easier for Ali's people at the other end to take off the furniture or even to deliver it to a retail shop. The containers are bulkier, and we have to take them back to the port empty. Why?"

"I imagine once our friends are expecting an arrival, they will be watching the port and your people," he said.

Rollie spoke up. "Good point. The last thing we want is for them to get the bright idea to hit the offload at our facility."

"No. That would be a disaster," I said. "Great catch. Yes, sometimes we will take an entire container right on a truck. This should be the case here. That way they'll think they have the target all in one spot. In theory, the cavalry could scatter once they get to our property."

"We'll need another location that is a plausible destination," Rollie said. "Someplace out of the way, and one where a container won't look out of place."

Charlie and William grinned. "Oh, we have just the spot, and it's right in the neighborhood."

"Where?"

They named a nearby salvage yard, one I'd suspected was buried under a bunch of shell companies but likely owned by the Irish.

"That's perfect," I said. But I saw Rollie frowning. "What?"

"If the target, as far as they know, is all crammed in one container, why wait for it to get to the junkyard? Why not hit it on the road?"

Everyone was looking at me, which was a compliment, I guess, but I didn't feel it at the time. I thought for a moment that seemed like an hour under their collective gazes.

"Two things," I said, finally. "First, if they think they know where the container is going, it makes it easier to plan a trap." I saw the doubt in their eyes. "Think about it. Going after a moving truck out in the open is tricky as hell if the goal is to wipe everyone out. And it'd attract a great deal of attention. But a junkyard, tucked along the Delaware River? Makes a nice ambush spot."

William thought about it. "Would it be difficult to be certain which truck leaving the big port was yours?"

"When we carry something like that, we don't typically have branding on the side of the truck. For this job, we certainly wouldn't," I said. "The Port of Philadelphia workers would know, and the paperwork will be legit, but I don't think an outsider would know for sure."

"Are you willing to bet the driver's life?" Charlie said.

"Since I'm going to be the driver, I guess so," I said. "But even if they know it is coming from my company, they have to be sure it's the right truck. We get more than one container in an offload. Usually more like three. Remember, they also only get one shot at this. If they hit the wrong one out in the open, they're screwed."

William nodded. "Plausible. Best for them to make sure, especially if they want enough privacy to finish the job."

Rollie spoke up again. "How is a scrapyard, in the middle of the city, in any way private?"

"It's on the edge of the river on one side," Charlie pointed out.

"Yes, and a small neighborhood not far on the other side," Rollie said. "Whatever we do, especially me, might be rather loud. I don't think a suppressed .22 will cut it."

I thought for a moment that Rollie had stumped the brothers. They leaned in to each other again, this time Charlie nodding as William spoke. When they broke their huddle, William spoke to us. "I don't think you'll have to worry about the neighbors." He said this with such confidence that I figured the people living there were either fans or afraid of the O'Briens. Probably both.

"As for noise," Charlie said, "we'll handle that. You just make sure that they get to the yard."

"What about after that?" Rollie said. "Kyle here is part of our baited hook, remember?"

"Kyle is tough. He knows when to duck. Right, son?" William grinned. "And he will have a guardian angel with a rifle, won't he?"

"I'm no innocent bystander. We all know what we're talking about." Rollie stared straight ahead. "I'll do what is necessary, but you understand I can't do it all, even if I wanted."

"Understood," William said.

"We have a few tricks up our sleeves," Charlie said. Then, producing a smile that dropped the room's temperature by ten degrees, he added,

"And I'll be damned if I don't get a chance to thank them for this experience." He held up his wrapped hand.

I opened a laptop and found the incoming shipment schedule for the next batch of imports. A week. I showed William. "Will this do?"

He peered at the screen. "Perfect. We'll set a meet for a couple days after this, and Charlie and I will plant the seeds with Red. He's going to be a very busy fellow."

CHAPTER 27

Kyle's place, one week later

I was always astonished at the difference activity could make on the perceived passage of time. When we had to wait for an operation to ripen, or for an anticipated attack, the time dragged while the tension built. Not so the past seven days. We'd all been busy, and while we considered the ongoing threat of the Albanians making a move at the house or on the O'Briens, it hadn't happened and it appeared they were playing along with what was claimed to be the capitulation of the Irish.

We weren't involved directly with the "baiting of the hook," as the O'Briens called it, but we'd worked closely with them on preparation of the scrapyard.

Rollie tapped on the front door, more to let me know he was there than to be allowed inside. He had keys to everything.

"Anything I need to know before I leave?" He took a seat at the dining room table.

"Sandy is going to be with VP at the site," I said.

"You caved?" Rollie laid on the shocked bit rather thick.

"We needed an extra pair of hands out there, and the spot you prepped ought to be safe enough."

"I guess, but you know anything can go wrong once it all kicks off," he said. "I thought you were going to ask Bishop to help."

"Bishop is out on this one. I asked William, since he does more with the Irish than us, and he point-blank said to keep him in the dark."

"They don't trust him?"

"Something about how they didn't think he'd have the stomach for what comes next."

"Maybe he wouldn't, but I don't doubt his balls," Rollie said.

"No, but we're probably doing him a favor. He is still a real cop, and he doesn't have to keep a secret if he doesn't know about it in the first place." I was relieved, actually. He wasn't one to take orders, and we all needed to be on the same page for this to have a chance to work.

"Does Sandy know what to do?"

"Yes, and she'd wanted to help already. She wasn't going to sit in the bunker and just monitor." I laughed. "It was a small price to pay to talk her out of riding in the truck with me."

This time, Rollie's shock was real. "Jaysus. Really?"

I nodded. "I kept it from being a courage test when I explained that she's not credentialed to go to the Port Authority loading area, not to mention that it would look odd as hell leaving the site with her next to me."

"Hey, you didn't even have to lie."

"Nice when it works out like that," I said. "She's been going stir crazy, hiding out and not being able to run her office."

"Didn't Beet and her people have that covered?"

"Yeah. Beet has been amazing. But it's not the same."

"I get it. This'll be over soon enough. For better or worse. Anything new from VP?"

"After she first spotted those scouts scoping out the site, what was it . . . the day after the seeds got planted with Red?" The days were running together.

"Yup. And they're still circling?"

"Tapering off. Guess they don't want to tip their hand." I gave a small smile. "Looks like we're going to get our fight."

Rollie stood up. "Be careful what you wish for and all that." He paused long enough for the awkward to creep in.

"We do get caught up in some shit, don't we?"

Rollie stuck out his hand. I took it and pulled him in for a quick hug. "Cold beer's waiting for after."

* * *

Port of Philadelphia

I brought up the rear of a three-truck "convoy" taking delivery of containers of furniture bound for our port at Global Imported Crafts. The first two would make the short drive for GIC. Once we were past our port entrance, I would make a conspicuous turn toward the direction of the scrapyard. Anyone watching would have to assume that I was now the truck to follow.

Easy to say, but I didn't know what I'd do if something happened to one of the other drivers. Both of them had been longtime employees at the old company working at the port and now were some of my best drivers under the new import company. Neither had anything to do with my side gigs and definitely had no connection to the Irish Mob.

But I had no choice. I needed everyone on my team waiting at the scrapyard, and they weren't licensed truckers anyway.

Still, I was sweating while we queued up at the inspection station. The early evening was still warm, and the Customs night shift was checking and waving through loads. I wasn't worried about getting inspected. Anyone watching wouldn't be able to see this part, and even if the officers opened my container, the contents matched the manifest.

As it turned out, they did check the first driver's container and after a quick once-over sent him through. The second driver and I got through faster, and the lady working my lane waved. We were regulars and she'd been on the job forever.

The quick haul to our port, the warehouse facility across the street, was so familiar I almost autopiloted the turn through the main gate behind the first two trucks. I'd already told my guys that mine needed to go direct, after all, so they wouldn't worry when they noticed I wasn't right behind them. I'd also made them promise to let me know as soon as the loads were delivered, not just because I was a diligent manager but because I needed to make sure they were safe. I was going to need all my focus for the task at hand.

I slipped on my earpiece and radio from VP. I also maintained my ritual of mirror-checking and so far saw nothing more than the usual traffic.

"Quarterback on the move, cleared port."

"Roger." I heard VP's voice and smiled a little. She'd been so reluctant at first to use certain radio terminology, at least until Rollie had convinced her that when working as a team being "different and glib" could lead to confusion and get people killed.

Not too many people could render VP speechless, but Rollie in "business mode" commanded respect from anyone.

VP had planted cameras around the immediate area of the scrapyard, but not this far out. If I got hit out here, they might ruin their big chance, but I'd probably not live through the experience. So far, so good. I was taking a simple and direct route with as few turns as possible. I wanted my drive to appear oblivious to any dangers. However, the one downside was that a simpler route meant that cars I might notice following could just be coincidence, unless, of course, they started shooting at me.

When I reached a long street, a six-block straight shot just before the last turn to the scrapyard, I knew that VP's camera coverage had begun.

"Coach"—that was VP's handle—"how's my six?"

I was sweating again. This was a dangerous time. I had to make it to the scrapyard for this plan to work, and by now anyone paying attention would know I wasn't heading anywhere else. I felt naked out there. I also had to be careful on the tight residential streets. Parked cars were easy to clip with wide load on the truck. Tinted windows looked darker under the streetlights now that night had fallen.

VP came back. "Nothing behind you. Hang on, let me see on the other street." She was calm over the air. All business. "Whoa. QB, pick up the pace, looks like fish on the line and moving to intercept from a parallel street."

"What is it?" I sped up and kept my eyes on the road. There was little traffic, as everyone in the neighborhood was either home already or out for the night and the businesses had closed up. I skipped the last few stop signs and got lucky on that front.

"Not it, they. Two fish, a mini-bus and an armored car."

"You sure?"

"The name on the side rhymes with stinks," she said. "Sorry, that was glib. Yeah, very sure."

I could imagine Rollie grimacing. He was on the net as well. So were Sandy and Steve, but everyone was supposed to keep quiet until their turn.

"Still got me?" I asked. "I'm coming in hot, an open gate would be nice."

"You got it. Looks like they are slowing down. You should beat them inside."

Icy fear knifed into my chest. Had they sniffed out something? "Are they stopping?"

"No. I think they're speeding up again."

I'd just made the last turn. I could see the scrapyard entrance ahead and still no vehicles to play chicken with before I turned inside the crushed car walls of the scrapyard.

"Places, everyone, and stay cool," I said. "Quarterback coming in." The truck's brakes hissed as I worked to bleed speed off for the turn into the unpaved scrapyard. The chain-link fence gate had been rolled back, as promised. I had to be careful not to hit the walls, which resembled something out of a post-apocalypse fortress. Mashed cars had been used like giant metal bricks to form an impressive wall. Old cars in various states of decay decorated the grass next to the sidewalk, and beside the entrance sat a faded orange school bus with no windshield and most of the side windows broken out.

Just inside the open yard I could see to my right a towering pile of scrap metal and several large containers being filled before they'd carry the metal to some distant recycler. Bright lights lit the interior like it was going to be the site of some dystopian high school football game.

Maybe "arena" was a better way to describe it.

To my left, I could see the dirt road that led to a two-story building. The unpaved course doglegged from there to the right, where more containers were stacked and several pieces of heavy equipment sat dormant. The lights made it hard to see the farthest edges of the yard.

A dark figure rolled the gate back into place behind me. It wasn't one of mine, had to be either with the yard or the Irish.

I drove the truck halfway to the equipment, where, along the back part of the wall, a pair of doublewide mobile homes sat. I knew the Irish had made Red outfit them with sleeping bags, food, and toiletries, enough for twenty or so weary travelers.

"Quarterback landed." I opened the truck door and stepped to the ground. No sooner had my boots hit the earth than VP was in my ear. "Company inbound. Look out!"

I heard a turbodiesel engine whine as it revved, and an instant later the fence gate blew off the tracks and out of the way. Just as VP said, it was a Brinks armored car with a reenforced bumper. The truck turned left toward me before skidding at an angle to a stop. I was very aware of the gunport on the side that now faced me. Right behind it came the mini bus, which also veered left and stopped at a right angle and about ten yards behind the armored car.

"Angel?" That was Rollie's codename, and I knew he was perched on the office building's roof overlooking the scrapyard. I scurried toward the front of the truck where I hoped the thick engine block would provide enough cover.

"Eyes on."

"Your call." Meaning it was up to him to decide if or when to shoot.

"My call." He sounded as calm as if it was him agreeing to buy the next round at a bar.

My heart was pounding as I peeked around the big front tire. I could see that the back doors of the mini bus were open, and bulky guys with rifles erupted from the bus like a kicked-over anthill.

They were using the armored car as cover and the men fanned out.

Then I noticed Tank. The huge bodyguard had been in the front seat of the mini bus and he hopped out. He looked even bigger with heavy body armor protecting his torso.

In a single, fluid motion he reached into the bus and pulled out an old nightmare.

Tank limped forward a couple steps and, with a clear path to the container (and me), shouldered and aimed an old Soviet rocket-propelled grenade launcher.

The stretched Coke-bottle shape of the rocket was the last thing truck drivers in the Sand Box wanted to see. My legs wanted to lock, but instinct and old training kicked in. "RPG!"

Time turned thick and syrupy. I tried to turn and run back away from the truck toward the back area of the scrapyard. I was still in the middle of the move, staring at that evil cone shape, when Tank's body jerked like he'd suffered a back spasm. I heard the single crack from Rollie's rifle, the round that must have hit Tank's vest. More importantly, the rocket leapt from the tube, and I could see right away by the angle it was a miss high.

I paused at the front of the truck as the rocket streaked out over the Delaware River. Soon after, I heard the blast as the round self-destructed at nine hundred yards. I knew more than I wanted about the damn things, but it came in handy sometimes.

I got low and glanced around the front of the truck. Tank still had a clear field of fire to the truck, and all the Albanian men were on the other side of the mini bus working their way up to the armored car and better shooting angles. I saw Tank on one knee by the front of the mini bus. From his position, I could tell he wasn't sure where the shot had come from. He pulled out another rocket. Just as he began to fit it into the tube, the backside of his head blew out, and he collapsed. An instant later I heard the shot. The next moment, the truck tire by my own head burst and the distinctive chatter of an AK-47 ripped from the armored car's gun port.

Too close. I rolled away and stood only when I knew I once again had the truck's engine block between me and the Albanians. Then I ran straight toward the back of the scrapyard. At first, I heard the thuds and smacks of bullets hitting the cargo container. Thankfully, the Albanians still thought the box was full of seasick IRA, so it drew most of the fire.

What the furniture inside didn't stop punched through the thin metal walls of the container, and I heard them zip past.

A second later, I didn't hear anything but loud whistles and explosions. The sky behind the scrapyard had erupted with commercial-grade fireworks. Shells burst and flashed, and the display was super-heavy on reporting fireworks. Their loud bangs masked the insanity on the ground of the scrapyard.

"Quarterback, Locker Room yet?" Rollie's voice crackled in my earpiece.

"Almost, Angel." I was making my way toward a big crane at the edge of the back portion of the yard. "Teacher, close the door. Coach, lights please."

"Door's closed." I heard Tom's voice. He was "Teacher" and had been hiding inside the not-as-dilapidated-as-it-looked school bus. At my command, he'd fired up the engine and pulled it right across the entrance, replacing the broken chain-link fence with about 25,000 pounds of dead weight.

I knew VP heard me when several blinding spotlights mounted along the back wall of the yard pinned the Albanians so they looked like center stage at a rock concert.

By now, I'd reached the crane and climbed up into the cabin. Between the bus and the lights, the shooting in my direction stopped for a moment. I let Rollie know where I was and grabbed the first of two body armor sets waiting for me inside the cab. I felt a mixture of déjà vu and PTSD as I geared up and readied heavy equipment while under fire.

Just keep going.

The barrage of fireworks that continued unabated from the nearby neighbors didn't help my nerves, but they covered the rest of the noise like a charm. William and Charlie hadn't been kidding when they said not to worry.

I set the second vest at the windshield to give me something to duck behind. Not perfect, but better than nothing.

One of the spotlights guttered out and flared with sparks and smoke. Shot, I presumed. Luckily, they weren't manned. We'd figured they might not appreciate the blinding beams.

VP cut in. "Quarterback, some of them are heading your way."

Now Rollie. "Eyes on. Will discourage."

I knew the old guy was working a bolt-action rifle. I heard shots ring out at a measured rate. Even so, a figure broke from the safety of cover to charge. A round hit high on my windshield. Above my head, but I felt glass fragments sting my cheek.

The guy was running and firing, which ruined his aim. I started the big diesel motor on the crane. All the dash lights indicated nothing important had been hit, yet, and the crane was ready.

I glanced up and reached for the Beretta pistol Rollie had provided. The Albanian slowed down and raised his rifle. He paused and I knew that was so he could hose down the cab properly with bullets. But what helped him aim, helped Rollie even more. The guy never got another round off and dropped from a headshot.

"Angel dry. Standby."

I racked the slide on the pistol. I didn't see any others, but this had to stop. "Coach and Marionette, begin the play. Salamander, ready?"

Starving Steve replied, "Salamander is green."

Now one more spotlight dazzled the main group of Albanians. A loudspeaker crackled to life, emphasis on LOUD, to be heard over the din: "NO SURRENDER!"

At that, dark figures sat up in and around the scrap metal mound. VP had rigged up a set of pulleys connected to mannequins at the scrap pile on the right side of the yard. Sandy was able to pull on them to simulate basic movement, all from a safe dugout behind the back wall.

The blinding light made it difficult to see more than vague shapes, but a moment later, flashes and reports made it look like troops in makeshift pillboxes had sprung a perfect ambush.

From my vantage point, all the Albanians ducked their heads, and then I could see them whirl around and reposition themselves to meet the new threat from the opposite direction of the truck and decoy cargo container.

I knew some of the automatic weapon fire sounds were piped in though the loudspeaker, but in all the confusion, it was hard to tell. The flashes were pipes with blanks set off remotely. Good thing.

I guess I wasn't the only one with frayed nerves. The Albanians began pouring return fire at the scrap pile. Now I heard the louder sound of Rollie's high-powered rifle. A window or two on the mini bus shattered and the Albanians trying to work in closer to the new enemies thought better of it.

Finally, the guys in the Brinks truck decided to do more than act like a giant paperweight. The truck made a three-point turn and drove around the mini bus. The driver tapped the horn, which I supposed was meant for the guys on the ground to follow the leader.

I had a better view once the truck moved and saw the Albanians. Had to be fifteen or more of them, crowded in a squat-and-crawl formation behind the perceived safety of the armored truck.

The problem was that with this many men, the truck wasn't wide enough. To their credit, they were brave, but they weren't real soldiers and their movement showed it.

"They're bunched up behind the Brinks. I don't think we're gonna get a better look," Rollie cut in. He had the best vantage point.

"Cut the puppet show." That was Sandy's signal to stop yanking on the pulleys and get back to Steve. "Salamander, make it rain!" I said.

Steve had a safe spot behind the back wall along with a laptop that showed a camera feed. But he also had something much more important.

Steve had brought a modified firehose pump now designed to spray more than just water. "Sprinkler on!"

I watched in amazement and terror as a heavy stream of liquid arced over the top of the back wall and showered the cluster of Albanians. The men jumped at the damp shock, and they stopped shooting the instant they were able to smell what was soaking them.

"On target," VP said. "Holy crap."

Steve swept the stream across the group once more, and at the same time, VP stopped all the shooting sound effects from the scrap pile. Now the loudspeaker boomed a set of instructions in Albanian. I knew the script already, and if we needed to adlib, we could do so in English. I'd figured not many of the neighbors spoke Albanian, and the less they understood, the better.

"Don't move. Don't shoot." The words echoed across the scrapyard. Near Steve, Sandy crouched at a hard point by the top of the back wall. She lit and held up a road flare so the doused Albanians could see the flame. Most of them. Some were screeching and rubbing their eyes.

Don't push it guys, it can get a lot worse.

"Teacher," I said into the mic. Tom lit his own road flares and began to toss them out of the school bus across the scrapyard's front entrance. Soon he had so many going, it would be hard for any of the men to leave the yard that way on foot without risking catching fire.

The wind shifted, and the pungent stench of gasoline reached the cab of the crane.

Time for the next part of the script. "Throw weapons away and get on ground."

VP paused the recording. I could see nobody wanted to be first.

"Or burn," the recording added.

Sandy waved the flare. It would be an easy toss to land it among them, not that she'd ever be willing to do anything like that. The key here was that they bought the bluff.

Now I heard more Albanian, but this time, it was coming from the Brinks truck. I didn't have any script, but I was pretty sure it was something like *Don't listen, Get up and fight,* stuff like that.

The bravado might have been more effective if the men giving the orders had left the safety of the armored car.

A tense moment stretched out, and I was really beginning to think we'd have to follow through. That meant me. I even had a few flares in the crane. I'd been very clear that if it got that bad, I would do it. The idea turned my stomach. Self-defense was one thing, but mass incineration was a different ballgame. I prayed the Albanians were more afraid.

Maybe it was the god of high octane, or the realization that they were going to die for leaders who considered them disposable, but one of them shouted "Wait!"

He tossed down his gun, raised his hands, and sank to his knees. The yelling continued from the truck but fell on deaf ears as a few more followed, then all of the men assumed the same submissive posture.

When the last rifle hit the ground, the Brinks truck shifted into reverse and would have run over one of the men if he hadn't rolled out of the way.

With a snarl, the truck's engine revved and launched the heavy truck at the entrance and the blocking school bus.

VP radioed a warning, but Tom had a front seat to what was coming, and I lost sight of him scrambling to exit the back of the bus.

The truck hit the school bus broadside, and I saw it dent and shift out of the way, but not enough. Some of the flares Tom had tossed got scattered. The Brinks truck backed up again, and the surrendered Albanians moved only to avoid being crushed.

I put the crane into gear, and it lurched forward. Between my time with heavy trucks, rigs overseas, and handling work at the port, I was familiar with most types of mobile equipment. But that wasn't the same thing as expert. I moved carefully because I might only get one chance.

The truck backed up and made another run at the bus. I couldn't see Tom. The truck hit harder this time, and the dent made the straight side of the orange bus more of an obtuse angle. It moved the bus farther, but still not quite enough. One more hit would probably allow them to escape.

I got the crane closer and began to work the controls on the arm. This one used a powerful electromagnet. I wasn't worried about the lifting power. This one had plenty. It was all about the balance. No time to screw around with the deployable feet; I'd just have to wing it.

As the truck began to back up for a final push, I jammed the controls to lower the heavy magnetic disc. It looked like a giant manhole cover with steel cables and power cords attached. I hadn't had time to practice with it, and the controls on this rig were more sensitive than I expected. The big magnet came down in front of the truck like a giant foot. Dust erupted from underneath.

I'm sure the driver must have been surprised, but he tried to go around. I lifted it up, which was much slower than the drop. The driver went to correct his angle and get through the entrance opening. The magnet rose, and I moved the levers to swing it to the left.

The truck hit the underside of the rising magnet, and I eased up on the lift. The vehicle rammed the disc, which kind of bounced and gouged the hood and then smashed against the bulletproof windshield. As the truck pressed forward, the magnet elevated and scraped along the roof of the boxy cabin. Soon it was going to slide past and off the truck and that would be that.

I hit the switch for the electromagnet and felt it bite down on the back part of the truck's roof. The truck's momentum had already slowed from fighting to get past the bulky magnet. The disc now had the back of the armored car in a firm grip. For now. The crane tipped with the initial shock. When it righted a second later, I began to ease the magnet upward. The rear tires of the truck fought the magnet, but as it exerted more and more lifting power, they started to slip, spewing dirt and gravel while scrabbling for purchase.

My plan was to hoist the truck up in the air and repeatedly drop it until it broke open or the goons inside surrendered. Instead, I was only able to lift enough weight to prevent the back tires from gaining any traction. After that, the crane would begin to tip again. Maybe if I could get the crane's feet deployed, I could lift from a more solid position.

The crane's windshield cracked, and one of the vests in front of me jerked like it was alive. No sooner had I pushed it back than more fire came from the back of the armored car. The vest jumped again and so did I when one got past a gap and slammed into my chest. The only reason I didn't scream was because it knocked the wind out of me. After I ducked down, I worked a hand underneath until I touched the ache, then pulled my fingers back. They were clean.

Too close.

I rocked the crane arm right and left to spoil their aim, but that made the crane wobble.

"Kinda stuck here," I said, "and taking fire."

Rollie came on before VP could answer. "Quarterback, are you hit?"

"Vest stopped it. I'm okay, but I feel like a goalie under siege. One's bound to get through sooner or later."

VP came on. "We still need to secure the prisoners."

She was right, but it didn't help if our team had to worry about getting shot in the back.

"Teacher on the case," I heard Tom say.

I jumped on the radio: "Angel, stand down."

"Roger, I see him," Rollie said. "Crazy bastard." He broke his own protocol about chatter.

Chancing a peek, I saw why. By squishing down as low as I could (not very, with all my gear on), I could see that Tom had run in with a pair of his road flares and crawled under the truck. As I watched, he stretched his arms out to apply the flames against the tires. If the magnet gave out or slipped, he'd be crushed.

"There go the tires." Rollie had the best vantage point. "But they'll be run flats."

"Bloody, flaming run flats when I'm done," Tom said.

"Just watch those gunports," I said. It seemed they'd brought plenty of ammo.

"Not a problem. I've got you covered," Tom said. "Them too."

I had no idea what he meant by that until a saw Tom scoot under the rear drive axle between the still sometimes spinning tires. He looked like a crazed gymnast as he pulled himself up and climbed the back of the truck.

I didn't need to warn him about the two gunports, which were making my life miserable. Just above the ports were bulletproof rectangular windows that the guys inside were using to spot targets. The glass was one-way, and then I realized why Tom was trying this stunt.

He reached into a jacket pocket and came out with a spray paint can. He struggled with his grip when the steel can leapt up in the magnet's pull. "Sod all, magnet near took it right out of my hand!"

We sure as hell didn't script this.

Like an experienced graffiti artist, he began to coat the windows, turning them into no-way glass.

The guys inside saw what he was doing, and my heart skipped a beat when the back door swung open. Tom reacted in an instant by hopping off and scrambling back under the truck. I reached for the pistol, not certain what I'd do next.

One heavy-booted leg made it to the diamond plate steel atop the bumper, and I saw the guy holding on to the door. At the truck's current angle, this was an uphill movement for him. He was holding a pistol in his other hand, so he had to pull himself out of the truck with one hand.

"Sending," Rollie said.

By the time the message hit my ear, I saw a puff of mist from the guy's calf. The guy fell back into the cramped space. I knew there could only be one or two more in the back area plus the driver and passenger in the main cabin.

The door fell to the open position. For a moment, everyone stayed inside the compartment, and I got an idea.

I could hear the wounded guy screaming and could only imagine what a mess his leg must be. That and the blood would make the tilted floor inside the truck slippery.

I grabbed the pistol and some road flares I had with me and lit one as soon as I'd climbed out of the crane's cab. It was only a short distance to the truck, and I saw one head begin to appear at the opening. I raised the gun and fired. The shot went high, striking off the ceiling inside the truck.

The guy ducked down, but I heard a fresh scream of pain.

"Skip-fire. Great idea, Quarterback." Rollie didn't realize that was an accident.

Deliberate or not, the guys inside hung back, so I flung one flare and then another into the opening.

"Brilliant," I heard Tom say, but didn't see him until he popped out from under the truck farther toward the front, spray paint in hand. "I'll get the windscreen. Mind your aim, yeah?"

Smoke began to billow from the truck, then one flare flew out the door followed by the second. I fired another shot, this time into the air, then lobbed the flares back in.

What followed was a bizarre game of hot potato where I would throw the flares in only to have them get tossed back to me. Nobody wanted to expose themselves to gunfire, and I'd hear more yelps when the flare singed someone before they could grab it. The other effect was that in the time the flares were inside, they added to the smoke already contained in the steel box.

It wasn't long before the guys inside were coughing nonstop. I waited out the din of a robust sky-burst of firework reports and shouted to the men inside. "Enough! Throw out the guns and come out one at a time or it's gasoline next."

Nothing wrong with their English comprehension; they'd seen what happened to the others. It didn't take much imagination to picture the interior as a makeshift kiln.

"Okay, okay!" Rifles and a couple pistols flew out only to leap into the air and clank against the big magnet holding the truck at bay.

"Send the wounded guy out first."

"Which one?"

Oh yeah. I almost felt bad, except for what they'd planned to do to us. "The leg wound."

I got on the radio. "Standby to secure prisoners. On my go, as soon as we're clear."

Tom jumped in. "Windows done. I'm covering the exit doors." I could see him under the truck. Now he'd replaced the paint with a pistol. If the driver or passenger tried to exit, they'd get an instant surprise.

"Marionette, can you join me at the gate with twine for a tourniquet?"

VP replied for Sandy. "On the way."

The first guy came out like the others were pushing him up and over. He dropped a couple feet, and right away I saw the fight was out of him, along with a ton of blood. To his buddies' credit, they had tried to tie off the leg, but in the end, these weren't cross-trained soldiers; they were glorified gang-bangers.

"Angel covering, advised of Teacher location." Rollie's way of saying he'd try hard not to hit Tom if he had to shoot. It gave me more freedom to help with the prisoners.

The second guy reached the opening and showed his hands. I noticed these guys weren't armored up, but of course the truck had been their armor. Now they were turtles out of their shells. This one had a blood-soaked T-shirt wrapped around his upper arm. When I looked at his face, I knew I'd seen him before. I pointed for him to lay on the ground and raised the pistol to cover the truck.

I heard grunts and stifled cries of pain. Finally, the last one pulled himself over the edge. His hands were empty and when he flopped to the ground, I saw why he'd had trouble getting out. Both of his knees were heavily wrapped. I also realized where I'd seen the second two men.

"These guys look familiar," Rollie said. They were the two guards from when we rescued Charlie.

"Teacher, stay put," I said. "Securing rear passengers." I took a handful of zip ties from my pocket and quick-cuffed the two more alert men. The other guy looked like he might lose his leg, if he made it that far.

"Landlord, I think your guests are ready to meet you. The last two are holed up and covered. Can you assist?"

"Thought you'd never ask." I recognized Charlie's voice. One of my biggest concerns was keeping people we didn't know well from "helping." That they listened told me how impressed the O'Briens must have been with our plan.

Now I had to trust that Charlie wouldn't just lob a lighter into the crowd when he got out there.

CHAPTER 28

Fishtown Scrapyard

I felt a chill when I looked at the two guards from the other site. I was glad I wasn't them, knowing Charlie was on the way. Would I feel any different if it had been my hand they'd helped to mutilate?

Sandy ran across the yard, making sure she avoided the gasoline-soaked ground and saturated prisoners. As soon as I'd given the word, the remainder of the O'Briens' muscle, which was only three or four guys and Cullen, stormed out of the building with pistols and shotguns and plenty of zip ties.

I'd been hyper-focused on the armored truck and trying not to get shot, so only now noticed what Steve was doing. I had to smile at the sight of him standing on the back crushed-car wall holding a bow with a flaming arrow notched and ready to fly. He looked like he was ripped straight from a *Mad Max* flick, but I couldn't argue that the message he sent wasn't clear enough. Everyone down below, disarmed and covered in gasoline, could figure out what would happen if he landed a burning arrow anywhere near them.

Sandy arrived carrying a medical kit. She'd insisted and I was grateful we'd held down the casualties as much as we had. "You're bleeding," she said to me.

"I am?" I'd reached under the vest to confirm that all I had was a bruise on my chest.

"Your face." She took out a gauze pad and wiped a patch of blood.

"It's fine. Just some glass spall from a windshield hit." I pointed to the guy with the wrecked leg. "He's in bad shape."

193

"Oh, wow. Okay, hold him still." Sandy knelt down and took out a pair of scissors and sheared off the pant leg. The belt tourniquet wasn't holding well. With the pants cut away, the leg looked much worse. I felt my stomach hitch, but I didn't look away. I had to own it all.

Sandy injected morphine into the guy, and he stopped his feeble struggling. Then with my help we cinched heavy twine just below the knee.

"You're getting good at that," she said.

"How long before we need to loosen it?" I asked.

Sandy glanced at the guy, who was in and out of consciousness at this point. She just shook her head. "I saw enough bike wrecks," she whispered. "That leg is gone."

"Best we can do is get him stable." I looked at the guy. More than likely, he'd been on the trigger when I got hit in the chest. "You shouldn't have gone after my man."

I doubted he heard me, but I know Sandy did.

"Coach, how we doing with the guests?" I said into the radio.

"Almost all secure."

"Let me know when they reach the accommodations." Ironically, we had a cargo container waiting. It wasn't the tricked-out imaginary version we'd conjured to fool Red, but it would keep them all in one place for the moment.

I looked and saw that the men were beginning to march the prisoners.

As if by magic, the continuous barrage of fireworks slowed and stopped. I expected the sound of sirens to replace the din. Nothing.

Now Charlie and William were coming over to the armored car with a couple guys who I was told worked at the scrapyard. One wheeled a portable welding torch. Charlie pointed to the open back door. "Make sure they can't get out this way." The men went to work, and I heard a hiss and saw the blue flame reflected off the walls of the interior.

Charlie gave me a wink and then he did a double take when he noticed the other men. He recovered and walked past them like he didn't recognize them. They were face down so they didn't catch the moment.

William glanced at my scratched cheek and seemed to satisfy himself that I'd make it. He moved alongside the truck, avoiding the side port on the driver's side.

I heard Tom mutter from under the truck where he was still braced to take on either the driver or passenger if they made a move. "Take your time, blokes. I've all day to stay under here. Mind the magnet switch."

He had a good point. The thing drew power while the engine was running, but something could have been damaged for all I knew.

"Teacher, class dismissed. Come on out."

"Right." He scrambled out and joined me.

Charlie took the right-hand side. He'd drawn a huge revolver that he held at his hip one-handed.

William pounded on the side and leaned his mouth close to, but not in front of, the gun port. I realized that was the thinnest part of the door. "I see you wanted to have our meeting early." He smiled at me.

Now that the fireworks had stopped, the two diesel engines were the loudest nearby sound. "Let us go," the driver yelled through the open port.

"I wouldn't dream of it," William said. "This truck is a mess. We can't have you driving around with your head hanging out the window like a dog, can we?"

"Your mother is a dog!"

William chuckled. "I can't say I like your negotiating style, but I admire your spirit," he said. "Oh, those windows won't open at all, will they?"

Charlie wasn't about to let his brother hog all the fun. "You'll have to come out," he called in to them. "Toss the guns and hands up. If you don't, we'll weld the rest of the doors and then take a bigger crane and drop the whole thing in the river."

"All your men are caught and sealed up in a container," William added. "If I say so, we'll take it and send them to the bottom of the ocean."

Sandy, who had been working on the guard with the arm wound, much less serious, looked up in horror. William could see her, and he just smiled and shook his head. She mouthed "Bluff?" to me.

I sure as hell hoped so. The O'Briens' glib attitude masked volcanic anger.

"Promise you won't kill us," the driver's side voice said.

"That's entirely up to you. We have to settle business." I heard steel in William's voice. "Now get out here before you make everything worse."

I tried to imagine the guys inside and what was going through their minds. They couldn't move, they couldn't see, and with all their fighters out of action, they were alone.

The pause grew. I began to wonder if we'd hear shots from inside. No.

"We're coming out."

"Guns first." Charlie raised his revolver.

The driver's side door opened a crack. The hair on my neck rose, and for a second, I was back in Iraq just before we got hit. A pistol dropped out. Then legs, as the driver lowered himself to the ground. William and I both pointed our pistols at him. The open door blocked our view of his upper torso and, most importantly, his hands.

"Very easy," I said. "If we see a gun in your hand, you're a dead man."

William aimed a small snub-nose revolver. No matter, he wouldn't miss from three feet away.

"No gun," the driver said. He stepped to the side, and we saw he wasn't lying.

Instead, his hands were clasped together as if in prayer and cupped between them he held a fucking hand-grenade. The guy smiled and stuck out his tongue to show us the pulled pin balanced on it. The tongue slipped back inside his mouth. "Let us leave," he said, slurring a little as he worked around the pin, "or we all go boom."

William was closer and he dropped his revolver like it burned his fingers. The big guy nodded and his gaze shifted to me. If I shot him, he'd drop the thing. I placed the gun on the ground.

"Sandy, get behind the crane," I said over my shoulder.

The guy shook his head. "No, San-deee. You stay right here."

"I'm trying to help your own men," Sandy said. "Now you want to blow them up?" She stayed where she was. She didn't even sound nervous. More than I could say.

As for her "patients," they became quite agitated at the thought of dodging a grenade.

The one with the lesser arm wound tried to get up but seemed to forget by this time that we'd zip-tied his legs as well.

The leader looked amused at the antics.

William pounced on the distraction. In a move faster than I would have thought him capable of, he leapt forward and clamped his own hands over the Albanian's. "Charlie!"

The guy was surprised, but started to struggle almost immediately. William held on like a bulldog, but the size difference between the men gave William little chance.

I ran forward but Charlie beat me to the punch. He already had his pistol raised. I put one hand over my good ear, anticipating the loud gunshot, and hoped Sandy had taken my cue.

Instead, Charlie reared back and used the heavy revolver as a club to the back of the Albanian's head. The guy was bigger than Charlie, covered in muscles and tatts, but he and Charlie were at least closer in weight class. At any rate, Charlie knew where to strike, and I doubt he'd held back. The guy collapsed like a puppet with its strings cut. He fell awkwardly and tumbled into William so they both went down in a heap of tangled arms and legs.

I looked at the ground in desperation, confident neither had been able to hold the grenade in this latest scrum.

I saw it roll right between William's legs.

Time seemed to slow, and I saw the handle, known as the "spoon," flip away from the grenade and land a few feet away. I knew enough that that meant the clock was ticking, and I wasn't about to get a chance to do anything other than what I did.

I snatched the grenade and tossed it into the open door of the Brinks truck cab. The moment the metal ball left my hand, I slammed the driver's side door closed. It felt like shoving the door on a safe.

I heard a terrified squawk from the passenger just before the door shut. Then I heard him open the passenger door and leap out. He moved quick for such a big guy and then an instant after the sound of the other door closing came the muffled blast from the grenade. The black-painted windows all flashed with a galaxy of cracks and the doors flexed, but held. I heard some swearing from the back where the two men had been welding, thankfully the curses were lively and out of surprise rather than injury.

"That's as far as you go, mate." Tom had moved faster than anyone else and now covered the other cousin with his pistol. I wasn't sure who was who, but at this point didn't think it much mattered. Negotiations were out of my hands, and I can't say I was sorry about that.

Sandy about tackled me in a hug, and her whole body was shaking like a leaf. "I thought . . ."

"Me too. Glad we were wrong." We held each other up for a while.

* * *

I met with William and Charlie inside the scrapyard's main office. "I guess we have some time to work," I said, "since we haven't had the cops and the fire department kicking down the doors."

William turned his palms up. "Maybe they got tipped off about the celebration up the street and everyone was assured that it was all safe, so they needn't worry about a few illegal fireworks."

"A few? Sounded like a preparatory artillery barrage."

"So dramatic," Charlie said. "I doubt anyone in the area complained."

"What you and your people did tonight hardly seemed possible," William said, "yet here we are. We couldn't have done this without you, but we like to think we have enough influence to hold up our end for the aftermath."

"So, all those guys in the container," I said. "You *were* bluffing, weren't you?"

"They won't drown," Charlie said. "We'll just toss in some smokes and let them figure it out." He found that idea hilarious.

"*I* wasn't," William said. "They killed my men and came here to do the same to all of us." His eyes were like ice chips.

"It's one thing to fight back in a shootout—" I stopped when he held up a hand.

"BUT," he said, "I am glad it didn't come to that. And I can thank you and your team. Those men are foot soldiers, nothing more." William looked at the floor, like he'd needed to hear it out loud again. "So, we are giving them a pass, on the condition they never come near Philly again. If that's too much to ask, we'll have standing orders to kill them on sight."

I felt enormous relief flood my body. I also got an idea. "I think VP can help drive that point home."

They listened and approved.

"What about the leaders?" I asked. "And Red?"

William met my gaze. "Kyle, we've been through the strangest few months of our lives. You've earned our trust in more ways than I think you understand."

"But?" I supplied.

"There's still such a thing as too many questions," William said.

"Even for you," Charlie added.

* * *

Outside in the yard it was like workers appeared by magic. The Brinks truck was already in the back area and being concealed. A dump truck and backhoe poured a mixture of kitty litter and baking soda on the gasoline-soaked ground.

The wounded went into the main office building and Sandy had politely but firmly been relieved of her impromptu nursing duties. I knew she wanted to know what would happen to them, and the best I could do was let her know that was the O'Briens' call. We'd saved many lives tonight, especially our own. That didn't exactly satisfy her, but I was happy she'd let it go for now.

I reached VP and she liked my idea. "You got it. It ought to mess with their heads. But maybe when they're dressed again, huh?"

I saw the O'Brien crew had rigged makeshift showers and decontamination in another container and a shiver went down my spine. Boxcars, showers. Either the Albanians weren't history buffs or they were so eager to get the fuel off their bodies, they'd overlook the ambience.

The cleaners, masked to a person, worked quickly and soon all the Albanians were no longer flammable and, in their white coveralls, resembled attendees at a painter's convention.

I realized all these workers couldn't be with the scrapyard and that I was seeing the infamous Shamrock Sanitation crew hard at work. True to their reputation, the crew made Tank's body vanish. So did the other guy, who'd hit me while I was in the crane. All the gore that went along with headshots from a rifle, gone.

I hadn't seen Rollie but knew he was somewhere in the building. He'd been very clear that he didn't want the Albanians to see his face. Some of them may have been related to Tank. For all we knew, half of them were. Better if they didn't figure out his role and have a face to go with the reputation. I thought the same thing should apply to the rest of the team, although they knew who I was and the wounded had seen Sandy.

When all the Albanians were lined up, they were clean but were still cuffed. One or two had been allowed to have their hands free. Several people held guns on them, and the Albanians didn't have as much as a nail clipper among the group.

A few minutes after VP told me she was ready, William came out like a victorious general to address the vanquished troops. He strode forward, and the men looked at him like they still couldn't believe what had happened. Despite the scrubbing, they still reeked of high-octane.

"I'll keep this simple," William said. "Your bosses threw you away like trash. You all saw it."

Right there it was easy to tell which men in the group spoke English by the expressions of disgusted agreement. William paused and gestured to give the English speakers a chance to translate.

I got the feeling that the Albanian leaders had pulled out all the stops to assemble this force, including recruiting directly from their home country. No wonder they believed the Irish had done the same thing.

When they were all scowling, William continued. "They knew all we needed was one match." William struck a kitchen match with his thumb and held it up as he spoke.

I pictured him onstage doing Shakespeare in an alternate universe where he wasn't a brutal mob boss.

"And while you burned, they would escape."

More nodding.

"But they didn't escape." William let that sink in. "And you didn't burn, did you? I say there's been enough killing, and there's nothing here for you now. Toward that end . . ." William signaled me, and I tapped my earpiece for VP.

The men looked up at the buzzing sound. They looked nervous as the little quadcopter drone came to hover in front of William, facing the group.

"Look up at the camera." William's voice made clear this wasn't a request.

Now the drone drifted toward the group and flew back and forth laterally. When it had captured all their images, it flew away. I keyed my mic and whispered so not even William could hear, "That was kind of spooky."

"Thanks, dude."

William resumed. "Here are my conditions: You leave Philly, tonight. With nothing. Don't go back to your place in Camden either. We are watching."

There were a couple expressions that said "How did he know that?" in any language.

"Leave tonight," he repeated. "Never come back. We know all of you now, and if we ever see you again, you will be killed on sight. Simple. Does everyone understand?"

Satisfied that he'd made his point, he allowed the group to exit single file out the front where their bus was waiting. The bullet holes were patched or disguised. The glass from the broken windows had been cleared, and they could enjoy the late-night air.

William faced me and spoke in a low tone for my ears only. "Let me guess, you have a tracker on it?"

"Not bad." I smiled. "Don't tell me you guys put a bomb on it?" I was only half joking.

"And spoil the surprise?" William smirked. "No. Besides, quiet and dead would have been far simpler."

"Where do you think they'll go?"

"Does it matter?" William said. "New York, if they will have them, but I imagine the families up there won't want anything to do with the whole affair."

I knew I shouldn't ask, but felt bold. "Are you going to be okay with your own families up there?"

"Thanks to you, we look much stronger than they expected. That will buy us time to rebuild." He shrugged. "There are always tensions." He started back toward the building. "But the New York Irish won't be getting too many favors from us for quite some time."

"Painter's club is on the move," VP told me.

* * *

Once the camerawork from the drone was over, VP and Steve worked to "strike the set" and remove the tricks and traps. The mannequins that were stand-ins for imported IRA still looked realistic at a distance, though I noted bullet holes in several of the dummies.

With the Albanians rolling away, Rollie joined me. "Look at that. Even in the fog of battle, those goons hit their targets enough to prove they had some skill. A stand-up fight would have been a bloodbath for both sides."

"I'm glad it didn't come to that. At least not more than necessary."
I could still see Tank with that rocket launcher. I imagine I would for a
while. "Thanks. Are you going to be okay?"

"Me?" I could see Rollie was about to play it off, then thought better
of it. "Sure I am. Maybe it wasn't sporting at such close range, but if the
big goon had landed that rocket anywhere close, you were done. That
wasn't a choice. Same for the other one."

"Even so." But the painful bruise on my chest reminded me Rollie
was right.

"All of them turn up sometimes along Memory Lane. But every one
made sense at the time. What are you gonna do?" Rollie switched the
rifle case to his left to give the right a rest. "Let's get that drink tomorrow.
I need some serious rack time."

I went to go help the rest of the team clean up.

CHAPTER 29

Kyle's place

Something woke me up.

Sandy and I had gotten home after midnight, and we crashed almost as soon as we were in the door. In the bed, she'd rested her head on my chest, and I was asleep before I had a chance to ask her to watch out for the bullet bruise.

I craned my neck to see the clock. It was 3:30 a.m., and before I could wonder why I was awake, I heard the buzz of my phone.

It could wait.

It rang again until voice mail. And again.

Sandy barely stirred when I moved her head and climbed out of the bed. I picked up the phone and the jolt of adrenaline worked better than a pot of coffee.

It was Cullen.

I moved to the bathroom and hit the button. "Yeah?"

"You awake?" Definitely Cullen's voice.

"I think so."

"Get over here right now." He gave me an address in Camden just across the river. "Did you get that?"

"What's going on?"

"One more time." Cullen gave the cross streets. "Say it back to me."

I did. "Now what—"

"Shut up. Come now, and alone. No phone either." Cullen hung up.

I doused the light and opened the door.

Sandy's voice startled me. "Are you okay? What happened?"

"It's fine. Well, I *think* so. I have to go out."

"Now? Where?"

"Yeah, I know. I can't tell you now, but I will later if I can. But it's important. I think it's safe."

"You *think*?"

"No lies means I just can't say sometimes, all right?" I pulled on a pair of pants and found my shirt on the floor.

"Not all right, but okay, I guess. Get back here as soon as you can. In one piece."

"Of course." I decided to grab a pistol from downstairs instead of the one in the bedside table. I didn't want Sandy to worry or anything.

* * *

Traffic across the bridge was light as expected this time of night. I was fully awake and felt bad because I knew Sandy wouldn't sleep until I got back. But Cullen hadn't called to spike the ball after the scrapyard battle. One of the Albanians or maybe Red must have been forced to reveal their hideout. I shuddered at the thought of how that must've gone down.

Once I reached Camden, I drove nice and slow so as not to attract attention. This was one of the rougher parts of a rough town. Even so, the streets were quiet. Muggers, dealers, and junkies had bedtimes after all, it seemed.

When I got to the intersection, I thought that I'd misheard the address. It looked like an old paper warehouse, long since closed. Graffiti ringed the lower parts and dotted the walls next to a rusted fire escape. I didn't see any cars along the building, but I did notice a fresh metal hasp and lock mounted on an exit door. And the lock was cut.

I parked around the corner and made my way back. The hackles on my neck began to stand. I wished I'd brought my phone, but Cullen had been clear. I glanced around and didn't see anyone. I slipped my hand under my shirttail and gripped the pistol.

With all other doors boarded up, this appeared to be where I was supposed to go. As I got closer, I saw something folded under the chopped lock. I took the cardboard and opened it.

It was a baseball card. Former Phillies pitcher Roy Halladay grimaced in mid-pitch back at me. I wasn't sure if the fact that he was deceased before his time had meaning, but a Topps card meant one thing for sure.

Cullen.

Now all I needed to know was if that was a good thing or not. I went inside.

The stairwell was dank and smelled like piss. I took out the gun. God only knew who could be in here, but I doubted any of them liked surprises. The fire door for the second floor was sealed, but when I reached the third, my eyes had adjusted to the streetlights filtering in through the grimy windows. This door had been pried open and propped so that it wouldn't close and relatch.

I listened but heard nothing. I crouched and opened the door with one hand while pointing the pistol with the other. The door squealed on the hinges so I went through fast and scanned the darkened hall for movement. I wanted to call out to Cullen, but if he was around, he knew I was coming. I passed several closed doors, pausing to listen each time. At the corner of the hall, I swept the gun around and peered after it. About twenty feet away I saw I door with light spilling from the edges.

I approached and the door was slightly ajar. As I got closer, I heard faint music, like from a radio.

I got a whiff of Chinese food, but under that, something smelled off. I peeked through the space and saw a row of mattresses on the floor. All empty. Still no other sound besides the radio from another room. I touched the door and opened it a little more, waiting for a screech. Nope.

Another few inches and I could see more mattresses on the other side of the room with a narrow path between them.

I pushed the door open enough to slip inside and kept the gun trained in the direction of the next room with the radio. I was sweating more than the warm room warranted. I stepped between the mattresses trying not to make a sound.

Then the lights went out.

I felt, more than heard, a large shape come from behind the door. I pivoted with the gun, but before I could complete the turn, flesh smacked the side of the weapon and my wrist. Huge hands gripped my arm and the gun. Before I could pull the trigger, one hand pushed the slide back just far enough to eject the round unfired. Then my arms got yanked forward, sending me off balance, and my wrist twisted hard enough to make me lose my grip on the gun altogether.

"Shhh." The lights snapped back on and Cullen, dressed all in black, loomed in front of me. He released my arm but kept hold of the pistol.

"You could have just looked out and waved," I whispered.

Cullen released the magazine and ensured the chamber was still empty, then tossed both back to me. "You don't need it." He spoke in a normal tone of voice. "Don't forget the one from the pipe."

I found the cartridge on the floor. That he wasn't being quiet anymore told me we were alone, or at least anyone else who might be here was in no shape to sound the alarm.

"I didn't know it was you," Cullen said.

"But you called me here."

Cullen took out the burner phone I'd given him a while ago and snapped it in half. He set the pieces on the floor and crushed them under his heel. He scooped up the pieces and handed them to me. "Bullshit. I didn't call anyone. I have to check in with the boss in fifteen minutes."

I didn't fully understand. "Anyone else here?"

"Not really." He took out a cigarette and held it unlit. "Not anymore."

That last word lingered. I tried to imagine a benign interpretation and came up empty.

"Oookay. Since we haven't spoken, I guess I'm not here?"

"How the fuck should I know? I was sent to sweep up the crumbs and look for stolen property. I need to stay alert, so I'm taking a smoke break."

I started to get a better picture. "If you wanted to go home early, where do you think you'd start looking?"

That didn't get me a smile. More like his face went from scowl to scowl-light.

"Me? Well, what if I ran into a mutual friend who thought he could get the better of me once the guards were out of the way?"

Who was still in the wind? Then it hit me. I whispered, "Milosh?"

"Don't need a name anymore. Chatty dork, might've told me not to bother looking, that the property was long gone." He shrugged.

I realized what the other smell was coming from another room. Blood. I felt my gorge rise and willed it down.

"So that's that?" I moved toward the door.

"Is there an echo in here? I'm going to have a smoke." He faced away from me but continued to speak. "Then I'm going to search the place anyway, just in case. I'll probably start under the kitchen sink."

I got the picture. And yet . . . "Thanks, I guess. But why?"

He took a deep breath, still facing the wall. "They've always been good to me, but I never liked that side of the business. Sounds fucked up, considering what I do, but we all have our lines in the sand." He cleared his throat. "Mostly cause I owe you one."

I didn't know what to say to that. "Didn't see that coming."

"If word ever gets back . . ." he began.

"Understood." I left it at that.

Cullen stepped out the door.

I figured five minutes was long enough for a smoke. I moved to the kitchen area with the radio and used my untucked shirt to open the cabinet under the sink. There was a large green duffle bag crammed in the space.

I pulled it out and opened the top. It was stuffed with plastic-wrapped packages of white crystals. How many dead couriers to build up this stash? The street value of this poison had to run in the millions.

Yeah, Cullen. We're square for sure.

Did I want to check the next room? Nope, whatever had happened was over, and I already had plenty of fodder for my nightmares. Everyone who might be in that room had known they were playing a dangerous game. So did the couriers, for that matter. But the Albanians took things a lot further than just a rip-off. There wouldn't be a trace of evidence in a few hours, I was sure.

So why couldn't I walk past the door without seeing for myself?

Own it all.

I may not have done the act, nor ordered it, but that wasn't the same as saying my hands were clean. Not at all. I was part of everything that happened, especially tonight, whether I liked it or not. One thing always led to another. The story of my life.

I opened the door with a cloth, making sure I didn't leave any fingerprints. Didn't want to own it *that* way.

The odor intensified, blood, and all the other things no longer held back by working muscles. My stomach clenched again.

I'd seen worse in the Sand Box. I probably looked worse when my truck got clobbered by the IED. Maybe it was a more personal connection to the violence, or even just the aftereffects of the whole night seeking a release, but it shook me.

Three men lay on an old king-sized mattress staring at the ceiling like they were wondering where they'd gone wrong. Two of them I'd never seen before, but on the side closest to me, dwarfed by the other two, lay Milosh.

He looked different without his glasses on.

That wasn't it. And it wasn't just that he was dead. The other two looked asleep with their eyes open, if that makes any sense. Milosh was shirtless and had marks on his body and a gag in his mouth to stifle screams. The smell of sweat and fear lingered under the other odors.

He'd died hard.

The bigger guys must have been the guards left behind to watch over the stash and the hideout. The rest of them had all gone to the scrapyard. If Milosh had been watching the place, biding his time, he would have seen the group leave. When Cullen showed up, he must have thought it was his big chance, let Cullen take them out and then surprise him. Underestimating Cullen was a once-in-a-lifetime mistake.

I closed the door, satisfied that I'd seen what I needed, and hoisted the duffel bag, still amazed at the sheer weight.

CHAPTER 30

Off the coast of New Jersey, two days later

Twenty miles off the coast the small swells tried to work their magic despite my taking half a dozen seasickness pills. Rollie piloted the boat. We both had fishing rods and gear, but for our purposes hoped we'd selected an unpopular spot.

Rollie throttled back and scanned the sparkling surface of the Atlantic. "Okay, kid, nobody here but us chickens."

"Chickens of the sea." I confirmed we were the only boat for miles. Good enough. "Thanks again. I haven't steered a boat in so long, I'd have gotten boarded by the Coast Guard before I cleared Barnegat Inlet."

"I'm happy to help."

I handed Rollie rubber gloves and a mask and put on the same. My hands began to sweat immediately inside the thick latex.

I'd cut open the package earlier to confirm its contents: an enormous sack of high-grade crystal meth. It looked like a cross between rock salt and broken glass. I left the top open, picked up a heavy aluminum ice-scoop, plunged it in, and flung the first scoop into the sea. It sounded like a handful of gravel hitting the water. I felt my blood pressure come down. I did another. Even better.

"It's faster if you just dump it out in one shot," Rollie said.

"Yeah." I tossed another scoop. I held it out to Rollie. "Try it."

He did. I saw tiny crinkles around his eyes above the mask and hoped it was helping him.

"How are you sleeping?" he asked.

"All things considered?" I took the scoop and kept working while I talked. "Better than I expected. You?"

209

"I'm okay. I see them all, sooner or later. Action wakes them up, you know? But I like to think they know it wasn't personal." He took the scoop back. "Hang on." He fired up the boat and we crawled along the water for a moment. "We don't want to give a whale a heart attack."

I laughed harder at that than it warranted. Pressure valves venting the stress all over, I guess. "You think this will make a difference?"

Rollie cut the motor and rejoined me. "In the big scheme? Like on the street? No."

"Then why are we bothering?"

"Would it do more good if you let your prosecutor friend find it for a big score?"

I'd thought about that quite a bit. "I think that somehow, some way, this shit would find its way from storage back to the street. A clerical error. Awful screwup, something." I took the scoop and sent some more to the bottom of the sea. "And then I could look forward to the O'Briens figuring it out, and you know the rest."

"It's not too late to sell it yourself. Think of all the good you could do with the money." Now he was just messing with me.

"Great idea. Put it under one roof, Sisters of the Poor Crackhouse."

"I like it."

"I know, I'll let Tom bring it to Ali and tell him we're square on the loan for the port." We both laughed. "If one of us had gotten hurt or killed, maybe I'd feel different, but I'm not even pissed at him."

"Are you sure about that?" Rollie faced me. "You put a lot of stock in him coming to the rescue."

"What would you call it? Tough love? Whatever. But if I'm going to get us into messes, I damn sure better know how to get out of them."

"You did okay," Rollie said.

"With a hell of a lot of help. I guess I also learned that, outside of you guys, I can't assume I can always just call in the cavalry when I get myself in over my head."

"I suppose it all depends on what you're willing to do in exchange for that help." He pointed to the sack on the deck. "Everyone has their limits. You do, I do, and so does our crew. And sometimes we get to make a difference. Like today."

"Sometimes we do at that," I said. "Even so, with this, what's the point? They're going to start up that side of their operations again no matter what, right?"

"I'm sure," Rollie said. "The question is, are you going to help them?"

I took a big scoop and flung it overboard. "Right after you do."

Rollie winced. "Once was enough, even if I was never sure about that package. I still wish I'd never let them force me into bootlegging their garbage."

"They threatened your wife."

"They did more than threaten her. Pack of cowards. Big Dan Sheehan gave the order and said not to leave any marks. Mary never told me what really happened."

"Mary's sister wrote to you, right?"

He nodded. "After Mary and Sheehan had both passed," Rollie said. His face had turned red, and I knew it wasn't from the sun. "She knew I would have killed him, then you know how *that* would've ended." Rollie dug both hands in the bag and lashed two fistfuls into the sea. Then he did it again. "That was about the size of the package."

"That was the Sheehan side of the mob. The O'Briens wouldn't try that with civilians. But we damn sure can't control what they do."

Rollie nodded. "And even if we could stop them from smuggling, they're just one stream feeding the ocean. Have you been through Kensington Avenue lately? It looks like a casting call for the living dead. Junk is coming in from everywhere."

"Not from right here, at least." I had to dig deeper in the bag now. "Not from us. But are we still civilians after all this? We protected them."

"We did. We also protected ourselves."

"But can we say we're better than they are, with all that happens, that we allowed to continue?" I felt like I was rambling, but I didn't want to shut it down just yet.

"*I* can. And so can you, if you'll take your head out of your ass for a minute." He flung another couple of fistfuls into the drink. "What about that old guy Penney getting ripped off by that scumbag lawyer?"

"Prosecutor Whitman told me that said scum LeSuer is already trying to talk deal, and front and center is restitution for Mr. Penney and the other victims."

"And the liquor store guy's sister with cancer? And the families in those slumlord rental properties? And the dopey loans you overlook collecting when the locals need more time? And on and on." Rollie took a turn with the scoop.

"All good points," I said. "But I just wish . . ."

"Wish what? That you could play Robin Hood and never get your hands dirty?" Rollie poked me in the chest, right where the bullet bruise was just starting to fade. "Doesn't work like that. It's messy. Maybe we aren't civilians after all. We damn sure operate outside the law."

That landed harder than if he'd punched me. "Maybe I'll be okay as long as I have an old fart sniper around to tell me when I'm lost in the weeds."

Rollie lifted the near-empty canvas bag and shook the remainder of the contents into the Atlantic. "I think the tide is plenty high now. Let's go home."

The End

ACKNOWLEDGMENTS

I want to thank my first reader (and wife) for her constant support and keen eye for detail and story. She keeps me and the characters honest.

I also want to thank the terrific group of editors starting with David Downing of Maxwellian Editorial Services all the way to the proofreading and wonderful cover design from Ebook Launch.

Note from the Author

Thanks so much for reading. If you enjoyed this book, I would greatly appreciate a review on Amazon or Goodreads. These can go a long way to help reach new readers.

You can find out more about new books at my Amazon page here: https://www.amazon.com/J-Gregory-Smith/e/B002VW9IIU/ref=dp_byline_cont_pop_ebooks_1

Made in the USA
Las Vegas, NV
06 October 2024

96368586R00132